OF BATTLES AND COVENANTS

PANDEMONIUM COLLEGE KNIGHTS 2

MONA BLACK

OF BATTLES AND COVENANTS

Copyright © Mona Black 2025

Published by Black Wing Press.

SYNOPSIS

With the dome covering the College, preventing any side from interfering, Frankie has to deal with the five supernatural hunks – when each one of them is determined to take her for himself.

And for his party, of course. The four Houses and Heaven all want a piece of her and the boys have made deals whose details she doesn't know.

Truths are coming to light about the boys' motivations in befriending her, and though her heart is broken, Frankie must accept that they never really cared for her and move on.

As much as one can move on in a College-turned-prison.

With five gorgeous and unavailable roommates.

While still trying to figure out who her dad is and why she is on the Most Wanted list.

Could it be that small incident of bringing someone back from the dead? Surely it isn't that important?

As if dealing death with her scream wasn't enough, dealing life seems to be the final straw for everyone in power.

As the boys' betrayal feels like the last straw for her heart.

When things get tough, that's when you discover your allies, or so they say. Will the boys come through in the end and will it be enough to save her?

*OF BATTLES AND COVENANTS is book two in a next-generation series following the events in Pandemonium Academy Royals. It is a full-length paranormal reverse harem romance, meaning the main character has more than one love interest. This is book one of four, and it ends on a slight cliffhanger. There is a happily ever at the end of the series. All four books have already been written.

This novel contains enemies-to-lovers/love-hate adult themes, foul language and humor as well as explicit content with darker elements. May contain possibly triggering themes. By book 3 there will be mm scenes. For 18+ only.

This book uses alternating points of view – one boy point of view chapter for every two of the heroine.*

THE FOUR ROYAL HOUSES

House of Water (vampires)
House of Earth (shifters)
House of Fire (demons)
House of Air (fae)

What to expect in this book/series:

Academy romance
Five supernatural hunks
Dynamic heroine
Friends to enemies to lovers to mates for life *ha*
Developing M/M relationships
They fall first
Characters forced into sharing a room situation *wags brows*

Heroine with evil mom
Found family
Multiple point of view

1

TIR

You fucked this up, T.

I know that. Things aren't going as planned. And that's the understatement of the century.

Frankie fights me at first. The portal I opened is incomplete, the edges fading into nothingness, the destination unclear as I haul her through it. She's shrieking or sobbing, kicking and pushing. It's like holding a wildcat in my arms. No matter how much demonblood there is in my blood and how badly I'm bleeding—and I'm bleeding badly—somehow it's not enough to break through the wards protecting the College.

She's strong, her moves good but also kind of wild, as wild as her eyes are right now, and I'm too weak. Bleeding out. I don't have the strength or the time to formulate a more complex spell, and I'd need to put her down and smear my blood all over the ground even in the hopes of getting out of here.

Despite my weakness, I wrestle her under control as I slam through the fabric of time and space, holding her tightly against me as I drop on my side and roll onto my back, protecting her more fragile body.

Is it fragile? Is she? What is she, anyway?

Why did I have this strange feeling from the first moment I saw her that I knew her from somewhere?

But of course, I never knew her before and I can't think straight.

To make matters worse, even through the pain and light-headedness, having her pressed against me, fighting me, sends signals to my dick that we're about to get it on.

Not die here on the grass, hoping that at least I did well enough and my deal won't be annulled, that it will go through.

If I deliver her.

Have I delivered her?

Where's the Wild Hunt? Why are they taking so long?

"Let me go!" She elbows me and my vision goes black for long moments, pain radiating up my torso. Just my luck that she managed to hit one of the wounds square on the head.

The wound where the arrowhead is still buried.

I groan, roll back onto my side. Blood seeps out of my mouth. It drips onto the grass. It feels a little like home, I think, threading my fingers through it. It's been so long since I lay on the green grass, free of worries, free of pain.

I hope the Wild Hunt gets here fast, or I won't even know if I succeeded.

Iron is still coursing through my blood, so I'm not healing as I normally would, and let's not forget the drugs we were given, though maybe losing so much blood is a blessing after all, cleansing my body from both poisons.

If I survive it.

Not looking likely, so don't get your hopes up, you idiot.

Though I'm gritting my teeth to keep quiet, I must have made a sound, because she gasps.

"Tir," she whispers, a broken sound, her eyes wide, as if she's just properly seen me.

And then the fight goes out of her. Kneeling in the bloodstained grass, she bows over. "Oh God, what have I done...?" she breathes.

"It wasn't you," I say, blood bubbling out the corner of my mouth. "We were attacked."

Why am I trying to make her feel better even now, when I'm about to deliver her?

"They came for me," she breathes. "And then I killed them all."

I don't understand her reaction at first. The men she turned into piles of ash were trying to kill us and not doing such a bad job of it either.

"They came for me."

I should have guessed. That scale-ball came at her—it goes for magical creatures. Sure, someone freed it, let it loose, and yet the signs were there.

"What are you?" I whisper.

A shake of her head, blond hair flying. A miserable twist of her pretty mouth. "I don't know."

With a groan and an effort that sends darkness through my vision, I struggle to sit up. Planting my elbows in the dirt makes my head spin.

She flinches at my movement. "So finish it," she whispers. "Finish me. It's what you were told to do, right?"

"I don't have orders yet," I manage, falling back down. Let's face it. Even if I did, I couldn't lift my head or my hand to do so, but I don't say that.

Her head shoots up. "What?"

"I'm waiting to be told what to do next. Our initial orders were to befriend you, protect you."

"Make me think you liked me," she says.

I grimace. Not sure why it feels wrong. "Yeah. That was the mission."

"Ryu told me the truth right before it all went sideways," she goes on, "after Rook walked out. It's what he and Asa fought about, isn't it? Outside the dorms. You lied to me. Pretended to be my friends, no, not just friends, but to want me."

"Those were my orders."

She doesn't look at me. I try not to think about kissing her, about how hard she gets me. It's ridiculous where I'm lying, dying here, but what's more, it wasn't in my brief. That was all her. But it doesn't matter. Never did.

"You lied to us," I say.

A shrug of her slender shoulders. "I couldn't go around telling every random person about my abilities."

This feels wrong, too. Of course, I was a random guy. But it makes my chest hurt, hearing the words from her mouth.

Get your shit together, T.

Haha. A little late for that. Or just right? What better time for a reckoning than your deathbed, right?

"And it's not like I'm proud of it," she goes on, oblivious to my inner turmoil and rising hysteria. "Being a killer. Being like this."

"What else haven't you told us?" I think I ask the question but she's just staring at me. Maybe the words never left my lips. And who am I to accuse her of hiding stuff when we failed to inform her that our flirting and courting was all fake.

Next thing I know, my head is resting on something soft. Smells sweet. Hair tickles my face.

"Tir," she whispers. "Stay with me. Don't fall asleep."

I almost laugh, but my chest is a mass of pain. Asleep? It's worse than that. Not just tiredness. This isn't good at all.

A feather-light touch on my forehead. I'm so dizzy.

"Where are they?" I breathe, trying to lift my head. It weighs a ton. "What the Hell happened?"

"Who? Who are you expecting?"

"The Wild Hunt. I called for them."

"Called them, how? Is there a celestial telephone line or something?"

I really shouldn't laugh. It fucking hurts. "They embedded a piece of Arawn's horn in me. To track me and contact me when needed."

"Like an electronic chip," she mutters. "Only that wouldn't have worked here."

"Hm..." I try to nod but my mouth is full of blood, earth, and death.

"Tir," she whispers, another broken sound. "What's wrong? Why aren't you healing? I thought the Fae were famous for their fast healing."

"Iron," I mumble.

"Oh God. The arrowhead?"

Fuck. I had forgotten about that. *Awesome, Kraish. More* iron. As if I didn't have enough in my veins already. No wonder I'm fading.

"What can I do?" she asks, that feather-light touch moving to my cheek and I realize suddenly that it's her hand. She's stroking my face.

Why...? Why would you want to do anything after what we did to you, I want to ask her but it's getting harder to speak. Or breathe.

"No! Tir, no. Stay with me."

Something's wrong, I think as black swirls through my mind. *They should be here by now.*

Something's changed.

Not good.

I'm fucked.

Twice over.

2

FRANKIE

I killed.

Again.

All those men coming at us, hurtling knives and Heavenly shuriken, dealing death.

I dealt it right back, like a mirror, throwing their intention back at them.

And it should be the one thing making me reel right now, reel on my feet, reel in my mind, but it's other things that keep my mind in a panic.

Finding out the guys—the ones I lusted after, the ones I'd reluctantly started to care for—had only pretended to like me. I was a mission.

And the fact that Tir is dying.

This last one I'm trying very hard to block from my thoughts. I have his head in my lap, my hand on his cool face, and my body feels just as cold.

What am I going to do?

Can't let him die.

How can I stop it?

What the Hell does one do in such a situation?

Yeah, he betrayed my trust. He pretended to like me—heck, he kissed me and touched me and I almost gave into the impulse to have sex with him—only to admit he had used me.

I'm still not one hundred percent sure as to what is going on and who he really is, but one thing is for sure:

I don't want him to die.

Because then I won't have answers, of course. That's the main reason.

Right...

"Hello!" I call out. "Is anybody here? Please help!"

The impromptu portal that Tir opened has spat us out in a part of the park surrounding the College that I've never visited.

"Tir, wake up!" I pat his cheek. "Come on. We have to move. Find people to help you."

"Too... late," he rasps. "No message... at the crossroads. No gifts..."

He's rambling as if with a fever. It scares me.

"No, it's not too late. I won't accept that. Then I'll go find someone." I scoot back, and lay his head on the grass. "I'll be back."

But his hand shoots out and grabs my wrist with surprising strength. "Can't... leave."

"I need to find someone who can help you."

"No."

"Then tell me." I kneel beside him, my wrist still encircled by his slackening fingers. "Tell me how to save you."

His lashes lift enough to show the pale green of his eyes. "I have a family," he whispers. "Tell them I tried."

My heart sinks. "Tir, no..."

"I tried to get back to them."

Tears are slipping down my face. Dammit, that's not okay. Not fair. Those wounds are still bleeding. If I could seal them, somehow... Stop the blood...

"I need to take out that arrowhead," I say. Which sounds

stupid, because everyone knows you shouldn't just remove jagged things from someone's body unless a surgeon is beside you to patch up whatever is inside. But the iron is seeping into him, killing him as surely as the blood loss, and not letting him heal.

Oh God, this is hopeless.

His fingers tighten around my wrist again. "Why aren't you running away?" Blood bubbles out of his mouth with every word.

That's a bad sign.

His lung is hurt.

"I'm not leaving you to die," I tell him.

He's watching me from under his pale lashes. He hasn't transformed, I think, as he lies there bleeding out. He's as beautiful as a pale statue.

"Do it," he says, releasing me.

"Take out the arrowhead?"

A faint nod.

A magical being, I tell myself as panic crowds in more. He's a magical being. I wouldn't try this with a human. A human would already be dead. I need to take the arrowhead out, make sure he's alive, and then... Then run, before the Wild Hunt gets me, and then...

Granddad. I have to get through to Granddad so he can take me away from here.

Because it's slowly dawning on me that not only the five guys are out to get me, but also the people behind them.

The empires behind them.

Faerie, Hell, the vampires and the shifters, all of demonblood.

And Heaven, too.

This was the worst scenario. Not only do people know where I am, and who I am, but the four Houses and Heaven already had their suspicions the moment I was enrolled and sent out five handsome guys to scope me out.

Scope me out and seduce me, while trying to figure out if I am as awful as they suspected.

Hence all the questioning.

Oh God. Now it's all falling into place.

The gifts.

The kisses.

The touches.

They did it so well. They deserve a prize for acting.

And I deserve a prize for my naivete and stupidity. In my defense, I never had a steady boyfriend. Don't have much experience in relationships. So I imagined we had one.

That I had a relationship with all these gorgeous guys.

What girl wouldn't have such a fantasy?

I almost laugh at myself, but now is not the time for falling apart.

I put my hand on Tir and shove him. he rolls onto his back with a small groan.

His chest is covered in blood.

His face is pale as death, his eyes closing.

Gritting my teeth, I lift his soaked shirt—up his flat, hard stomach, his impressive pecs, my hands and eyes shouldn't be registering such things at a time like this, I know—my fingers slipping in blood.

What a strange moment, a strange picture.

Me, kneeling in the grass, my hands on the torso of this handsome Fae, a sea of blood between us, a chasm between life and death and another dimension where he looks at me with hope in his eyes and I believe it—

My fingers find the gash in his chest. The broken shaft of the arrow is sticking out a little, scraping my palm. He makes a small sound and I realize I've jostled it.

I almost throw up.

I can almost imagine how that feels.

How that hurts.

He used you, I remind myself. *His pain should please you.*

I wish it did.

In the dappled light passing through the foliage of the trees, I can see the gash in his neck where an ophanim disk got him dribbling more dark blood into the grass. I wipe some of the blood away from the arrowhead gash and I see that his chest, beautifully sculpted as it is, is riddled with wounds from the werewolves that bit him, the flesh torn and hanging in strips.

More bile rises in my throat.

That green glimmer under his lashes is still there.

He's still conscious, if barely.

Watching me.

I dig into the wound with my fingers, digging into warm, soft flesh.

He jerks up, legs kicking in the grass, but makes no sound. I don't dare look at his face anymore as I dig deeper, feeling around the broken shaft, feeling the edges of the arrowhead.

Am I killing him, too, like I killed those men who attacked us?

What am I even doing? Only a few days ago—has it been a week? Two?—I was living with Granddad, training in fighting and researching magic, sitting at his table at night with his lovely live-in concierge serving us warm food. It was relaxed, easy. Cozy. I knew this terrible power was in me, I knew I was in danger and everyone around me was in danger because of me, but I never imagined I'd find myself in this place.

In this situation.

In this doubt, this dilemma.

I killed already today. *Please, dear God, don't take this one, too.*

I'm sorry, I whisper under my breath. No matter what he did, why he did it, how he hurt me, nobody deserves to be in such pain.

I manage to grip the arrowhead's base.

I tense my arm, draw a deep breath.

And yank it out. Or try to.

It takes a second, it takes an hour. His flesh resists. Tears more.

I yank harder. Ripping through flesh that resists. Ripping through blood vessels so that warm blood sprays me.

He makes a sound.

I'm crying.

He's shaking as if he has a fit.

I throw the dripping arrowhead away from me, wipe my hands frantically on the grass, on my pants, my heart hammering. Then realize what I'm doing, and press them against the wound to keep more blood from spilling out.

"Tir," I say, choked. "Tir!"

His face is white and slack. A long breath shudders through him.

And then stillness.

"Tir?" I swallow hard. "Tir! Come on, open your eyes. Tir!"

He's not breathing.

Tir isn't fucking breathing. His chest has fallen still. He's gone.

No. He has a family out there.

"Tell them I tried. Tried to get back to them."

That's why he told me.

No!

Gripping the stems of grass, I scream, the sound tearing out of me. I expect the trees to crumble into ash and dust, the birds to fall from the sky.

They don't.

I think about pulling life from the grass and the earth, from the elements, as my mother might have done. I try and try, and the grass breaks off in my fingers.

No...

I let the clumps of grass fall from my hands and press them to Tir's chest. Press my cheek to his bloodied skin.

Have I run out of tears? My eyes are dry now.

My chest is so tight I can't breathe. "Come back," I say, startled by the roughness of my own voice. "You can't go. Come back."

I lift a hand to his slack mouth. The other one I rest on his still heart.

"Come back," I say again. "This isn't the end. It can't be. I still don't know why you did this. I still don't know you. You bastard! I hate you! You sold me out. You can't die on me, too."

Something wrenches inside my chest. It feels as if my heart is twisting like an animal trapped behind my ribs.

It hurts.

Distantly, I hear running steps and twigs cracking. People are moving about the park, probably looking for us.

I should be running away, hiding until I manage to contact Granddad. He has drilled into me what to do in case of danger. Taught me that running is not for cowards but for those with a brain who want a chance to live and fight. Taught me that sticking around to be caught is dumb. That what I need to do is leave him a message and he'll find me.

Only as I start to get up, I feel breath under my fingertips.

I feel his lips move.

His chest, too.

I jerk away, gasping.

He's still alive.

Then why did he look dead a second ago?

3

FRANKIE

*T*ir is alive.

His handsome face is still slack and pale, but he's breathing. His heart is beating under my hand, his muscular chest rising and falling under my palm. I couldn't feel it before, but I feel it now.

Alive.

The thought alone fries my system and I kneel there for a long moment, watching him breathe, unable to believe it, caught in a state of joy and shock. It's like witnessing a miracle.

His eyes haven't opened, and he's smeared in blood. His bloodied shirt is still rucked up, but the bleeding from the arrowhead wound has slowed down.

What just happened?

His accelerated Fae healing must have kicked in.

He probably never stopped breathing, or his heart beating. I just thought it did, because of my panic.

And I can go now.

I *have* to go.

Getting up on shaky legs, I start to run, roughly in the opposite direction the sounds of pursuit are coming from.

But my shock has delayed me, and the delay costs me.

Whoever is crashing through the park—several someones —is bad news for me. Whether they be the guys—my guys, oh crap, when did I start thinking of them that way?—or more killers after my hide, I'm almost out of time.

I hate that I'm leaving him alone—because what if the others find him and hurt him more, what if they're not on the same side anymore?—and I hate him for all he's made me feel, that punch of emotions straight to the heart, the progression through hope and affection to shock and disappointment, then fear and despair.

And now back to anger, at what they did to me, how they used me for their own purposes.

They fought for you against those men! Took arrows and blades and teeth to their flesh for you!

Yes, but for their own objectives, not for my sake. Not because they actually cared about what might happen to me, but because they needed me to deliver to their bosses. Whoever those might be.

Stop thinking about that and hide, for Heaven's sake, a voice says in my head and it sounds like Aunt Mia's. *Hide!*

Sounds seem to be coming from all directions are once— steps and crashes and whispers and thuds.

Which way to go?

Away from the buildings?

Or back to them to try and call Granddad? With all this magic affecting technology, the only reliable phone is in the administration offices.

I press my back to a tree trunk and struggle to catch my breath.

Choose, Frankie. Choose. And quick.

You can run in the park and hide in the branches, I tell myself, *but until when? Sooner or later, someone will find you, and you don't even know anymore if anyone in this College is on your side, if even a single person wants to help you and not hurt you, kill you, or deliver you to a greater baddie.*

Oh God... I close my eyes, draw a jagged breath that hurts my chest. The air is made of thorns and pain.

I'll have to make a break for the admin offices. Getting out of the College campus and back to the human world is my best bet.

My *family* is my best bet. They are the only ones I can truly trust, the ones who truly love me and want me safe and sound.

Take the risk, Frankie.

Take risks or you'll never find out what's going on here and who you really are.

Or give yourself up, confess to your crime, and be done with it. Maybe Heaven already knows who you are. Maybe everyone at the top does, except for you.

I bite my lip, breathe out, open my eyes.

"*I have a family...*" The softness in Tir's voice when he spoke those words, the softness in his gaze...

And so do I. I have a family, too. My aunt, my uncles, my cousins. My granddad.

Not giving myself in before I even get a chance to say goodbye.

So take a risk it is.

Patch up your broken heart with a Band-aid, Frankie, and make it quick, because you seriously fall too easily and way too far.

Now run for your life.

———

And run I do, among the trees, slinking from trunk to trunk, trying to gauge where the noise is coming from. Whoever is coming after me is more careful now, as if they've realized I'm nearby.

My sweater is covered in Tir's blood, and so are my hands.

It's drying, flaking off. It smells of rust and death. It turns my stomach. It's the fear I felt, thinking he'd passed away, that I couldn't save him.

That bastard.

God, I'm so pissed with him. With all of them. But first of all with him, because he whisked me away and then almost died and I still don't have a full explanation as to the why.

Why I cried over him, thinking he was gone.

Why he kidnapped me, why he took on this mission.

And I don't know if I should be grateful he hauled me away from all the other gorgeous, dangerous, duplicitous guys I've been falling for, or upset. Did he save my life by doing that?

Why didn't he take me far away but only to the park of the College?

Was it because he was too weak?

Why didn't the Wild Hunt come, as he apparently hoped it would, to take me?

Something's going on.

A laugh almost escapes me. *Oh yeah, Frankie, ya think?*

Dry leaves whisper and rustle, and I make myself move. If I stay, I'll be a sitting duck. Keeping low, I cross to another tree and hold my breath, waiting, straining to hear more sounds.

I have my knives with me, but how much damage can I do? It all depends on who I come face to face with, what weapons and magic they have, how many of them come at me.

When I must not use my magic again.

Not ever.

Not even if I fear for my life. What if by mistake I kill people I love? Like Juliette or any other member of my family?

How didn't I kill my guys?

Stop thinking of them as your guys, I scold myself. *They're not and never were.*

You know that now.

Should have known from the start.

Should have seen it coming.

But it felt good, didn't it? To think you had all these gorgeous men panting after you, liking your company, desperate to hold your hand, kiss your mouth, possess your body.

Stupid little girl.

You're a grown-up but your heart is still that of a child, latching onto anything you see as affection, as attraction.

You slipped.

They were too pretty.

A girl can lose her mind and heart easily.

Now you know.

The mistake always stings, but the memory of the sting lingers, teaching you a lesson.

The buildings loom behind the tree trunks as I slip from bole to bole, crouching behind shrubs and rose bushes. I'm getting close. Sweat is running down my back despite the cold.

Evening is falling over the College like a dark cloud, blotting out the stars and making the lights in the dormitory windows twinkle. It looks incongruously pretty in the gathering dusk, a picture from a cozy bedtime story, and for a moment I pause, drawing in the scented air. It smells of pines and flowers and wet grass. Like Summer. It reminds me of home.

Wait... We're in the dead of winter and the rosebushes had no flowers. In fact, I only thought they were rosebushes because of the scent...

Ryu.

Shit.

Abandoning the cover of the trees, I sprint toward the buildings, my breath rattling in my lungs. If Ryu shifts into a fox, there's no chance I can outpace him. My sheathed knives dig into the small of my back, strapped discreetly to my belt, but I hope I won't have to use them.

Not on my boys.

Damn. My brain just won't accept the memo.

That these aren't my guys. They only want to sell me to get their hands on money or whatever it is they want.

Mercenaries, the lot of them.

And Asa? What does Heaven want with me?

I pound alongside the main path, still using the trees as cover, stumbling over roots and rocks. The admin offices are closed at this time. I'll have to break in. What was the security lock on the door? Granddad would be horrified. How many times he'd tested me to see if I noticed that sort of detail?

This College managed to distract me in the worst way.

Oh God, were they all chosen to be so handsome for this precise reason? To stop my brain and make me mindlessly follow them wherever they wanted?

Beauty.

Sex appeal.

Charm.

Talk about a weapon of mass destruction.

Mass distraction, too.

And I was caught like a fish in their nets.

Fear is a cold surge in my blood. I'm thankful nobody is around in case another scream tears its way from my throat without my permission. I'll gag myself, I think. Tie a scarf around my face. Is it the sound that causes the magic? Is it the volume or the act itself?

Still no answers.

I'm almost at the offices. My steps echo on the paved yard, just as my breath echoes in my ears, jagged, asynchronous beats. Almost there, almost...

Then another scent slams into me—wood smoke and hot dust and the alluring musk of a sexy man that hits you right in the guts.

Oh no.

It's Rook.
He's here.

4

ROOK

From the moment I realized Tir hadn't managed to take Frankie away from the campus—because the fucking angel trapped us here—I went on a hunt.

I'm a Hellhound. Hunting and fighting is what I was bred to do.

That fucking angel and his connections with Heaven. I've seen angels fight before, seen their Radiance and Glory, the impossible powers they wield when Heaven sanctions their actions. Good little soldiers, peons in the game Heaven and Hell have played for millennia, placed on the chessboard, moved around without permission.

But their part was always small. Heaven doesn't like to interfere, to dip its fingers into the messy pie that is Hell and Demonblood, not since the Coalescence which brought demon-blooded races to the scene of the human world and probably not before that, either.

Aloof and squeaky clean, that's the image it cultivates.

And this angel, hot damn... Never seen a sexier representative of the High Kingdom.

Wouldn't have minded doing him one bit.

But now he's pitted himself against all of us, throwing this dome over the College, trapping us all inside.

I wonder if Hell will find a way around it. If I can contact them.

Can't fucking contact them without catching my prey first.

Fucking Tir. That motherfucking bastard.

I streak through the campus, ignoring wounds acquired in the fight with the assassins sent against us.

Against her, I correct myself.

But who wants her dead? We've barely been around her, barely seen what she can do.

Maybe that's enough for some.

I'd think it was Heaven, only Asa is with us—was with us—and didn't whisk her away the moment he touched the ground. In fact, he didn't send the Heavenly hosts after her and Tir. Only trapped us here.

As if awaiting instructions.

Like the rest of us.

What in the ever-loving fuck, right?

My mind has cataloged and dismissed my wounds as non-fatal. Two scratches from arrows, one shuriken cut in the back, a knife stab in the side.

Non-fatal and hopefully not life-threatening, though the blood trickling from them all is a concern I will have to address at some point, before the world darkens more than the nightfall guarantees.

I can run. I can swing my staff. I can fight.

That's all that's expected of me.

Surviving isn't part of the contract.

I weave among the trees, jumping over fallen branches and rocks—*you'd think they'd have an army of gardeners in a place like this, fixing stuff, or maybe just use magic? There's a thought!*—as I follow her.

But dammit, I'd like to survive.

I have no fucking clue what the others were promised if they succeeded, but I'm a selfish asshole. I want a good life. And that's what I intend to get.

I hear you can have cocktails on the beach or by a pool, served by pretty girls and boys. And that you can spend weeks without fighting to survive in a bloody war you were cast into. With time to lick your wounds and watch movies. Books are apparently fun, too.

I'm literally dying to give it a go.

Fucking life.

Where is she? I sniff the air, stop, and turn in a circle, following the air currents. The others are close by, both a nuisance and a sign I'm on the right path. Not that I need them to know it.

She's near, so near.

I can almost feel her, a whisper against my skin. Makes me shiver. Never felt anything like that.

Never met anyone like her.

Yet I feel as if I've always known her.

And there she is, running toward the college buildings, her long pale hair blowing behind her like a tangled gossamer banner, and fuck, my eyes devour her as if I haven't seen her in an age.

Her curves, her legs, the flashes of her skin, the fucking smell of her.

Predictably my body tightens, and yet it fucks me up. I shouldn't want her and yet I want her so fucking badly. I've never wanted anyone like this, with this visceral need, this tangle of body and thought

Goddammit. Is it my nature? Being an incubus is a damn disaster sometimes when you're at war. Whoever thought I'd make a good bloodhound was missing a few brain cells. But nobody ever volunteered any information about my origins and

I never had a chance to find out how I ended up in the mercenary ranks.

I storm at her, my inhuman speed impossible to beat—except perhaps by a shifter, or who knows about the angels, secretive motherfuckers that they are—and catch up with her right outside the door of the admin building.

Right in time.

I grab her arm and swing her away from the door, and she lets out a cry. I tense, anticipating a repeat of that lethal scream she let loose on our attackers, preparing to crumble into a pile of ash and dust—but she just starts kicking at me. I'm so startled, I release her and she steps back, breathing hard, her dark eyes narrowed.

She's flushed and pretty and fucking scared. I can smell it on her. I can hardly imagine what it feels like to be her.

"Come here, girl." I make my voice a low purr. I have no instructions yet so I can't go about hurting her. That could cost me, if Hell wants her whole and I want those cocktails on the beach, dammit. "Come to me."

She doesn't come to me. She's strangely immune to my magic.

Well, after seeing what she's capable of, not so strange after all, perhaps.

Instead, she starts running again, this time toward the dormitories.

Loosing a curse, I leap after her, grab her again.

This time she pulls out her knives—so fast it's a blur and I want to know who trained her—swiping at me.

Not bad. A part of me marvels at her moves, is fascinated by the surety of her movements, the strength in her lithe body, and the lust nips at my heels, making my mouth water and my dick hard as iron.

But I have the experience of decades behind me. She's just a girl.

A sexy, dangerous, stupidly attractive girl.

I knock her hand with the knife aside, grab the other, and haul her against me. I sigh when her curves press to my chest. "Enough."

She struggles against me, whiffs of sugar and some flowery soap, and if she doesn't stop, I'll come in my pants. "Let me go. Let me go, you... brute... ugh!"

"Go where?" I tug more, making sure she feels how hard I am, and she gasps, eyes widening a fraction. "Anywhere you run, one of us will find you. Lucky that I got to you first."

"Lucky for whom?" she spits out, but her breathing is even more uneven now.

"For me, obviously." I grin down at her, lick my lips. "What about Tir? You're running around on your own. Where is he?"

"Wouldn't you like to know?"

I chuckle but my chest tightens. "What happened to Tir? Did you kill him?"

"As if you care," she spits.

"I care to know what the fuck happened. That *elshat* Fae didn't manage to get you out of the College, huh? The angel fucked all of us over."

She blinks those long dark lashes. "The angel? Asa?"

"Why, do you know more angels? Oh, right. Your granddaddy."

She doesn't take the bait. "What did Asa do?"

"He imprisoned us in this place, though I bet my ass that Hell will find a way to get us out of here in no time."

"Is that why...?" She frowns.

"Why what?"

"Tir said..." She's frowning harder now, and damn she's lovely. Holding her in my arms is an experience I don't hope to repeat. I realize with a strange pang that no matter how many other girls I'll get to fuck or kiss, it will never be one like her.

It will never be her.

"What did he say?" I ask to get my mind out of the weird loop.

"He expected the Wild Hunt to show up but they never did. He was wondering why."

"Ha. What a mess. Is he..." I'm gazing down at her pretty face, those winged brows and long lashes, the rosy cheeks and the small mouth, and I lose my train of thought, only... "Is he dead? He was pretty banged up when he took you through that portal. Kass even cast a spell to make him bleed more."

Her gaze swings back up. She's looking right at me now, her gaze meeting mine boldly.

"You are all assholes," she says flatly. "Trying to kill each other over me, no, not me, over a prize. What prize did they promise you if I spilled all my secrets to you?"

A hot feeling starts in my chest. A feeling that has no job being there. I'm not human. I have no morals. I owe her nothing. I don't owe anyone. I've long paid my dues.

But suddenly telling her the truth feels like a blow to my pride.

"He'd have done the same," I end up saying. "And you haven't replied."

"Find out for yourself." She lifts her chin, grinds herself against me, lashes low over her eyes.

Lucifer's balls, she's a wildcat. And I fucking love it.

Way to make me lose my chain of thought yet again.

But I'm a Hellhound above all and I didn't survive this far by thinking with my dick. Well, mostly not.

Grabbing her, lifting her over my shoulder in a fireman's carry, I stride away from the buildings, so I can contact my handler.

She's cursing a blue streak now and it makes my smile wider. Hell dammit, if she wasn't the mission, I'd be deep inside her by now, making her scream in quite a different way.

But here we are, and she's not worth more than my safety.

"Sorry, girl," I mutter. "I wish things were different. I wish I didn't have to do this."

"I don't believe you! Fuck you," she hisses, squirming in my hold.

Yeah, I wish that, too. I wish we could just fuck and nothing more.

I cast a quick spell with one hand as I go, coating my fingers in the blood seeping from one of my cuts, calling for Forcas, my handler.

The Hellish words scrape my tongue, the back of my throat, make my eyes burn. Flames jump on my fingers. They burn. The pain makes me even harder.

The spell jerks me to a halt as a projection comes through.

An unexpected monstrous face appears, flaming eyes and a mouth full of black smoke.

Yeah, Hell ain't pretty.

"Oh *shit,* what was that?" Frankie breathes and renews her struggle, hitting my wounded back with her fists and kicking at my chest. "Put me down! Asshole, let me go!"

"Be still," I manage, grabbing her more tightly, trying to gather my wits faced with one of the cruelest dukes of Hell. "Gemory. I mean, your Grace. I was expecting Forcas."

"Forcas is a useless imbecile *shashukra.*" Duke Gemory belches smoke and I cough although he's not really there, the spell convincing my mind that he is. "I have taken over this little project."

Smug ass.

"I have her," I say, kind of needlessly as he can very well see her slung over my shoulder, still kicking and cursing. "Can you get us out of here?"

"No. Keep her hidden until the fucking Celestials decide to sit at the negotiations table and let go of this nonsense."

I force calm and acceptance into my voice. "Yes, your Grace."

"Did you know they initiated the Raziel protocol?" His ugly face twists in a sneer. "Hasn't happened in centuries! I had to get out of my pit of filthy orgies and deal with this, and for what? A girl who can kill with her screams? As if she's the first one?"

"Put me down, I said!" Frankie manages to dig slender fingers into one of the cuts in my back and I hiss, half in pain and half in pleasure. "I'm not the first one? Who else was there? Put me down, I need to talk to him?"

"Talk to Duke Gemory?" I almost laugh out loud.

"Put her down," he says. "I want to look at her."

With an inward sigh, I let her slide down, keeping a good hold on her in case she makes another break for it. "I present to you Francesca, your Grace."

She draws a sharp breath when sees the dreaded face of one of the most powerful demons in existence. "Your... your Grace," she manages.

"Hm... I expected to see signs of her power on her face." Gemory sounds dismissive. "She's pretty. How boring."

She chokes a little but recovers. "Do you know of more people who kill others with their screams?"

I'm fucking impressed. Most people, when faced with an actual high demon, shit their pants, puke and pass out, usually in that order. They don't stand and talk to them.

Respect.

"I've lived countless lives," Gemory says, still sounding bored. "I've seen it all. Think you're special, Francesca? Well, you're not."

"I don't want to be special," she says. "I just want... to stop being like this. Reverse this magic."

"Reverse it? You were born with it. You can't stop it unless you reverse yourself back to death and nothingness."

But she doesn't shut up. "Who else?" She sounds desperate. "Who else is like me?"

"Oh, there have been cases throughout time. Various causes. Various demonic and angelic lines combining. How would you expect me to remember?"

I frown at that. He sounds so dismissive. Too dismissive.

"Then why do you all want me?" she demands to know. "Why not leave me the Hell alone?"

"Everyone wants a weapon."

"If you wanted a weapon, you'd have used me by now. You'd have taken me with you. Why did you wait? What do you want?"

"Don't overestimate your importance," Gemory says, starting to fade, his voice growing distant and yet there's something like worry on his face.

Or maybe I'm getting used to human faces. It would be a mistake to judge a demon's expression through that lens.

Fuck. He's given me no instructions, no orders. Just... hold onto her until further notice. What am I to do with her? Assassins are out there trying to kill her and every supernatural House is after her.

A weapon. I've had enough of weapons and war but I'm still stuck in the middle of it.

"Let's go," I grind out, already lifting her off the ground. Her weight is negligible to me, even though she's not a tiny girl, but she manages to elbow me in one of the wounds and I grunt, tightening my hold on her convulsively.

Can't let her get away. Got to find a hidey hole and wait this quarantine time with her until the dome is lifted off the grounds.

And then a rock crashes me, felling me to the ground. Frankie cries out even as I do my best to roll and not crush her, keep her alive.

No, not a rock, I think, my senses taking longer than they should to make sense of the situation. A man.

It's the damn vampire.

Fucking *Kass*.

5

FRANKIE

"*K*ass. Let me go." I squirm over his muscular shoulder, my stomach bruised. "Why do you all insist on carrying me around that way? Put me down. I can walk."

He says nothing, his silence stony as he limps through the campus.

Shit. Fine.

I didn't expect him to release me, and right now I'm not seeing the benefit in fighting, either. Night has fallen, I'm exhausted, and at least I know that there isn't much he can do.

Sure, the situation is getting out of hand. Rook didn't seem inclined at all to let me go—and if what he's saying is true, then I'm trapped here, with them. And now Kass has me.

Good news is, that means they can't carry me away anywhere.

Not at the moment.

I still have a chance. I need to contact Granddad, or anyone in my family. Find Juliette and tell her everything, beg her to help me.

Not sure how she can do that, but if she tells Aunt Mia

and my uncles, if she can contact Granddad for me, I'm sure they'll think of a way. If there's a way out of this, my family will find it, I'm sure. They wouldn't let me die here, or be taken God knows where to be used in a war I didn't know was still raging.

My breath hitches.

A weapon.

I shiver at the memory of that demonic face, twisted in a sneer, telling me I am nothing special.

But he did say that there have been others like me.

So why haven't I been able to find any mention of them until now?

If I'm nothing special, why is everyone after me?

It's not like I'd like to be an ordinary girl. My family is far from ordinary. And let's be honest, every girl wants to be special and different. Chosen.

Only being chosen to mete out death isn't what most girls dream of.

Not my preference, either.

I have to laugh about it, not to go crazy.

Ash is still sticking to my hands, mingled with Tir's blood.

"Where are you taking me?" I ask at long last. The lights around us have faded. We've moved far from the center of the campus and its buildings again. Juliette must be asleep, peaceful in her room. She probably has no idea any of this has happened.

I bet most students don't.

I wonder if the administration has been informed.

It feels like the end of the world to me, but behind me, in the dormitories, people slumber rolled up in warm covers and bright dreams, without worries and self-doubt. Without nightmares.

Without the fear that they might turn out to be themselves the nightmares they abhor.

He stumbles, cursing under his breath. Despite the cold, his sweater is clammy with sweat, and maybe also blood.

"Put me down," I say again, quietly. I can walk and your limp is getting worse. "Kass, stop."

He stops.

Puts me down.

He folds down to the ground beside me, panting. Sits back on his ass and lets his hands hang between his knees.

He's pale as death, blood running down his neck. He's covered in it.

"Oh my God, Kass..." I reach for him, then let my hand fall before I touch him. "You look like shit. Are you all right?"

A bitter chuckle leaves his lips. His gray eyes are bloodshot, his mouth white.

"I should bind that wound on your neck," I say. "If you let me..."

"Why...?" He shakes his head. Tightens his jaw. "Why pretend you care now that you know what we were after?"

"Because I... I don't want you to die," I whisper and it's the truth.

"It won't fucking change anything," he says harshly. "You being nice to me. I still have to deliver you to the House of Water to do with you as they will."

"And why are you doing this?" The pain in my heart is too great for the amount of time I've known him. Pain for seeing him in pain, for hearing him say he will just give me up, no hesitation. "What are they holding over your head?"

"You're wrong," he says, his voice a mere breath. "They aren't forcing me to do this. I'm doing it of my own free will. I volunteered for this mission."

A stab in my chest.

"So you did." I bite my lip and look away, not to see his handsome, loathed face anymore. "I see."

After a moment, he makes a noise. Clearing his throat. Shifting on the coarse grass.

"You're crying," he says.

"Am I?" I hadn't noticed the tears coursing down my cheeks. When he lifts his hand to wipe a tear from my cheek, I flinch. "Yeah, you are."

"It's just fear," I say. "Fear of myself. And for myself. Aren't you afraid of me?"

He tilts his head to the side. "Should I be?"

"Yes! I killed all those people today."

He settles once more. His eyes are mere glimmers in the dark, and he's a handsome ghost in the light of a half-moon hanging in the sky like a lantern.

"Say something," I beg. I feel shredded inside, my feelings all over the place.

From the start, I felt closest to Tir and him. Tir almost died, and now Kass is silent and bleeding, and I don't know what I'm supposed to do. Run? Where to? How do I get out of the reality of what I've done?

"Fear is nothing to be ashamed of," he says after a while.

"What I did is shameful and horrible. I'm a killer."

"All of us are," he says.

"How can you be so calm about all of this?" I demand. I'm shaking, the adrenaline turning to ice in my veins. I wipe angrily at my cheeks. While I ran, it was easier not to think about everything that happened today, but now... "Let me go."

"Can't do that."

"Then take me to the dean. Put me in prison. Make me pay for my crimes."

His gaze hardens. "You're going to the vampire den. That's what I signed up to do. Deliver you to them."

"You don't have to! You can deliver me to justice. You can—"

"No. I can't be seen to fail. Can't be seen not trying to succeed."

"Or what? I thought you said you volunteered for this."

"I did. But the small print on the contract is always a bitch, isn't it?"

I stare at him.

"The others will find me," I say when he falls silent again. "You're in no shape to fight. Let me look at that wound in your neck so you at least have a fighting chance."

"Who says I'm your safest bet?"

"Nobody, but I'm not letting you die, Kass, dammit!" My hands shaking, I pat my pockets for anything I can use to staunch the blood, but I have nothing.

His dark brows arch. Something shifts behind his gaze but I can't read it. Not with everything rioting inside my own head.

This time, when I reach for him, he doesn't move. I touch his neck, swallowing down bile as I examine the jagged wound.

"We have to get it disinfected," I say, and bandaged. "You may need stitches. It's a werewolf bite, isn't it?"

He turns his face, lips parting as if to speak, but instead, they brush against mine. His hand finds its way over my neck, over my jaw, my cheek, calluses scratching lightly as his mouth presses more firmly, taking away my breath.

For a moment, I forget where I am, what has gone down. I'm caught in the spell of his beautiful face, the feel of his lips, his long fingers sweeping into my hair, tugging. His tongue swipes against mine and he tastes like a forbidden fruit, sweet and spicy and mindblowing.

Can't believe how much I want him.

How much I want my enemy.

With a gasp, I pull away. "Don't do that."

"You wanted it."

"Not with you. Not anymore."

He licks his lips. "I'm half incubus," he rasps. "I need energy to heal."

"So I'm to let you fuck me now, is that what you think? Or drink my blood?"

"You wanted to help. Wanted me to survive. You just said so."

"Oh, fuck you, Kass."

Unbelievably, the hint of a smirk teases his lips. "I thought you said no?"

"Incredible." I jump to my feet, relieved that I can focus on annoyance and forget my shame and fear for a moment. "And here I was, thinking you were one of the nice ones."

"A common error in judgment," he says, and it fuels my anger more.

"Well, thanks."

He doesn't seem to be paying me any attention anymore, though, trailing his fingers over the bloody wound in his neck, then staring at the viscous crimson coating them.

Why? I want to scream at him, at the world. *Why did I let myself care for these guys? How did I let myself be so stupid?*

"Amon," he says, the quality of his voice changing and it takes me a minute to realize he's not talking to me. "Finally, you answer."

"We have had issues with Heavenly interference," a dry voice replies. "I'm sorry, did I keep you waiting?"

Kass frowns.

The air in front of him seems to turn into a mirror, droplets of water trickling over the surface. This time the face in it is attractive, its coloring similar to Kass'. Pale eyes. Dark hair. An arrogant kind of beauty.

It's his handler, I realize, just like that terrifying demon had been Rook's. His contact to his clan in the House of Water, the vampire faction of this new world.

I glare right at the asshole. "What do you plan to do with me?" I ask the face in the mirror. "Did you send the assassins after me?"

"Oh, she can speak." The face dons a long-suffering expression. "No matter. Shut her up and keep her safe, Kassander. We shall speak anon."

"Wait, wait..." Kass makes an abortive movement toward the mirror. "The emissaries of the other Houses, not to forget the angel, are after her, too. I've lost blood and haven't fed in—"

"Not interested, soldier. Lick your wounds and complete your mission. If you fail, there will be consequences and you know what I'm talking about."

"No," Kass says harshly, his mouth tightening. "You can't... You won't."

"You want to test me, Kassander? Keep the girl with you until an agreement is reached with Heaven, or he will suffer. I promise you that."

I turn to face Kass. His gaze is raw, all that arrogant veneer stripped. "No," he says again.

The air ripples in front of us and the image blips out.

"Fuck..." Kass bows his head and shoves his bloodied fingers through his wild black hair. "Fuck!"

"Kass?"

He closes his eyes for a long moment. His face has gone ashen. "We should get moving."

"But—"

He rises from the ground with a deep groan, swaying a little. "Come on."

"What will happen if you fail? Who will suffer? What did this Amon guy mean?"

"He won't do it," Kass mutters, grabbing my wrist and starting in the direction of the lake. He's slow, his limp so bad it makes me wince in sympathy. "He won't."

I don't think he's talking to me. He sounds like he's trying to convince himself.

"Will all of you get punished?" I voice my thoughts—concerns?—as we make our way through the trees. "If you can't keep me. Does that mean Tir and Rook are getting punished right now for losing me to you?"

"There can only be one victor," Kass grinds out.

"What is this, the Roman arena? Why can't we talk about this like civilized people?" I almost choke on my own words—I'm a menace to the world, not a civilized anything—but he just keeps walking.

Limping.

Dragging blood and pain and a fear deeper than mine in his wake, driving home yet again how little I know about these young men who've surrounded me and are now hunting me.

"I don't know if they will be punished," he says, pulling on my hand hard enough to make me yelp, hauling me behind a trunk. "Now be quiet."

"But—"

His hand slams over my mouth hard enough to bruise and he drags me against him, my back to his chest. He's breathing hard, and no heat comes through. He's cold.

Because he needs blood.

And sex, apparently.

And because he's bleeding.

But I'm not going to concern myself anymore about him, or any of them, I decide. I have to turn my heart to stone because that's where the problem lies, after all. I engaged my heart. Went past the lust into emotional territory.

And it had to be with the guys who are getting paid—and threatened, talk about every possible motivation—to grab me and sell me out.

He stops again. He's panting.

"Kass? Dammit, talk to me, just—"

"*Minchia,*" he breathes, pulling his hand away from my mouth, then turns around. "We're being followed."

Why isn't he running away with that superhuman vampire speed? He must be pretty bad off not to attempt it.

And yet, I don't care, I remind myself. *I don't give a damn.*

"What did you expect?" I mutter. "Come on, Kass... I told you, you stand no chance like this."

He doesn't reply. Collecting blood from his neck—it's smeared on my side and I can't bear the thought of having more of their blood on me, blood on my hands, blood on my conscience—he hums something under his breath and forms signs on the air.

"What are you doing?"

"We need to hide you," he says.

Another mirror forms in front of us but it feels different. It feels like the portal Tir opened earlier today. "You can't go far."

He hauls me against his side more tightly, weaves a few more patterns that I recognize as space-shrinking symbols, and rushes us through the slick slippery interdimensional void between worlds...

...and into a dim, dusty space with long benches along its walls and a strange musty smell of fur and animal.

I gasp. "Where are we?"

"Below the arena." He lets go of me to close the door and bar it. He shoves his hands through his wild black hair. Then he presses a palm to it and starts whispering under his breath again.

More spells. Securing the door against intruders. Despite his obvious exhaustion, Kass is thinking more clearly than Rook. Or maybe he's just not that arrogant.

Hm. Doubtful.

I walk around the room, not because I think I can escape anywhere but to get a feel of the place. Distract myself, too.

Piles of ash. Screaming faces as a wind blows through them.

No. I trail my hands on the wall. *Not real.*

Then the door rattles.

I open my mouth to shout—not sure what, a name, a plea?

—but Kass is on me like the wind, slapping his hand over my mouth again.

"Quiet," he breathes in my ear and I shiver. "The spell will hold."

It doesn't, though.

The door implodes with a deafening crash, pieces smashing into the walls and ricocheting like bullets.

Something hot slices through my arm and I jerk.

A huge red fox lopes into the room, and I make a sound behind Kass's rough palm.

And then a more urgent sound when the fox rises on its hind legs and shifts into a handsome red-headed man.

He grins at us. "Miss me?"

"Ryu," I breathe as Kass hauls me to the side, pulling out his lash. His grin is unsettling. Manic. Half-crazy. Gone is the sweet guy who spread his beautiful stationery around him during class and gave me gifts.

"How did you break through my spell?" Kass demands, his voice hoarse.

"It may have escaped your attention but I'm not a simple fox," Ryu purrs, ambling toward us, his teeth glinting white and sharp. "I don't only cast illusions. If you had really thought about it, I wouldn't be here if I wasn't capable of more."

"Fuck off," Kass says succinctly, snapping the lash. His eyes are turning red, his fangs sliding out. "You can't have her."

"And yet," Ryu says. He doesn't even seem winded, though dark splotches on his colorful clothes look like blood. His grin is now a vicious baring of teeth, his eyes hard. "I can't lose her. It's my only chance to get what I want."

"I don't care what riches they promised you." Kass takes a step back, pulling me along. "You can't be thinking my lash is my only weapon, either."

"You're not old enough to manage compulsion. Someone like you." Ryu steps closer. "Who craves sex but whose brain translates touch into pain. So touch-averse and yet holding onto her because you need her."

"Her touch doesn't hurt me," Kass says. "But my touch on you will, if you come any closer."

"You're mixed race. Your magic is mixed, too. You're no prince of the vampires. Can't talk to the dead or shapeshift. Do you have bat wings? I'd like to see that. Can you perhaps control the weather?" Ryu walks around us. "No water in here for you to manipulate. Except for my blood."

"Want to try my blood manipulation?" Kass growls like a caged animal, hauling me along as he turns to keep Ryu in sight. "Come a little closer."

Ryu stalks around us, round and round, making me dizzy. With his red hair and those deep green eyes gone flat like an animal's, with the sharp grin and the bushy tail swishing behind him, against the back of his muscular, green-clad thighs, he looks like a vision from an adult fairytale.

God, Frankie, stop it.

These guys are over-the-top sexy. Their fault. I mean, they were chosen to seduce me. And I'm in shock. My body is confused.

Jesus, girl. Focus!

I squirm in Kass's hold and hiss when my arm screams agony at me.

"Poor Kass," Ryu says, stopping, eyes narrowing. "You're weak, aren't you? No matter what powers you have, you can't properly use them against me. You're wounded, leaving a trail of blood behind you. And now she's wounded too."

"What?" Kass turns to me, eyes wide. "You're hurt?"

"I..." I don't know what to make of his expression and the fear in his crimson eyes, in the lines of his handsome face— until I remember that he's supposed to keep me alive and safe, apparently, for the vampires to decide what to do with me.

But his distraction is enough.

Ryu falls on us, wrenching me away from Kass and lifting me up in his arms. Like a lover's embrace, I think, dizzier than ever, as he jumps away and to the door, his inhuman eyes bright. "Gotcha."

"NO!" Kass howls, leaping after us. "You can't take her."

"Watch me." Ryu lunges out the door with me in his arms and races becomes the wind. Our surroundings blur as he practically teleports up the stairs and through corridors, a gust streaking through the underbelly of the arena and bursting out into the naked night. "Sayonara, baby."

6

FRANKIE

I knew shifters can be fast. All magical creatures are superhumanly fast and strong, and I always thought vampires were the champions in speed.

Being in Ryu's hold as he runs is like riding a bike on a highway at two hundred miles an hour, with no helmet and no controls.

He carries me out of the arena and into the park, zooming between trees, his arms turned into unbreakable bands around me, crushing me to his hard chest. I'm nestled in his warmth—a shock after Kass's cold skin—and have one hand bunched up in his shirt, the other curled around his neck.

Like a child.

Or like a bride.

Neither fits and yet his speed has me pressed to his body so snugly I might leave some skin behind when I unglue myself in the end.

I'm too stunned to speak, or even breathe. A senseless fear grips me that we'll smash into something and die.

Join the race.

A one-way ticket to Hell—because I doubt I'm going to Heaven.

And what do you do with concepts like that now that Heaven and Hell are actual places, when angels and demons live and die among us? Where do souls go?

Other, higher spheres, I was told growing up. Other planes of existence. Different dimensions of the afterlife than the worlds we have seen pictures of.

Purgatory, I think. Transitional states.

Are Asa and Rook reborn souls who reached their destination? Are the Heaven and Hell we know the end of the line? Did my family get it all wrong? Or were they trying to protect me?

My mind swirls with colors and images.

Ryu is still running.

I close my eyes, bury my face against his chest. The fear melts away as I listen to the strong beat of his heart. It shouldn't feel so comforting.

When the wind stops and all I can hear is his ragged breathing, I lift my head at last and find that we're inside a building once more.

"What is this place?" I whisper, my voice hushed, my ears still buzzing from the mad race that got us here, from the events and conditions that inexorably brought us to this place, this position.

My naivete.

My evil magic.

My inability to control my emotions and my power.

"Hm?" He's still standing where he stopped, his arms still wrapped around me, holding me to his chest. His heart is pounding madly against my side and his eyes have lost some of their manic brightness. "Oh. The library."

I turn in his arms and he lowers my feet to the floor. "What do you intend to do? You can't take me out of the College grounds."

Floor-to-ceiling shelves filled with books about magic, looking sinister in the emergency lights, nothing like the day when I came in here searching for answers about my magic. It feels like ages ago.

He shrugs. "Sooner or later, the dome will collapse and then I will."

"So we'll stay here, in the library, until that happens? Eating books?"

"I thought you liked books," he says.

"Not as snacks."

"More like full meals, I suppose."

"I like big books and I cannot lie," I whisper as I peruse the shelves closest to us, barely making out the letters on their spines. It gives me something to distract myself with, take a moment to settle my breathing. It's no use, though. My heart is skittering about my chest like a frightened animal, looking for a way out.

I hear him step closer to me. "There are more entertaining ways to pass the time." His voice has deepened and then his fingers brush through my hair

I jerk back. "What is wrong with you?" I demand.

He looks startled. I think. It's hard to read his face in the dimness. "I want you. I thought you wanted me, too."

"And I thought you were nice," I breathe. "Was it all a façade? Coming on to me now is something I expected from Rook or Tir."

"Does wanting you make me not nice?"

"Wanting me after betraying me? Yes. It makes you a big-ass bastard."

"Betrayed you? Look, I haven't been in human form in ages and... and let's forget about that. But your powers are off the charts. The whole world is holding its breath, waiting to see where you will end up. One side would have gotten you in the end. I only made sure it was the shifter side, the House of Earth."

"Is that supposed to make it right? To make me feel better?"

"No," he says. "I won't lie to you. You're dangerous and I don't see any good outcome to any of this."

"Except for you. You'll get what you were promised. Right? A big house with a pool in the suburbs? A nice park attached to it so you can run in fox form and hunt rabbits? A harem of pretty girls? Or boys? I mean, what do I know? I know nothing about you. Maybe just a hefty bank account?"

"You have no idea what I asked for," he says, his voice going flat.

"No? Then tell me. I'm dying to know!" I throw my hands up in the air. "Enlighten me."

He shakes his head, red hair flying.

"Kass is afraid for someone he cares for. What do you have to lose? It's all a game to you!"

His jaw clenches. He steps away from me, hands curling into fists by his sides. "You wouldn't understand."

"Seriously? Try me. I may prove to be less stupid than you think."

"Christ, I don't think you're stupid, Frankie, I just..." His muscular shoulders hunch in. "It's complicated."

"Then fucking *summarize*."

But he stalks to the far end of the room, checks the door. Locks it. Leaving me there seething and feeling lost.

Lost and losing it. I've tried to keep my cool but how the Hell am I going to keep my wits about me when it's all falling apart, taking away any semblance of control? I press my lips together, willing them not to tremble, and hug myself.

You'll be fine, I tell myself. *They can't fly you out of the campus, at some point you'll escape and you'll be fine.*

I sound escapes me. It's not a laugh or a sob but something in between.

"What's wrong?" he asks, returning to stand before me.

I look away and snort softly. "Seriously, you're gonna ask me that? Any more dumb questions?"

"I mean apart from this mess."

"What makes you think it's something else?"

"Your expression."

I hate that he can read me that easily, even in the dark. Probably shifter supernatural senses. The eyes of a fox. Whereas his face is in shadow, mine seems to be in the spotlight.

"My family," I mutter. "They'll worry about me. I want to contact them. I have to call them. I'm not able to contact them like you guys contact your people with a spell. I just need a landline telephone—"

"No. I don't think I can allow that."

"You wouldn't understand. Do you have a family? Do you know what it's like to be afraid of hurting them? Of having them worry over you? Ow." My sudden twist away from him reminds me that I have a gash in my side.

"Frankie." He grabs and lifts my arm, his other hand ghosting over my side. "You're wounded."

I flinch and he lets go. "Don't touch me. You asshole." The pain mingles with the uncertainty, the guilt, and the panic, choking me. "You've done enough."

"I didn't mean for you to get hurt," he says softly.

"And what did you think? That you'd flirt with me and then deliver me with a bow on top to your buddies? And you thought that wouldn't hurt me, using me as your ticket to something better?"

"Fuck." He gazes at me for a long moment, saying nothing more, and I'm working myself up to a real rant inside my head, because, besides the shock of what I did and what I thought was going on, resides the hurt of their deception.

Deflating, I press my back to the shelves and let myself sink down to the floor. "Please let me contact my grandfather. Or my aunt."

"No."

"You're heartless."

He turns his back to me and silence stretches between us. Eventually, he says, "If you want to know, I lost people. People I cared for."

"So you do understand!"

"But I still can't let you contact them, not yet."

"You lost people. Is this the reward you hope for? Did they promise to bring them back?"

He laughs, a bitter sound. "Nobody can bring them back. They're gone forever. You said it yourself, you know nothing about me, so stop making fucking assumptions and sit tight. Sooner or later Heaven will take its thumb off us and I'll hand you over. Then I'll be done for good."

"Done? What do you mean, done?"

7

RYU

*F*uck, I let that escape my goddamn mouth. Hadn't meant to.

"I don't mean anything," I grind out and go back to the door, listening for any sound from outside. "Just done with this mission."

"And what will you lose," she whispers, "when you fail?"

"I'm not going to fail," I snap, turn, and press my back to the locked door. Fold my arms over my chest. "What do you know about that?"

"What Kass told me."

"Yeah? And what did the damn vamp say?"

"You act like you don't care about him, about what he'll lose in this mess. About Tir almost dying, either."

"Tir almost died? I thought he was fine when you..." I catch myself before I blurt out more. "Just tell me what the Hell Kass said."

"He said there's small print on your contracts. That if you fail, you'll get punished. Or don't you have anything to lose?"

"You're right. I have nothing left to lose." I gaze at her from under my lashes, drink in her annoyance. And no, I don't enjoy her pain, sorrow, and anger, but I need to reset the boundaries, put some distance between us because...

Because if there's anything I might regret right now it's her, and I can't afford that.

Not when I'm so close to getting what I want, after centuries.

She feels so familiar, so achingly dear, this girl I've barely met, it fucks with my resolve.

"So what's in the small print for you?" she asks.

"Small print?" I watch her annoyance morph into a deeper emotion I can't quite read. "What are you talking about? I think Kass was leading you on."

"He was telling the truth. I heard it straight from the mouth of his handler."

"Handler?"

"The vampire he reports to. Don't you report to someone?"

"Sure I do. Everyone does. What sort of punishment was Kass expecting?"

And I should contact my people right now, only her talk of failure is a reason to hold back. What if she's right? In that case, better not to report success until I know it's for real. No success, no failure. At least let them think I'm still chasing her.

I'm buying myself time.

"Someone he knows would be punished in his stead, if I figured it out correctly." She tangles her fingers together over her knees, her long pale hair curtaining her small, thoughtful face. "He seemed... distraught."

"At least he has a living person he's concerned about," I snarl, the heat of anger coming without warning. I didn't expect it. By now my anger has cooled into a vague sorrow, but since returning among humans, it seems that my emotions have woken up, too.

Not what I need right now.

Small print, all right.

What more could I lose?

I lied. There's always something we want, right out of reach. We strain for it, do everything in our power to get it. The moment we desire something, we have everything to lose.

And I desire her, but that's not my concern, because I've lost her already. Lost her the moment I found her.

No, what concerns me is *time*.

How much more time will I have to wait until the end, until the last of my memories fade, until all that's left is a vague pain where my heart should be?

And what if the *end* is taken away from me again?

———

She likes books.

I knew it from the start, from the way she regarded my notebooks and pens, from the way her small hands caressed her books as she took them out of her bag in class.

I watch her wander the shelves, touching the spines, reading the titles, head cocked to the side. She's wound her long hair into a knot at her nape, and my mouth waters at the sight of the fine skin there, and the way her back cinches into a narrow waist and flares at her hips. Her ass is heart-shaped and I want to press my body to hers.

It was true, what I said. I hadn't inhabited a human body in a long time, and my time as a fox is a blur.

This body has cravings. It wants food, it wants drink. It wants sex and it wants this specific girl.

Damn stupid, this human body.

Then again, the problem is the brain, isn't it? That primal part of it that singled her out from the first fucking glance, picked her out from all the girls before I even knew she was my target as pretty and sexy. As the one I want.

When she's the last girl I should be wanting.

When I should be done with wanting, period.

What's a dead man walking got to do with a breathing, living girl?

A girl who is a weapon encased in a hot body and a face like an angel's, with those dark eyes and that golden hair...

"Ryu? Did you hear me?" she says.

"Hm?"

"I said I think someone's outside."

"No way, I'd have... heard it. Of course I'd have heard it."

But distraction will be the death of me, because now I hear a noise, too.

If only it were that easy to die.

But no, I have to work for it. Snarling, feeling my ears twitch and my tail lash against the back of my thighs, I slink closer to the door and whip out my katana. My shuriken are a reassuring weight, stuck in the back of my belt.

My senses sharpen as they do whenever I go into a half-shift, my body remembering the ways of the fox, the days and months and years I spent in animal form, roaming, hunting, killing, nesting.

Foxes are solitary creatures.

That's another word for lonely.

But it was easier to bear as a fox.

It's getting damn difficult now I'm again a man.

Not for long, though, I remind myself as something crashes into the door, crashing through my locking spell and the actual fucking lock.

Closing my eyes, moving the fingers of my free hand through a new spell, I cast an illusion outside the door.

Not many creatures can see through my illusions, which means—

The door splinters and a force throws me through the air and slams me into the far wall. There's a crack. I think it comes from me. Pain hits like a fist twisting my insides and I crumble to the floor.

Fuck.

"Ryu!" Frankie screams and starts toward me but someone enters, grabbing her around the waist, his gaze on me implacable.

"Of course it would be you," I breathe, blood bubbling on my lips, as the angel strides out of the library, leaving me there.

Asa...

8

FRANKIE

*A*sa drags me out of the library kicking and screaming. He lifts me off my feet with an arm around my waist, seemingly without any effort, as if I'm a feather, an insubstantial speck of dirt.

"Let me go!" At this point, it's frustration fear, and a general sense of unreality that has me shaking and yelling. "What do you want with me? I'm not going with you anywhere! Tell Heaven that!"

I don't care if anyone hears me. Who is left? If the others haven't come back after me, it means they can't, and I hate to imagine why. Are they so badly wounded? Did their contacts deliver the promised punishment? Is it physical, psychological, has it broken them?

Is Asa the last one standing, or is he simply the strongest?

"We have to go back!" I kick and twist, trying to relax his hold on me as he marches through the yard. "Ryu is hurt. You hurt him badly!"

"He'll survive. He's a shifter. He'll shift and heal."

"What if he can't?"

Asa hesitates, just a moment's arrest of his easy stride. It gives me hope, but then he seems to shake the doubt off. "He's demonspawn, full of accursed demonblood. Just like you. He'll be fine."

"And you're pure like driven snow, are you?"

He lifts his chin and manages to glare down his fine Roman nose at me even though he has to look up. I struggle in his hold. "I have no connection to demons."

"You just threw him against the wall! You're violent and awful."

"I'm a soldier," Asa says. "I follow orders."

"Bullshit! And fuck your orders!"

Never breaking stride, never even slowing down as I keep cursing him, he hurries into one of the buildings, shoving the door open and calmly walking into an office where he dumps me on a chair and dusts his hands off.

He actually fucking dusts his hands off.

Jesus.

And that's when it hits me that we're in the admin building. Figures that he'd feel secure inside the headquarters of the College. Looks like Heaven has the upper hand.

Nobody ever really speaks about it. The pink, winged, little elephant in the room.

Everyone speaks of the Coalescence and the rise of demonblood Houses and their integration into human society. How witches tried from time to time to bring the power of the elemental magic back but failed. Everyone recounts how the four Houses were at war for so long, both overtly and covertly, and how my aunt Mia and her four conduits, now her husbands, managed to become the Queen Witch and prevent my mother from taking over the world, suppressing not only demonblood but also humankind.

Nobody talks about the power of Heaven. Its hand behind everything. Granddad doesn't talk about it. Nobody ever does.

But Heaven is turning out to be the puppet master, holding all our strings.

At least that's how it's starting to look from where I'm sitting.

And it doesn't surprise me in the least when Asa opens a line of communication with his masters while I'm sprawled on the office chair, trying to get my breath back and sort through my jumbled thoughts.

He doesn't cut his palm or wrist or even finger open to use blood for the spell. No blood. I mean, what do I know? Maybe Heaven has open comms with its peons.

Then he curls one hand in the air and light erupts between his fingers. A hum surrounds us.

Asa seems to hum something in return, nodding.

The hum intensifies, rising into a whine, until I think my ears will start bleeding. I get to my feet, looking around, trying to see something, anything. Is this the angels speaking? My head aches and I'm gritting my teeth.

And then the whine transforms into words, breathy vowels soft consonants, and a voice like a flute.

"Asariel," the voice says, "identity verified. Nephal rank verified. Mission Pandemonium College verified. Raziel protocol implementation still in place. You may speak."

I frown. Wait a minute. Is it an angel speaking or a computer? I open my mouth to ask, when Asa opens his hand and the glow previously contained in his fist now forms a ball of light that floats in front of him.

Ooh. Pretty.

If only I wasn't in such deep shit right now, and annoyed at Asa, not to mention weirded out by the robotic volley of questions lobbed at him, I'd be excited to see this show and learn more about Heaven. We know practically nothing about it.

"Report on the whereabouts of the girl," the globe's fluting voice intones.

"She is with me," Asa says in that deep voice of his.

"And the demonblood house emissaries?"

"Out of sight. They have probably exhausted themselves running around. The girl will stay with me until it's time to hand her over."

"The girl? The *girl?*" I blurt out, unable to keep quiet any longer. "Seriously? I have a name. You know me. You went *down* on me!"

Quiet spreads inside the empty office. The orb pulses softly. Asa's face is still, his expression... *precious.*

Oh, I enjoy the look of shock on that gorgeous, perfect face.

"You understand angelic?" he eventually asks.

"Wow." I frown, doing my best not to smirk. "Wasn't I supposed to? And did your angel master understand me, too? Oh wait, I'm sorry. Was it a secret? Maybe going down on me wasn't part of your mission?"

"Going down on her?" the globe says in that same breathy voice and suddenly it's so funny I giggle. "My translator tells me it's a sexual act."

"Not really," Asa says, his voice frosty.

"Oh, you mean that putting your hands on my pussy to pleasure me, and at the same time I believe you touched yourself, too, that doesn't count as sexual for you?" I purr.

"You put your hands on her private parts?" the globe inquires after a moment. "That is a sexual act."

I have the pleasure of seeing Asa's face paling. "It was part of the mission," he says.

"Oh, fuck you," I mutter, annoyed to Hell. "Fuck you so much."

He ignores me. "What are my orders?"

"Avoid sexual acts with the girl," the globe says, "and keep an eye on the emissaries. We don't know what they are up to."

"You said you'd eliminate them," Asa says coldly. "I've done my part."

"Excuse me? What the fuck? Eliminate them?" I gape at him. "You agreed to something like that?"

"Language," Asa says, his jaw set in a hard line.

"You don't get to lecture me about language!"

"... is this the girl?" the globe asks.

"Yes." Asa's hands clench and unclench at his sides. "She is unruly and stubborn."

"Excuse you!" I snarl because fuck him.

"Tie her up for now. And find the emissaries. We still don't know who sent the assassins against her. They may have been sent against all of you to silence you."

"I understand," Asa says, though he looks like he's tasted something sour.

What a total jackass! I mean... angels. Demonblood is all bad boys, and I'd imagined angels to be full of goodwill and kindness. Like Granddad.

If Asa is kind, he's doing a pretty good job of hiding it right now.

He's hidden it so deep inside of him you'd need a drill to dig it out.

The globe fades and I'm left facing him. I'm ragey. They all betrayed me, but he betrayed them, too. He's an extra special douchebag.

"So what now? What will you do?" I demand. "Deliver me to Heaven to make mincemeat out of me? What?"

"I follow orders," he says, "I—"

"Oh, how nice. So you don't have a brain of your own."

"You're dangerous."

"Only when assassins are after me! Can you blame me?"

He blinks.

I rerun my words through my head. That is the truth... isn't it? At least so far. But that's because fear triggers my curse... right? And any fear might trigger it and that's no good.

No matter. I file that away for later examination.

"You don't care," I seethe. "You literally don't give a shit about others. And the other guys, you wanted them gone. You never cared whether they lived or died."

"We're not friends," he says. "They aren't here for pleasure. We're all doing our jobs."

Way to drive the point home once again, that none of them is on my side. Sure, I have been telling myself that same thing over and over since the attack, but I guess somewhere deep in my stupid little heart, I'd hoped that even one of them would care.

And somehow, I'd pinned my hopes on Asa. An angel. An angel who closed all escape routes, preventing the others from carrying me away. I thought that he'd care if I live or die, that he'd feel something about me, and about the others.

"So you're a fallen one," I say, "despite all your claims to the contrary. You're governed by emotions. Pride, arrogance, and the need to prove yourself better than others. Ring any bells?"

His eyes are chips of ice. "You think you know angels? Who told you that the angels are good?"

"But—"

"Those who fell, fell for love, or so they say. Those who stayed are true believers. So who's to say who's the better party?"

"So the angels are cruel fanatics, is that it?"

"Of course you'd think that. They believe in God's glory. They believe in the glory of the angelic taxiarchies, in Heaven's mission."

"Which is? To step on dead bodies and rise higher?"

"... that's not what Heaven's mission is."

"I don't care what it is! What you're doing doesn't sound like the job Heaven would give. I don't care what you say. If God is kindness, then what is this all about? To keep God safe?"

He's watching me, his eyes unreadable.

Saying nothing.

"Damn you," I whisper. "Damn all of you. Not that it matters to you, but I'm never going to forgive you for this."

"You are a killing machine," he says tonelessly.

"At least I feel bad about it," I mutter. "I guess magic or not, I'm still human. Unlike you. You're just one of God's many hands, aren't you? No will of your own. No heart. You sure are pretty to look at, but there's nothing inside of you. You're right, you're just an empty shell, a vessel for divine power. I'd take a fallen one over you a million times."

A flash behind icy eyes. A tightening of his jaw. He feels things, all right. Not pleasant things, not loving things, but my tirade wasn't to his liking.

Well, screw him.

"Rest," he finally says. "This might take a while."

"If you say so," I say, making my voice as cold as possible, to match the ice in him. I fold my arms under my boobs and sit back in the chair where he'd first dumped me. "I can't wait."

———

As time passes, my worry for the others grows.

Yes, I know I said I wasn't going to give a damn about them anymore. And yes, I am angry. Pissed as all Hell.

You're not worried, I tell myself. You're just curious to know what happened, what punishment they received, that's all. After all, you're busy enough feeling guilty and terrified about your curse, right? That should be taking up all of your headspace right now, together with the fear of whatever Heaven has in store for you.

Right.

Of course.

And it does, believe me. My self-loathing, the fear of myself, is taking up most of my mental capacity. It's a tortuous, never-ending cycle of self-destruction.

It's my scream. My scream kills. When has a scream ever killed people before? And why isn't any of these men scared of it?

God, I'm exhausted. The office is warm, the chair comfortable. Despite the adrenaline still pumping through my veins, my lids start to get heavy.

"Why haven't you gagged me?" I mumble as images flash inside my mind and sleep rolls over me. "To be on the safe side."

"There is no safe side," I think I hear Asa say before I sink deep into dreams.

Nightmares, not dreams. My nightmares are all real. They are memories of the last two incidents, and now I have a third one to add to the arsenal.

Just wonderful.

The images pummel me—men rushing at me, bullets and blades flying, death surrounding me, and then the feelings. The fear. The anxiety. The mind-numbing panic. And my scream shattering the world, snuffing out life just like that.

Favrash... Favrash... the voice whispers in my ear. *Remember them...*

The blond man is there, watching me, leaning on his staff, watching my every move—

"Frankie," a voice says very close to me, and my eyes snap open. "Wake up."

I flinch away from the handsome face bent over me, and that presses my hurt side to the armrest of the chair, which startles a cry out of me. "Don't touch me," I manage.

"Let me see that wound," he says.

I'm panting, bile in my throat, my stomach twisted in a knot, my hands sweating. I'm still caught in the nightmare, the memory, and I'm in real danger of puking on his boots.

"I said don't touch me!"

"I won't let you bleed out," he says, a crease etched between his brows.

"Why, will you be punished if you deliver damaged goods? Boohoo, poor angel boy. Will they take away your privileges? Your shiny sword? Will you have to stand in a corner up in the sky while the other angels spin around and giggle?"

"Angels don't giggle," he says stonily.

"Oh, I see, no sense of humor."

He's scowling at me. He has no right to look so gorgeous while glaring, and while he's being such a traitor. To sound so calm and rational while my heart is hammering its way out of my chest. "There has to be a first-aid kit in here."

I watch him limp away from me to rummage in the metal cupboards by the window, and see the shaft of a black arrow sticking out of his thigh. You wouldn't have thought he's wounded from the way he's been marching around, and from the amount of blood, it's serious.

Frigging angels.

Looks like they bleed red like the rest of us.

Good. Let him suffer, too.

He returns, crouches down beside me. "Here." His voice is gentle, some of the ice thawing. "Take off your top."

"You just want to see me naked," I snarl and it reminds me of Tir, and… and now I wanna cry. "Go away."

"Why won't you let me help you?" he snaps, frustration bleeding into his voice.

"Help me? like you've been helping me, pretending to like me, and all this time you were working for your own party? What did they promise you, huh? You all got promised a coveted prize. What was yours?"

"I don't…" He frowns. "I'm not sure."

Confusion fills his blue eyes, twisting his handsome face, and...

"Wait a minute. You don't know what you're doing this for?"

"I serve Heaven," he says.

"Bullshit."

More confusion. A hint of fear. "I'm doing this... to go back."

"Back where? To Heaven?"

"Yes." But he sounds unsure. He really doesn't know? Doesn't remember?

"Who are you? What are you?"

"Just... sit tight," he grinds out, getting back up. "And don't reopen that wound. There will be a decision soon enough."

"Fine. But no matter what you say, no matter if you like to think you're untouchable," I whisper, "a Heavenly angel, untouched by emotions... You're wrong. You do feel. Maybe gaining a human form has changed you. Or maybe you took over a human and that person is still in there?"

"Shut up."

I shake my head. "Asa... is it true there have been more like me before?"

"I don't know." Said through gritting teeth.

"Then find out. I know Heaven hasn't told you to dig into this, that you're a good little soldier, but... ask. For me. You owe me that much."

I don't get an answer from him, nor do I expect one as he turns his back on me. He won't do it. He's convinced he knows who he is and what he's doing, and I have my doubts, but at the end of the day, what does it matter?

I'm stuck here with him and honestly, I don't see a way out.

Unless you scream and kill him.

Jesus, Frankie.

I don't want to kill him, or anyone. I don't wish anyone's death, and here I am, a proven killer, a destroyer who then weeps like a coward over the destruction she's wrought.

But look what he's doing! How he treats everyone else!
Brain, shut the Hell up.
You're not helping.

9

FRANKIE

I fall asleep again at some point and come awake with the image of distorted faces and the sound of screams in my ears.

Thankfully the screams don't originate from me.

Even in the dream, I know that, and it's a relief.

Yawning, I rub my eyes and lift my head, wincing at the crick in my neck.

And find myself looking at a hot angel with icy blue eyes and light blond hair that's falling in unruly waves on his forehead. His broad shoulders draw my gaze next, his bulky biceps, his muscular chest that fills out the white, smudged T-shirt he's wearing to bursting.

It takes me that long a moment to remember I hate his guts.

And mine own, too, for my curse and my inability to stop fear from governing me.

It takes me another moment to realize that he's staring at me.

"What do you want?" I grind out.

"For you. Eat." He throws me a sandwich and a bottle of

water. They land in my lap. He probably got them from the vending machine down the hall.

I check out the sandwich. Ham and cheese. *Yum.* I wonder how long it's been sitting in the machine and how edible it is. "What about you? Don't tell me you feed on your own light and bullshit?"

His mouth twitches like he's about to smile, but he glares instead. "Eat."

I shrug and unwrap the sandwich. "This is probably carcinogenic. You know, long-life ham and cheese. Highly processed foodstuffs. White bread. Probably expired, too."

He grunts.

I take a bite and almost spit it out It is vile, just as I thought. "Looks like you need to get a haircut, soldier boy. It's about to fall in your eyes and impair your perfect vision." I wave with the sandwich. "Your hair grows fast, huh?"

He lifts his hand to shove it back. "I said, eat."

"I *am* eating. If I get poisoned, my death's on you. And speaking of death... What about the others? Any news?"

"I told you, I don't care what happens to the others."

"No, *I* said that. You only said that Heaven promised to eliminate them."

"And didn't."

"No, and that relieved you."

"You don't know what I felt."

"But you felt something."

"You're wrong."

"Am I?"

"What the Hell does it matter?" He stalks away from me and goes to check another closed door that probably leads into another office.

"Heaven can't provide you with any decent locking spells?"

He kicks at the door and curses. Then he rests a hand on it and bows his head, breathing hard.

"All right, now you're freaking me out." I get up, abandoning the half-eaten sandwich and the bottle of water on the desk. "Something has happened. Asa, what happened while I was asleep?"

He turns around and I notice instantly that a vein is ticking at his temple. His jaw works. "My orders are in."

"I missed the return of the snidey fluty voice?"

He blinks, pale brows arching. "What?"

"Never mind." I sigh, hold out my hands. "Put them on, then, sheriff, and take me away. But before we go, can I please at least get my phone call? Granddad is going to have kittens."

His brows stay up. "I'm not taking you anywhere."

I frown. "Come on, Asa. Don't mess with me anymore. Enough is enough. Please, let me contact my family. Kidding aside, they must be worried sick about me and I can't just wave my hands around and open a communication channel like you guys can."

"Are you deaf?" His hands clench into fists and his mouth becomes an unhappy line. "I said I'm not taking you away."

"And why not? If you have me, and you are Heaven's rep, why aren't you taking me away right now?"

"My orders are different." He looks definitely unhappy.

"You spoke to Heaven and they said... what, that I can stay here?"

He nods, a jerky dip of his chin.

"And you? Are you going back?" Something's off. It's too good to be true. "What exactly are your orders?"

"We continue as before."

"Come again? I mean, who? Me and you? Me, you, and the others?"

"All of us."

"Are you freaking insane?"

"We attend classes," he goes on as if I haven't spoken. "Do PE. Eat at the cafeteria. Pretend none of this ever happened."

"*Why?*"

"Heaven is in negotiations with Hell. We must remain inconspicuous while waiting."

"And what, let the bullies get on with their program meanwhile?"

"Nobody said anything about the bullies." A wicked glimmer enters his eyes before he turns away, presenting me with his broad back.

What was that?

"Well, thank God," I say slowly. "I mean, I'm happy for a chance to fight back the bullies, but you want to get back to Heaven, right?"

"Indeed." He seems to be struggling with something. Probably this situation. Hell, I'm still in such shock that I don't know what to say.

"Wait. Are you seriously going through with this?"

"What other choice is there? You can't run. Nobody can."

"This is it, then. We're all stuck here. And I'm not your prisoner anymore."

"Frankie—"

"I need to talk to my family. At least I can do that, right?"

"Nobody said anything about keeping you silent," Asa says. "You can speak to whomever you want."

"Gee thanks," I mutter. "So you can eavesdrop on my conversations? Something in his gaze shift, and I stiffen. Seriously? I thought everyone knew by now what I am."

"Nobody knows what you are," he says.

I take a step toward him. "It doesn't matter that you took me away from the others. You didn't win a thing."

"I will deliver you to Heaven," he grinds out, "the moment I am told to do so. You're still my captive."

"Open the door. I am getting out of here."

"You're coming with me."

"Am I? Where?"

"To the dorms."

"I don't have to be around you," I say stiffly. "I don't have to pretend to like you. So stay away from me."

"I can't."

"Beg your pardon?"

"I have to stick close, make sure no other assassins attempt to kill you."

"Or you mean, that I don't kill more people?"

His handsome face stony, he walks to the door and puts a hand on it. Light seeps from under his fingers and palm. "I have to keep you safe."

"I don't want your help or your protection. I don't care what Heaven says. Stay away from me or I'll gouge your eyes out. Just so we're clear."

"You're bloodthirsty," he mutters.

"And practically a demon, apparently, therefore vile and worthless, so hurry up and let me out before I lose my patience with you."

I'm not even joking.

At least my anger isn't dangerous, I think as he opens the door, turning to cast me a dark look. It swings outward with a creak and I long to step outside, soak in the fresh air. But I don't move.

"Come here. You stick by my side," he says, his voice a low rumble I feel in my bones. I shouldn't like it so much. It shouldn't send pleasant shivers through me. "We continue like before."

"Only I never stuck by your side before," I remind him, reaching for the phone on the desk because contacting my family is paramount and I won't be pushed around, not when he claims this is a truce. "And there's no way things can go back to how they were before. Not after I turned those men to ash and dust, and certainly not after your lies."

———

"Francesca, are you all right?" Granddad isn't much for endearments and cutesy nicknames, never was, but using my full name is a sure telltale sign of his concern. His voice is strained over the phone. "Did anyone hurt you?"

Out of sight, I place a hand on the bandage on my side that Asa applied and chew on my lower lip. "No, I'm good. How is the situation?"

"There was another incident, wasn't there?"

"Yes," I whisper.

I'm very aware of Asa watching me. He has closed the door and stepped closer to me. I turn and scowl at him, lifting my hand off my side and waving at him to move away.

Of course he doesn't. He props his hip against the wall, folds his muscular arms over his chest, and just... stares at me.

Not uncomfortable at all.

"Rumors are that there was an attack," Granddad says. "According to Juliette, there was shouting and many students ran to see what was going on, but all they found when they arrived behind one of the buildings, were piles of what looked like ash."

"Yes," I say again, my voice strangled. "We were attacked. Everyone was getting injured, trying to keep me alive, and I couldn't..." I draw a shaky breath. "I screamed."

He's silent for a few beats. "How many dead?"

I shake my head. "No idea."

He sighs. "Okay. Now, who is 'we' and 'everyone' you mentioned?"

I find myself chewing my lip so savagely I might draw blood. "Uh, just some guys I've become...friendly with."

"Franks. What did I say about keeping your distance until we figure this out?"

I wince. And I haven't even told him the best part yet, regarding who the guys are and what they were trying to do, but I don't want to be chewed out by Granddad right now, especially not in front of Asa.

"Anyway..." Granddad sighs. "We're at an impasse. Hopefully, Heaven will get its head out of its ass soon and lift the protective web over the College. I can't protect you like this, not the way I would like. I do know people in the College and have alerted them to the situation—"

"What people? Granddad? Whom have you alerted?"

"Friends," he says vaguely.

"I hate it when you do that. What friends? You have to tell me who to turn to if I need help, can't you see?"

"I can't tell you." His voice softens. "They will come to you if you are in need."

I want to yell at him that I was 'in need' just now, when I was carried away by one guy after another, but that would imply telling him more about the guys and Granddad isn't stupid. He'll put two and two together and come up with... five guys I shouldn't have been hanging out with in the first place. Not to mention the implications regarding my intelligence.

"Speaking of Heaven." I glance at Asa and then focus my gaze on the far wall that is covered in shelves stacked with folders. "I'm being guarded by an angel. "

"*Guarded.* You mean he's holding you prisoner?"

"He says we're supposed to just hang out and go to classes until Heaven decrees something else."

"Pass him the phone," Granddad demands.

"What? But Granddad, I—"

"I want to have a word with him."

"There's no reason, unless it is to tell him to fuck off!"

"Franks. Put the angel on the phone."

Sighing heavily, I hold out the receiver. "Asa, it's for you."

His pale brows rise. "Me?"

"Yeah, I'm as surprised as you are, trust me. I hope my granddad tears you a new one, but don't worry. If you're rude to him, I'll do it myself."

10

ASA

*N*issu *antadul saharsu sensan.*
Under the canopy of the sky, we will fight to the grave.

Gardar, zukesh asune asag, abad nili hedug.
Destroyer, disable the demon power, keep us safe.

Azas.
Let it be so.

I have her, ripped her away from the demonblood Houses to deliver her to Heaven with a bow on top. Raziel protocol is engaged, my mission accomplished.

It's over.

And then Heaven tells me to sit tight.

With her.

With the entire college full of irritating demonblood-pumped individuals.

Sit through classes. Breaks. Lunches. Mornings, afternoons...

Nights.

And now I have another angel on the line, a fallen one.

I could refuse the call. I don't answer to Barathiel

Evenstar, aka Francesca's grandfather and mentor. I don't answer to the fallen races or to anyone who isn't High Heaven.

But I take the receiver anyway.

I admit I'm curious to find out what Barathiel Evenstar wants to say to me.

"So you've taken my granddaughter," he says without preamble and I sit on the edge of the desk, trying not to roll my eyes. Angels don't do that. They are serene unless they are lethal.

"I have."

"Heaven told you to fetch and you did and then it told you to sit like a good boy."

I frown. "I don't get the reference..."

"Like a good dog," he clarifies.

"I'm not..." An image hits me—*sunlight on green grass, voices and laughter, and a white shepherd racing across the lawn, chasing after a thrown stick*—

"Now you listen to me, boy," Evenstar says and I have to blink several times for the image to completely fade—*how odd* —"you think you have this under control, you... What is your name?"

"Asariel," I breathe, "Asariel Nephal."

"Asariel. Listen to me. Make sure she's safe, you hear me?"

"Granddad!" she protests, narrowing her eyes at me—or the phone? "What are you doing?"

"Keep her safe. Those men who came after her, they will do so again."

"No way," I say, still stunned by the image of the dog and the lawn that had no business being in my brain. "The dome will keep any wannabe assassin out of the College."

"So you think. Every faction, every House, has people in the College. Do not assume that the danger is past, is that clear?"

"Crystal," I say, and stop.

Not an expression I would use. I'm not familiar with human expressions. That's more Tir's domain. That's...

I feel *weird*.

Being in the human world is screwing with my mind. Yeah, that must be it. I'm not used to it. No amount of studying could prepare me for the crudeness and shallowness of this place, the stupidity and pointlessness of all these people. The awful gravity, pulling me to the ground. The vile physical needs.

The unexpected, hard-to-control hints of feelings.

The strange feeling I've seen her before. Known her.

I can't wait to return to Heaven and its pure incorporeal joy.

Slender fingers wrestle the phone receiver from my hand and I blink at Frankie as she slams it to her ear.

"Granddad. Not cool, okay? I don't need his protection. I don't want him near me. What? No."

He's telling her that she needs all the protection she needs which I agree with—of course I can hear what he says, I'm a supernatural—and that the assassins may come back.

Of course I will guard her life. My orders are to deliver her to Heaven alive.

My contract says that. Only then can I go back to Heaven.

"Why, will you be punished if you deliver damaged goods?"

I frown.

"I know I'm stranded here," she's saying, gripping the receiver hard, her eyes glittering. Is that rage in them? Or fear? "I know you can't help me. Doesn't mean I need an asshole angel looking after me as if I'm a child!"

"These are special circumstances," her grandfather's tinny voice says through the receiver. "Take any help you can, Frankie. I'm serious. Anything to stop another incident while I try to communicate with Heaven."

Does he think he can get her out of here? A Raziel dome is impenetrable. Only Raziel himself can lift it and will only do so once the council has decided what to do.

Which is... one more unexpected thing to add to my list.

Why are they stalling? What are they waiting for? What is the confusion? Like she said, why not take her to Heaven right now and... do whatever it is they want to do with her?

What *do* they want to do with her?

Grabbing the receiver from her hand while she's still ranting at her granddad, I slam it down on the ancient set and haul her toward the door.

"Hey. Hey! What do you think you're doing?"

"I told you before. We're going to the dorms. We need to shower and sleep. It's back to classes tomorrow."

"Just like that? Seriously?"

"We have no choice," I say harshly, pulling her along. "Heaven decrees it."

"Screw Heaven," she grumbles.

"May the divine forgive you," I snap, "and save your soul."

"Whatever. Your Heaven isn't where I hope my soul will end up. Sounds like your Heaven is a giant military camp."

"You blaspheme a lot."

"Do I? What about free speech, huh? What about freedom in general? Let go of my arm."

I clench my jaw so hard my teeth grind together. I don't release her. I don't trust her not to take off running and my leg feels heavy.

The arrow. I have to deal with the arrow in my leg.

Damn. Never had to deal with a body before.

...sunlight dappling over dusty furniture, dust motes dancing in the air, and there's a house with a porch. A porch with a swing and...

"Asa. Hey." She snaps her fingers in my face and then takes a step back. "Asa!"

What in God's name happened? I don't remember releasing her arm. Don't remember her stepping out of the building while I'm still standing on the doorstep.

"What's wrong?" she asks.

"Nothing," I breathe, shaking my head to clear it—like a dog, I think, and the white shepherd streaks across my vision again, over the sunny lawn.

Why is it so vivid? It's as alive as any real memory.

"You're okay," she says. "So I'm going."

"Wait—"

She wiggles her fingers at me and takes off running.

I start after her but my leg drags. The pain can't be muted anymore. I have to get that arrow down, plug the leak.

I had guessed right. The moment she could, she ran from me.

But no, that's not entirely true. She stayed long enough to ask if I'm all right.

Why?

And what is going on with me?

Sleep. That's all. Lack of sleep and blood loss. I'm guessing this human body needs to keep all the crimson fluid inside instead of it leaking all over the floor, and it also needs sleep to sort through memories and thoughts. It's glitching, like a machine.

I'll find her. It's not like she can leave the grounds.

Nobody can.

Which reminds me that she's not the only one furious with me and I need to be on my guard. Assassins from an unknown source as well as four disgruntled emissaries—given that their Houses haven't killed them dead for their failure to capture and keep Frankie.

Just like my failure to do the same just now.

I hope they're dead... so they won't trouble me.

"I told you, I don't care about the others."

I frown.

"Is it true there have been more like me before?" she'd asked. *"Find out."*

It's none of my business, what she is, what she can do, and whether they've been more like her before.

Whatever happened to the others is of no consequence.

The others. Implying that we are a team.

We're not.

If they are alive, good for them and bad for me. I'd do Heaven's job and eliminate them, only my assigned task is only to keep her alive and like she said, I'm a good little soldier.

I'm Heaven's hand on earth and proud of it.

I *am* proud of it.

Still frowning, wondering why I don't quite feel it, I make my slow way toward the dorms.

———

It's afternoon, I note as I limp toward the dorms. Students are out and about—as if nothing monumental has happened, as if a girl hasn't reduced a team of assassins to piles of ash and Heaven hasn't closed off the campus from the rest of the world.

As if my mission wasn't successful.

As if my return to Heaven isn't all but guaranteed.

Such a selfish thought, I chide myself, passing by small groups of students who shoot me curious looks. Whispers fly as some of them notice the arrow sticking out of my thigh. A few guys laugh. Do they think it's a prank? Such a selfish, self-centered thought. What does the world care if you succeed or fail, if you return to your rightful place or remain stuck here, in this form, in this plane of existence?

My return to the Glory of the Divine.

That is what I long for.

To leave this heavy, cumbersome and demanding body behind, return to a state of free wandering and celebrating the light.

That's my end goal, and setting my jaw, ignoring the

burning in my leg, I open my stride. Students step aside to let me pass and I realize I'm giving everyone daring to stand in my way a glare. Why am I annoyed? Things are going well.

It's just the damn leg, I tell myself.

A lot of cursing happening inside my head since I landed here.

No matter. It's part of this elaborate disguise, this incarnation. Soon I'll be singing praises to the divine in the angelic choirs and all this will be behind me for good, it will be—

A woman's face, smiling, leaning close. Her smile is warm like sunlight. She reaches for me, her hand light on my face. "Come back," she says. "Do you hear me? Come back to us..."

I stumble, go down on one knee. Shake my head. A pain is hammering at the back of my eyes and behind my forehead.

What is this continuous bombardment with people and places—and dogs!—that I've never actually met or been? Are these fake memories another side-effect of wearing this body?

Of course it is. Must be. I wasn't warned this might happen.

It keeps throwing me off.

I mean, confounding me. Even these expressions seem to come to my mind out of nowhere. How does it work?

She said I'm wearing a body, but it never occurred to me that maybe... maybe it had belonged to someone before.

"Hey, man, you okay?" A hand lands on my shoulder. An unknown voice.

I shake it off and with surprising difficulty pull myself upright again, ignoring the random guy who dared touch me. "I'm fine."

"If you say so, dude. You're bleeding. Your leg, I mean. Did you know you have an arrow stuck in—"

"Yes."

"Oh. Better visit the medic. I heard you shouldn't try to remove arrows by yourself. You might bleed out."

"Get out of my way," I grunt and continue to the entrance of the dorms. I pause at the foot of the staircase, then start up the steps.

The campus medic should be kept out of this, as should the students not directly involved. Holding such a weapon is something we don't want the population to know about, magical creatures or not.

Discretion, Heaven advises. Always discretion. Let the world think that demonblood rules, that the angelic hosts aren't taking notice, but we're always there, ready to intervene and save the day.

Hopefully, most students missed the show, and if they didn't, they must be convinced they imagined it. That it was a game, a friendly encounter, a party, a small row.

Move along, move along. We're just students ourselves, nothing special, nothing different. Nothing to see.

I will assume that the demonblood Houses have instructed their emissaries to behave the same way. Everyone with great power prefers to keep its true extent under wraps from the masses. Everyone with great power only wants their opponents to know how great their power really is.

Basic facts.

Stopping halfway through the stairs, I reach back and break off the feather end of the arrow.

The fletching, a voice whispers in my mind and I throw the bloodied feathers away.

Shut up.

Black feathers on a black arrow.

All arrows shot during the attack were black.

Turning that little fact in my mind, I climb the rest of the stairs more slowly. The steps seem to sway and dip under my feet. The end of the staircase seems to be narrowing like a tunnel.

By Raziel's... swords. I slap my hand to the wall and find myself leaning against it, my lungs laboring to work. Black stars dance in my eyes.

Kind of pretty.

Need to get to the room, though. Can't stop here. This isn't good, somewhere deep inside I know that much. My body is trying to shut down and then it will be vulnerable here for the emissaries to kill.

I have to keep moving forward.

In my bag, I have a medic kit. Bandages. Antiseptic. Heaven has made it clear that magic alone can't keep this body functioning. It needs food and water, it needs warmth, it needs not to bleed itself dry.

Makes you wonder why they put me in such a weak vessel.

Shit. I stop again, lean against the wall, rest my face in the crook of my arm. Why am I questioning Heaven? They had to make me look like a student to get closer to her.

And why not just grab her and test her? Why this charade?

"Shut up!" I tell myself, anger warming my neck, clearing my head. "Shut up and do your duty."

Reaching the door to my room, I shove it open and stumble inside. Sanctuary, at last, a place to fix myself up and become functional again, sort through my thoughts, shut down any weird lingering feelings, wipe the weird images and sensations clean.

But... I'm not alone because, right... I forgot it's not just *my* room.

My shoulders tense when two people turn to look at me.

A man and a woman. He's tall and blond with pointy ears, she's small and pretty, her long blond hair caught in a ponytail.

Tir and Frankie.

Tir... is alive. And Frankie is okay.

Something inside me settles, something I hadn't realized was trembling.

"Tir," I say in greeting.

He glares at me.

"Oh, great, you're here," Frankie says, acid lacing her voice. "Yay."

Their anger doesn't matter. I just don't understand why my chest feels so light. As if a weight has lifted off me. What is this feeling?

I shove it away, shove all feelings away, and pull reason back inside my head.

This isn't a reunion of friends. I'm stepping into a den of vipers and can't let my guard down even for a second.

"Asa," Tir says. "Are you going to sleep here?"

I make my way to the bunk bed, reach for my duffel bag. Once I've taken this arrow out, "I'll spend the night here, yes. It's my room, too."

Frankie makes a sound, then says, "You will take out the arrow on your own?"

"Yes."

"And you'll sleep here?"

"I don't sleep," I say. "And I don't require help. You can continue... gallivanting if you like."

"Gallivanting?" Frankie echoes. "Are you for real?"

"Well, if we're having a truce, I'm going to bed," Tir says. "Some people may not need sleep, but these past twenty-four hours have been a bitch of a year."

11

FRANKIE

*W*hen I ran out of the administration building and away from Asa, my first thought was to check on the others. Just to check that they're alive, that whatever punishment their Houses chose to mete out didn't wreck them.

And then, I thought, I'll go and lie on my bunk and scream into my pillow, because what the Hell, world? Why am I even bothering? I have to cut this emotional link clean through. It's clearly one-sided and doing me no good.

Time to focus on my curse. Scream, yell, cry, yes why not? Then buckle down and do some more research—and decide what to do. Granddad said to stay put but can I? If I am a weapon, can I risk any of the four Houses claiming me?

Or even Heaven?

I have to find a way out of this College. Forget about living a normal life. That bird has flown. Deep inside, I've known it for years. Someone with such power doesn't get a pass.

But running through the campus I didn't see any of my gorgeous traitors, so I decide to go to my room anyway and scream into my pillow.

Only I find Tir there already when I enter and I swear, my

heart leaps in my chest, a fish in a glassy pond, breaking the surface, sending circles spreading over the water.

He's standing there, staring at me, alive and more breathtaking than ever.

It takes all I have not to rush and grab him in my arms.

But I don't.

I won't.

I plant my feet inside the room and stare back at him, panting with exertion and suppressed emotions.

"Frankie," he says, voice low and rough and I keep seeing him in my mind as he was the last time I saw him.

Lying on the ground, wounded and bleeding out, his face white, lips bloodless. I had his head in my lap, my hand on his face, the other on his chest, and I feel once more the despair in me when I thought he had died.

"Tir," I breathe. He's still covered in blood, hasn't had a chance to wash it off yet. His clothes are shredded and filthy, and yeah, his wounds are still in need of patching up. He has his medic kit open on his bunk, I realize, bandages spread out on the rumpled covers. Screw this. I start forward. "Let me—"

He lifts a hand, stopping me in my tracks. "I got this."

I nod, both stung and relieved. "Suit yourself."

He's not bleeding out anymore, at least. His fast healing has really kicked in, as I can see, the wounds in his neck and chest starting to scab over.

I could sink to my knees from the weight lifting off me. A paradoxical feeling. I should feel like jumping, or flying, but instead, I feel as if my joints won't hold me upright.

Locking my knees, I manage to keep my feet—and my head.

Remember what they did, Frankie. Remember you're not even friends, let alone anything more.

But I still need to know something. For curiosity's sake. That's all.

"Did they punish you?" I ask. "For failing?"

"I am unharmed," he says stiffly.

It's... so unlike Tir, this stiffness I've associated with Kass and Asa. A tightness in his face that looks less like pain and more like... sadness?

"That's not an answer," I whisper. "If they didn't hurt you directly, then they must have hurt what's important to you. Your family?"

He jerks as if burned. Curses under his breath. Stumbles over to his bunk and fumbles with the bandages.

Oh God.

There's no way I can't go to him. And yet, even as my steps lead me toward him, I know it's a mistake.

But screw that. We may not be entirely human but our emotions are. I understand love for your family. I'm scared to ask what exactly happened but I lay a hand on his forearm.

"I'm sorry," I say.

"None of this is your fault." His broad back straightens, the bandage clutched tightly in his fist. His profile is hard, a muscle ticking in his chiseled jaw.

I take a breath and plunge in anyway. "Did they harm—?"

"Or any of your business," he finishes.

Ouch.

"Thanks for the reminder," I breathe, lifting my hand off him and taking a step back. "I won't bother again."

I had wished so much for this to be real, for these charming, handsome men to be interested in me as a person, not as a means to something else. And I realize now that recovering from that won't be easy.

They were never mine, I remind myself. And it hasn't been all that long since I met them.

Still. My silly heart won't be appeased easily.

Your heart or your pride?

That squeeze in my chest is too deep for pride, unfortunately. I got invested.

Didn't take long.

No. It didn't. Then again these aren't random guys, remember? They were chosen for this task. Chosen to break your heart.

Damn.

And then Asa walks in.

———

Asa is limping, reminding me of Kass and making me wonder where he is and if he's okay. I'm instantly annoyed with myself, but really, I can't help it. Looks like I'll have to see them all alive and well before I can relax enough to call it a day.

Or a night, as it were.

I glare at him and open my mouth to ask if he's following me, then remember he's my roommate.

Again.

Which means, *oh crap...* that I should expect Kass to show up, too? Somehow I thought they'd all... move out or something.

I turn my back on Asa. He's wounded, but so what? I don't care. Let him deal with it on his own. The moment he walked in, the tension inside the room went through the roof, and I can feel my heart thumping against my ribs like a hammer.

And as happy as I am to see Tir alive and well, I can't let myself enjoy it any longer.

You got your wish, I tell myself. *He's fine.*

Without another word, I head for the door.

"Where are you going?" Asa grunts.

"Well, like Tir just told me, it's none of your business, but I'm going to check that the others are alive, Kass, Rook, and Ryu. After that, I'm done with all of you."

Tir draws a sharp breath as if he's about to speak, and Asa stills.

But the tension ratchets up a notch when the door opens and another man enters. Both Tir and Asa spin around, reaching for weapons.

"Kass?" I whisper.

But it's not Kass, and I realize my mistake the moment he steps into the light. It's Rook, and he's followed by Ryu, both of them bloodied and scratched, their clothes half-torn off their bodies. They stop and stare right back at us for a long moment.

Finally, I find my voice. "What are you two doing here?"

"We're bunking here from now on."

"Excuse me?"

"These are my orders, darling," Rook says.

"And mine," Ryu says, "green eyes dark and sharp. Doing our duty."

"Don't darling me," I seethe. "And duty? *Please.*"

"Come on, Frankie," Ryu says with that dark, raspy voice of his that does things to me. It shouldn't still be able to affect me so much. "We know you hate us. This isn't easy for us, either."

"Oh sure, play the martyr card," I mutter crossly. "Anyway, you can't stay, because... there aren't enough bunk beds."

"We'll make do." Ryu shrugs broad shoulders. "We're soldiers. we can sleep on the floor."

"Dammit," Rook mutters. "I really would prefer a fucking bed."

Ryu rolls his eyes. "Rook..."

"I'll bring my mattress over. I'm done sleeping rough and living like I'm already dead, you hear me?"

I'm gaping at them, haggling over where to sleep—in my room—when I don't know if I ever want to lay eyes on them again—

And then Kass enters, all but dragging his leg behind him, one hand clapped over his neck, dark blood seeping through his fingers, his eyes red and his fangs extended, though he only stops and gives us a look.

Jesus.

The feelings tangling inside my chest are choking me, and this is a terrible, terrible idea.

"No way, guys." I'm shaking my head and I can't stop. "No way are you all sleeping in here. No."

"We have no choice," Kass rasps. "Orders."

"Fuck the orders. Get out."

"I can fuck almost anything but those orders," Rook mutters. "Trust me."

I want to laugh, and I want to cry.

Enough.

Calling it a day right now.

Making my way to my bunk, I grab my satchel. "Then I'm out of here."

"You can't," Rook says.

I whirl about, pure murder in my heart. "What did you just say?"

"You have to stay where we can keep an eye on you."

"Or else?" I head for the door.

Kass moves to block my way, folding his arms over his broad chest, dark hair falling in his gray eyes.

I take a step back. "What is this? You said we're going back to normal and by that, you meant I'd be your prisoner. The prisoner of all five of you?"

They're silent, faces stony, eyes bleak.

Oh my God. I want to scream, and that's the last thing I should ever do again, ever.

Even in my pillow.

Holy shit.

My knees feel weak, the adrenaline seeping out of my system, leaving me shaky, and this last revelation knocking me completely off balance.

This is really happening. They are serious. These are their orders, and they will follow them to the letter. I have to live with five guys who betrayed me, who invited and then hurt my feelings, and are now only waiting for the first opportunity to kidnap me and deliver me to their superiors to do what they will to me.

I won't let them. No way. *It won't be for long,* I tell myself.

And I will escape from here.

Just play along for tonight, Frankie. There has to be a way out of this.

A prisoner of five gorgeous traitors, all sleeping in the same room as you.

This is nuts.

Turning back, keeping my mouth shut and my eyes dry, I throw my satchel onto my bunk and climb up the ladder, aware of their gazes on me like firebrands.

I can't think right now, can't figure this out beyond climbing onto my bunk and hiding under the covers.

I mean, there you are, Frankie. They are alive! And not in the process of dying, either. Wounded, sure, but obviously well enough to drag and make themselves comfortable here.

So you can stop worrying now and just be angry at them.

I snort and clap a hand over my mouth because that scream is still locked in my chest, behind my breastbone, trying to break free.

My book. I drag it toward me, plop it on my pillow, place my knives beside it.

I want familiar objects around me, things reminding me that there's goodness in this world, there is normalcy, there is my family who loves me, and that maybe, just *maybe* things will turn out okay in the end.

Ha. Fat chance. But hey, sue me. I need a minute.

Pulling the covers over my head, I grab a pen to write in the margins of the book, searching for a free space. After all the years of doing this, no matter how small my handwriting, how succinct my notes, it's getting full.

It's okay. For tonight I can indulge in an activity that has kept me sane for all my life.

I can pretend that beyond the flimsy tent of my blanket, I don't have five traitorous hunks keeping watch.

Keeping watch over the witch's bastardly daughter whose only power seems to be dealing death.

12

FRANKIE

rrows whistling past me, tipped with fire, acrid black smoke wreathing me as I run, trying to outpace the assailants...

A scream that seems to come not only from inside me, but also from everywhere, breaking trees and lampposts, felling men like a deadly wave...

I wake up with a gasp, my entire body trembling and jerking, as if I'm still running—and not lying on a hard bunk bed with my cheek mashed to the pages of my book, the pen still in my hand.

Shit.

Unclenching my cramped fingers, I let the pen fall on the pages. Slowly, carefully, I lift my head and wince at the gigantic crick in my neck.

Ugh.

I don't remember falling asleep and... the events of the previous day come rushing in, making me wince for a different reason.

I'm so screwed. The boys have camped in my room and

promised not to let me out of their sight. This is going to suck big time.

But right now... it's quiet. A strange quiet. There's an expectant feel to it that has the fine hairs on my arms rising.

Where are the Wonderboys?

With a groan, I throw the covers off me and sit up, turning to look around the room—and yelp, flinching back.

"What are you doing?" I gasp. "You scared the crap out of me!"

Five handsome guys are standing by the bunk, faces tense, gazes flashing like laser beams, muscular arms folded over their chests.

The Wonderboys in person.

Tir cocks his head to the side, a pointy ear poking out of his pale, chin-length hair. "You were having a nightmare."

"I wanted to wake you up but Asa didn't let me," Rook mutters, shooting the angel a scathing look.

"You were mumbling something about a wave," Ryu says, eyes narrowing a bit. "What was that about?"

"Shut up, Ryu," Kass says. "Dreams are just dreams. Are you okay, Frankie?"

I'm still staring at them but it's time to shake off the haze. I mean, what if they look good enough to eat, hair rumpled, jaws hard enough to cut steel, chests bare—*gah!*—and all but vibrating with protective macho energy?

"Well, it's none of your concern anymore, is it? If it ever was," I grumble, gathering myself, patting my hair down. It's like a rat's nest. "Your only duty is to keep an eye on me until it's time to hand me over. So off you go. Shoo."

They don't move from the spot.

Rook huffs what almost sounds like a laugh. "Go where?"

"I don't know? To piss, shower, fall off a cliff? Why do you ask me? I'm not your mother."

Kass chokes. He turns away and his big shoulders shake. I

stare at the back of his neck where those flaming black tattoos map his skin.

"Are you laughing at me?" I demand, gathering the covers to my chest. "What do I have...? Rook, tell me." When he only shakes his head, I turn to Ryu. "Why is he laughing? Do I have something on my face?"

Ryu's mouth twitches. "A note to yourself?"

"A note...?" Ink. From the book. I put a hand to my cheek, feeling my eyes go wide. "Oh crap."

"I'm sure it washes off," Tir says, stepping closer. "What is that it says? 'Ryu is the hottest man I've ever—'"

"Whatever." I roll my eyes.

"Wait, no, that's not what it says. 'If guilt was a lake, I'd be lying at the bottom with the fish—'"

"No," I gasp and scramble around, giving them my back. I need to get out of here.

What the Hell. These guys can read mirror script?

Elite troops. Probably trained in all sorts of insane things. They might look young, but that's the privilege and curse of supernatural races, isn't it? Well, one of them. They may look like they're twenty but could be hundreds of years old.

Would they tell me their real age if I asked?

Would they tell me anything real about themselves?

You shouldn't care, I scold myself. *What does it matter? It's not like you're going to be friends from now on. Yeah, for a hot moment it looked like there were feelings, but remember, it was all a ruse.*

You were well and truly played.

Beware of pretty, nice boys. They are thirst traps for stupid girls who don't know any better.

———

"Can I take a shit on my own," I ask, one hand on my hip, the other holding my body wash, "or do you have to shadow me in the bathroom, too?"

"I'll stand outside the door," Asa says, "if you need to take a shit. That's the time when your guard is down, I have to make sure nobody takes a shot at you while—"

"Fuck you!" I wave my bottle of body wash at him. "Fuck you."

He lifts a brow.

"Quite metaphorically," I add.

His other brow lifts too. "I thought you only wanted to take a shower. Aren't the toilets apart?"

"Go away!" I stomp into the girls' showers with my towel and close the door. "God!"

It's so weird to have them hound my every step, and it's only the morning of day one! How is this going to work out without me screaming my head off and killing them?

Though right at this moment, I'd gladly wring Asa's neck.

And everyone's. They kept watching me as I'd climbed off my bunk with my shampoo, conditioner, and shower gel, my towel draped over my shoulder, as I hunted for the shoes I apparently ditched at some point last night from on top of my bunk—I honestly don't recall—and put them on.

Their eyes were on me as I started out the door.

And then Asa got in my way and asked me where I was going. Got his answer, which for the record wasn't formulated very politely. Followed me here.

I'm still fuming at the thought that they won't leave me alone for five seconds. In theory, it sounds bad. In reality, it's even worse.

Another girl is already under the spray. She looks vaguely familiar, though honestly, every person looks different when naked and with their hair slicked back with water in the showers.

She turns her back to me and that's fine with me.

I make my way to a stall, placing my various bottles of cleansing liquids on the floor, hanging my towel on a peg, and pulling off my filthy, bloodied clothes. *Ugh.* Can't believe I slept in them—and I try hard not to remember that most of the blood on me came from Tir as he lay dying.

But he's not dead.

So stop thinking about him.

I hiss a little as I pull off my blouse and peel off the bandage that's a little stuck to the wound in my side. I examine the gash.

Doesn't look like it will need stitches. It's scabbing over already. But hey, would you look at the black and blue bruising all over my torso and arms? I guess rolling in the dirt and being slung over muscular shoulders gives you some serious-looking bruises. I look like I was used as a punching bag by someone.

Awesome.

I finish undressing, hang my clothes, and turn on the spray, waiting for the water to warm up before stepping underneath.

It feels good to let the warmth wash over me, seep into me. I bow my head, let it drench my hair. My scalp feels itchy with grime. And then I remember the ink on my face.

Pouring some body wash into my palm, I scrub at my cheeks furiously. My words, my private words of guilt and shame and anger, stamped on my skin for anyone to see. It's unacceptable. A horrible feeling. Feels like a violation but nobody is to blame. I should be more careful where I lay my head.

Or lay in general.

You know what they say, lie in the bed you made? That's me right now. Sure, I didn't choose my curse but I sure lost control of it a few times, and that's on me.

The guys figuring out what I am? That's on me.

And what, should you have left them to die for you? To die not even knowing that you were indeed what they feared?

Something in what I just thought strikes me as... off. What was it? Wait a minute...

If they didn't know for sure I was the one they had to capture... then why were they willing to die for me?

Something in their contracts most probably, I tell myself.

And let's be realistic here, the assassins were after me but they were not discriminating. They were shooting arrows and shuriken at all of us. They were just trying not to be killed.

Then why do I keep seeing in my mind's eye these five guys putting themselves in front of me, dragging me behind them, doing their best to keep me safe?

The contract. I return to that. Something about their contract and the possibility of me being the one.

Right.

Nothing else makes sense.

I soap my body, then turn into the spray. Research. I have to go back to that. Would it help at this point? And I still have to do laundry, do my homework and eat. My stomach growls and a hunger pang hits me.

Yeah, eating would be good. Might help my brain to work better.

None of those necessities have vanished while all of us almost died and then became deadly enemies. They only gathered, waiting for me. Hey, even if your friends abandon you, laundry will always be there for you.

Laundry and the Wonderboys, apparently.

I still don't know how they were punished. Apart from guessing they hurt Tir's family somehow, I know nothing about it.

And their injuries. Did they manage to disinfect and patch themselves up okay? Don't they need the college medic to look at them?

Franks, stop it.

Grabbing my shampoo, I breathe out, trying to center

myself. I feel scattered to the winds. I feel as if the water could wash me down the drain. I don't know who I am, what I'm doing. Everything feels out of my control and it's scaring the shit out of me.

Just the day before yesterday, I thought I could get to the bottom of this, find a solution, go back to my family.

Now it all seems impossible.

Outside the door, Asa is waiting. I don't want to face him, or anyone right now. I need five minutes to myself.

So I take my time, washing and conditioning my hair because I haven't done it in ages and I need to buy some time— time alone, to be able to think.

Because having all these hunks around me is frying my brain.

These assholes, I mean.

Yeah, that's what I meant.

Rinsing out my long hair, I run my fingers through it to detangle it. Maybe I should trim it. Cut it, shave it off, dye it black or blue to match my torso, to match my morose thoughts—

"Frankie?" a male voice says very close to me and I almost jump out of my skin. "Frankie, are you okay?"

I give a very undignified squawk and scramble to cover myself up with my hands. "What are you doing? These are the girls' showers!"

Ryu opens his mouth, then forgets to close it for a long moment. His gaze skims over me, then returns for a slower, more leisurely perusal.

"Ryu!"

"What? You were taking too long." His brows draw together. He's still staring at the general area of my chest, even though my arm is forming an impromptu bra, my other hand covering myself up between my legs.

"Get out!"

"Wait…" He reaches for me and this time he's looking lower. "You're hurt. Who did this to you?"

"Oh, you want to play?" I turn my back to him and grab my towel, wrapping it around myself, gathering the remnants of my tattered pride. "Play at caring? No, wait, I know. It's your duty to make sure I'm okay. Well, rest assured, kitsune, I'll live."

"Frankie." He makes the mistake of putting his hand on my shoulder.

I whirl about, shove him off. He stumbles, a funny, stupefied expression on his face, and barely avoids landing on his ass. "Don't touch me," I hiss. "I don't want any of you touching me ever again. Is that clear?"

"But we're supposed to—"

"Watch over me. Fine, then, watch all you want, but if you touch me again, I'll break your hand. Got it?" God, I'm so angry at him. And shouldn't find him cute when he's gawping at me like that. "And where is Asa? I thought he was the one standing guard outside."

"He's off on Heavenly business." Ryu rubs at his chin, his stubble rasping distractingly under his fingertips. "He had to talk with Raziel."

"Raziel? The archangel?"

"What can I say. You're our VIP guest. Only the best for you."

"For me? Just… get out!"

He bares his teeth at me and snarls like an animal, making me flinch, then he opens his hands and walks backward with a sharp grin. "You look so pretty when you're angry. It brings out the animal in me."

He's so confusing. I watch until he reaches the door and steps outside.

Finally.

I turn around and find the other girl watching me with big eyes. "Are you all right?" she asks in a tiny voice.

"Fine," I grind out.

"If you want, I can go denounce the guy to the dean—"

"No. I said it's fine." I sigh, soften my anger because she's being nice. "He's just teasing me."

"If you say so," she mutters and turns back to her shower.

She seems sweet. The first sweet person I meet in this College apart from my cousin, but I can't afford to try and make friends.

Speaking of my cousin, I need to see her, talk to her... find out how much she knows about me. The illusion Ryu sent yesterday to pull information out of me—he really is a bastard —got me uneasy and confused. I need to know what the real Juliette knows and thinks about me.

If she mistrusts me.

If she knows what I am capable of.

If that changes anything for her.

Which is... weak on your part, Franks. At this point, you should only hope she knows nothing and suspects nothing and is therefore not involved in any of this crap that could place her life in danger.

Right.

Dripping, still wrapped in my towel, I grab my things to go, juggling all the bottles and getting the bundle of my clothes wet. I march out the door...

And come face-to-face with Kass.

13

KASS

*T*his situation is getting damn ridiculous. Babysitting Frankie. *Merda.*

That should go on my resume. Babysitting a hot but dangerous-as-fuck girl who has just stepped out of the showers... only clad in a small towel and a glower that could put Asa to shame, but...

Small.

Towel.

Her tits, fuck... and her legs. Her waist. Her hips. And that mouth...

Damn, I'm so hard right now I could drill through steel with my dick.

"You," she says and that glower is now on me, turned to the max. "What is going on? First, there was Asa, then Ryu, and now you. Are you playing musical chairs or what?"

She's really pissed.

Then again so am I. "*Porca miseria,* do you think I like this any better than you do? You left so fast we're still in our fucking underwear and the whole point of this fucking exercise is to fly under the fucking radar until new fucking orders come in."

Her brows have gone up. "Don't limit your swearing on my behalf," she mutters as she resumes walking, heading toward our common room. "Do your worst."

My hands are clenched into fists. I limp past her and open the door of the room. "It's not funny."

"You're acting as if this is my fault," she whispers, her small chin lifting as she brushes by me to enter, her vanilla-and-cake scent wrapping a band around my chest—and yeah, my dick too, dammit.

I'm pissed at her, but I don't even know why. This is all on me. I failed Brody, failed myself, and wanting her so badly is the cherry on top of this epic disaster.

My dick is laughing at me, *il bastardo,* twitching inside my briefs. At least I managed to throw on a pair of sweats and a T-shirt before dashing out of the room, despite what I just told her.

Though 'dashing' is too grand a word for the sorry limping thing I've got going and the whole situation is getting me pissing mad.

I follow her into the room and run my hands through my hair, trying to center myself and not start punching walls—or other people. I stumble against a T-shirt and a pair of sweats lying about on the floor and I lose it.

"Tir!" I snap. "Pick up your goddamn things for once! If I fall and break my neck because of you, I'll hunt you all the way to Hell and use my Bitch on you until it breaks."

"Damn, calm your tits, *abesh.*" Tir doesn't deny the clothes are his. He ambles over but makes no move to gather them. "This isn't your goddamn room only, you know. We have rights, too."

"Rights?" I reach for him and he slaps my hand out of the way. "You're a walking disaster, motherfucker."

"And you think you did any better? No. Or maybe you decided you're our boss? Also no."

"Will you two shut your traps?" Ryu grunts. "Some of us have a frigging headache from your snoring all night."

"I don't snore," I growl. "And—"

"Aw poor baby, you have a headache?" Tir's smirk turns into a sharp blade. "Of course then we will shut up and let you rest, won't we, Kass?"

"All of you, shut up," Asa says, zipping up his duffel bag and straightening. "You're acting like children. Get ready for class and stop this farce."

"And since when are you our daddy? Who asked for your opinion, huh? It's your fault we're all prisoners here!"

Great, we're all pissed.

"Break it off, dimwits. It's dick measuring, Asa. Damn all this testosterone." Rook is rubbing his cock through his sweats but his eyes are on Frankie. "What's a man to do, right, darling?"

"Don't darling me, Rook." Frankie is glaring at us. "Take your bickering and fighting out of here. I won't have it in this room. This is a place to rest and study and sleep."

I see on Rook's face that he wants to say something— probably add sex to her list, but that would be stupid, and not only because she's angry. We still have our missions, but now they've changed.

None of us dispute her claim. None of us tell *her* to pack her things and go. After all, our mission is to be with her. And she's right, dammit. We have to stop fighting.

Minchia, she's sexy when she's angry. She's sexy no matter what she does.

What the fuck, brain? Just stop.

"Nobody said I have to obey *your* orders," Tir says, returning her glare, and turns around to limp to his bunk—still without gathering his clothes from the floor. "Only that I have to watch over you."

"And that gives you permission to throw your stuff all over the place?" Ryu snarls. "You have no integrity."

"Ooh, duty man is back." Rook guffaws. "I'm gonna need booze for breakfast, methinks. I need to be drunk for this."

"Really?" Ryu turns on him. "Want to knock yourself out? My fist can get the job done faster."

Whoa.

"What in all the saints' names is wrong with you?" Asa demands, striding to the middle of the room and placing himself between Ryu and Rook. "Have you all gone mad? Is it that hard to get along for a while?"

"Easy for you to say," I mutter. "You seem to have won this battle, while the rest of us are merely waiting for the other shoe to drop."

"I haven't won any battle!" Asa rubs a hand over his face. "I don't even know what this..." He lets out a breath. "Just like you, I'm following orders. I haven't tried to stop you from sleeping here together—"

"Yeah, good luck with trying to stop us," Ryu grumbles.

"—so would you stop being goddamn dicks about it?" Asa finishes.

And blinks.

"Do you sing God's praises with that mouth, cherub?" Rook gives him an appraising look. "Hiding a naughty boy behind that angelic face, are you? I knew it."

"I'm not a cherub," Asa says, "I'm..."

"Yeah, you're *what* exactly?" It's Frankie who asks him this and we all stare at her. She's been quiet all this time, still wrapped in her mini towel—I have to get her a bigger one or I'll have to hang it on my hard-on—and she's holding her clothes in front of her like a shield.

Asa frowns, something like uncertainty flitting behind his blue eyes. "I'm a seraph but..."

"But?" Rook gestures encouragingly. "Elaborate if you please."

"A seraph? But that's a high angel," Frankie mutters. "Why would they send a seraph here?"

"I'm going to class," Asa says after a pause. "And you'd all better start getting ready because Frankie is going to class, too, and if you want to be around, you'd better keep up."

What an ass of an angel. My fists are itching to hit him and sooner or later things will come to a head, I just know it.

Five guys and a girl crammed together in one room, doing everything together?

This thing would go off like a bomb even if we weren't supernatural creatures from opposing camps, all fighting to get the girl, somehow.

We're gonna level this place down if we're not careful.

The way I feel right now, might as well get it over it and burn in the crash like that fucker, Icarus, who he fell into the waves while reaching for the sun and knowing he was doomed already.

———

We're all way too slow getting dressed. We all move with grunts and groans like old men. Fast healing means we're not dead but deep wounds take their good old time to knit and bad bruises get worse before they get better.

Even Frankie moves slowly. She retreated up on her bunk to get dressed, demanding we look away, and I'm making an effort, only to find the others staring at her shamelessly.

Sadly, there isn't much to see, only her back where she's sitting and cursing, and wait, that's not good. Something's wrong?

"Frankie?" I ask. "Wait... Is that a bandage?"

"She's wounded," Ryu says.

The words echo inside my head. Time seems to slow, and yet suddenly we're all crowding the side of her bunk bed.

"Frankie? Show me that wound," I demand. "How bad is it?"

"Hey." She flinches back. "I said no peeking!"

"If you're hurt, we have to know," I insist.

"I'm fine. I told Asa already."

"You knew she's hurt and said nothing?" I turn to the angel, incredulous. "Want the imprint of my fists in your teeth, angel?"

"I bandaged her," he says, eyes narrowed. "I was supposed to deliver her to Heaven. At what point are you suggesting I could have told you about it?"

"Last night? Today? You knew about it and still said nothing? *Che cazzo, cherubino?*" I was distantly surprised by the jolt in my chest when I saw the bandage, the thought of her in pain, harmed, perishing twisting like a blade in my gut.

"Calm your fucking tits," Rook says. "We need to shut this down. Asa and Frankie are right, we can't keep bickering. It's been a long week. Let's just organize ourselves, yeah?"

She's staring at us over her pale shoulder, eyes huge in her face. "Meaning?"

"At least one of us is going to be with you at all times."

Her brows climb up. "What? no way."

"This isn't a negotiation."

"Are you suggesting I trust you near me?" I snarl. "Are you insane?"

"Well, apart from Asa, the rest of us do need to sleep, piss and shit," Rook says, and fuck, he has a point. "We were all told to be with her at all times, but that's simply not possible. We have to take shifts. So unless you have any more revelations for us, angel, like you shit out perfumed air and rainbows or, I dunno, you can sleep with your eyes open, I think it's time we put our heads together and thought of a way to arrange her protection."

———

Rook's idea is solid but implementation is the issue. None of us agree on the times. In fact, none of us agree to simply let her out of our sight for longer than it takes her to shower or take a piss, so that's a problem.

Also, halfway through our shouting match, she grabs her bag, shoots us all a glare, and marches out of the room.

Leaving us to scramble after her, still half-clothed and unprepared.

This isn't fucking good.

Minchia.

All this fucked-up mess, and for what? The reward promised to me could be snatched out of my hands at any moment, and it's already not going well.

Brody, I'm so fucking sorry.

I failed.

I failed you twice now and it's fucking killing me.

However, not all hope is lost. This isn't over yet. I'm going to fight for you.

Asa and Ryu are already striding out, following Frankie. Tir is having some trouble with bending over to slip on his sneakers, where he's sitting on his bunk, but though he's cursing and his face is twisted with pain, he's about to follow the others.

Which leaves me and Rook.

For some reason, he hasn't fucked off with the rest of them and is instead watching me, not so covertly.

"Listen... Your Bitch... that was your whip, right?" Rook asks. "Just checking."

I sigh. "Yeah."

"Hm…"

"You didn't stay back to ask me about what you already know. So what do you want?" I mutter.

"Waiting to see if you'll make it out of here. Can you even walk?"

"What the fuck are you on about? I just accompanied Frankie back from the showers. I can walk just fine."

He twists his long black hair back in a knot, tying it up somehow, folds his arms over his chest, and leans against one of the bunk beds, as if he intends to stay there until I move and prove him wrong.

What's his deal, huh?

How does he know that my hip is agony, my leg is stiff, and my knee is a mass of pain? I'm pretty damn sure I have a good poker face.

Nothing to do but give him the show. I push off the wall and yeah, my leg almost gives out from under me but I manage to keep upright. "Happy?"

"Why, are *you*?"

"Fuck off, Rook."

"You lost something," Rook says quietly, too perceptive. "It hurt you."

"Shut up. As if I was the only one to lose something. Didn't you?" Suddenly I need to know. "What did the House of Fire punish you with?"

"Hell, you mean? Let's call things by their names. House of Fire makes it sound like a lofty neighborhood full of mansions at the top of a hill. Hell is a filthy dungeon where you go to die."

"I heard some regions of Hell are beautiful, if you're into lakes of acid and rivers of Sulphur and shit."

He makes a disgusted noise. "Forget about Hell."

"Fine. Answer me, then. What did they take from you this time?"

"Opportunities," he snaps, "that's what. Now listen to me

Kass, you won't heal unless you draw from both sources you need. Sex and blood."

"I can't. Besides, this isn't from yesterday's fight."

"Oh? It certainly got worse."

Can't deny that, so I settle for a scowl as I make my slow way to the closet, doing my best not to limp too badly. "Why don't you run along ahead? I'll change my own diapers and come find you."

"Touchy, too."

"*Too?*"

"Stubborn *and* touchy."

My teeth are grinding so hard my jaw aches. "Fuck you."

"You know you need blood and sex to heal. That hip and the bite on your neck are no good."

"You telling me," I grumble.

"So what are you waiting for?"

I slowly pull back my lips, showing him my lengthening canines. "*Figa, mi hai rotto i coglioni.* Are you offering blood and sex? Just so I get this straight. Do you volunteer?"

"I bet you just insulted my ancestors but know what? Fuck my ancestors. And no, I'm not offering, Kass. Can't afford to give you sex energy I need for myself right now. See? We're not buddies. You can relax."

"Fuck you, if you think I can relax—"

"You need a blood donor, at the very least, man."

I turn to the closet, open it, grab some clean clothes. Note that the other shelves are now taken, but not with Frankie's clothes, probably still in her bag, but guy clothes. Rook's, or Ryu's.

"What's the matter, vampire?" Rook calls out. "Don't you like sex?"

"And don't you have anything better to do?"

"I could set your pants on fire. Would that help you change any faster?"

Still with my back to him, I slowly pull off my ruined shirt and let it drop to the floor. Fuck, I think I managed to bruise every single muscle in my name. Abrasions on my side and stomach from when I fell during the fight burn. I pull on the clean shirt, gritting my molars.

I start on the buttons of my pants. "Won't you take a fucking hint, Rook? Just go."

"You need to get laid, Kass."

"I can't," I grind out. "I find it... hard."

"Pun not intended, I assume."

"*Vaffanculo.* Just... fuck off."

Isn't it ironic? That my power is to give pleasure. I am actually part incubus, sex demon, and yet sex is an open wound for me.

That I need it and yet don't want it.

Sometimes the things we need and the things we want are different. Sometimes life fucks us over in a thousand different ways and we're left to pick up the pieces without understanding what happened.

"You know, I could make an exception for you." He sounds... pensive. "I like what I see. I'll make you come so hard you won't know what hit you and—"

"Shut. Up!"

"I see how it is. Poor vampire," Rook says. "Let me see if I got this right. Can't get anyone interested in your dick, is that it? Being part-demon is a woeful thing. Now let me tell you about myself. I'm a shax demon, incubus through and through, and I draw on others' energy to live. I'm a kind of sucker too. But I'm scarred and look like a beast. Now tell me more about your woes, pretty vampire. I'm dying to hear about how unfair your life has been to you."

The muscles of my back lock. Black anger burns in my chest. For Brody. For myself. For this leech of a demon who won't just go the Hell away and leave me in peace for one minute.

"If you're done telling me what a failure I am," I mutter, letting my pants fall, the scarring on my thigh and ass in full display, "then don't let me keep you, incubus. Go fuck someone and leave me the Hell alone."

14

FRANKIE

*M*y left bra strap is twisted, digging into my shoulder, and I think I've put on my tank top the wrong way. That's what you get when you get dressed as fast as you dare on top of your bunk with five hot men observing you.

Worst of all? I wanted their gazes on me. I wanted to turn around and let them look their fill, see their eyes darken with desire, see how much they want me.

If they still want me.

I'm furious with myself for my weakness when it comes to them.

And annoyed with their bickering as if I wasn't there, as if I'm some... *thing* they need to guard, snapping at one another when at some point I'd hoped...

Yeah, back to that. Your silly hopes and dreams.

Wake up, Frankie. It's about time.

I just... desire them. Can you desire someone you're supposed to hate?

I need to find Juliette.

There are things you can only discuss with your bestie, and

that's her. My sister, cousin, friend. Only, I don't know how much I can tell her. It's imperative to find out what she knows.

Only I currently have three determined clingy men on my heels.

I turn around and plant my hands on my hips, my backpack thumping on my shoulder blade. "Stop."

They come to a halt, confusion flashing over their handsome faces. They are so hot, damn them. I'm stuck with five supermodels who also happen to be experts in killing and who are ready to kill one another for the privilege of kidnapping me.

Go me.

"What's the matter?" Tir asks. His hair is tucked behind his pointy ears and he still has blood caking the lobes and tips where his jewelry was ripped off by the bullies what feels like years ago but is only a few days.

"The matter? The matter is that I'm not interested in sharing classes with you. Any of you. I'll change my schedule to be in classes with my cousin."

"If you do that, I will do the same," Tir says, matter-of-factly.

"Me too," Ryu mutters.

"I go where you go," Asa declares.

As if that wasn't enough of a nuisance, Rook appears, followed by Kass who's limping pretty badly—but I won't worry about him, like I said.

"What's going on?" Rook asks.

"We are changing our schedule to match Frankie's," Tir says.

"Well, obviously," Rook says. "Kass!" He turns back to the vampire who's making his way to us, his jaw clenched. "We're changing our schedule to match Frankie's."

"Got it," Kass says.

I stare at them, half-exasperate and half... I don't know what

I feel. As if I'm about to start laughing. "All five of you want to be in classroom with me and my cousin?"

"That's right," Kass says.

"Why?"

"To keep an eye on you." Rook sighs. "Wasn't that clear by now?"

"You've only said it about a hundred thousand times already, but what for? What do you think I will do?"

"We have our orders," Kass says quietly.

I gaze at their handsome, determined faces. I don't know if to scream or laugh or cry.

"Stubborn pigheaded men." And yes, I said that out loud. "Fine, do whatever you want. Can't stop you, can I?"

Turning in my heel, I start toward the administration office and they follow me, like ducklings imprinted on me, or like the rats led by the Piped Piper.

I shiver. That fairytale didn't end well...

———

"Miss Seymour..." The mousy, mustached secretary wipes his forehead with a white cloth handkerchief which he then stuffs into one of his pant pockets. "We can't just change your schedule around to fit that of your cousin."

"Sure you can," I say.

"And ours, too, pretty please," Rook says.

The secretary squints at my harem of men. "I beg your pardon? Like I said, we can't just—"

"If you need authorization," Ryu says, just call. "It's paramount that you get it done today."

"It's paramount that you all sit in the classroom with Miss Seymour and her cousin?" He blinks. His moustache trembles. "It doesn't make any sense. Why—"

"That, my friend," Tir says, stepping forward and placing his palms on the desk, "is above your pay grade."

"Um..." The secretary's gaze skitters from Tir to the rest of us. He gulps. "Really?"

I want to laugh. I feel awful because I'm sorry for him.

"Guys," I say. "Stop scaring our secretary. Tir... Give him some space."

"You're no fun, *elenyi*," Tir rumbles but surprisingly he does as I ask.

"It's not that difficult," I tell the secretary, "surely."

"Well, it is actually quite complicated," he protests, "to move around everyone's schedule for..." His mouth closes. "Um."

I turn to see what he's looking at and find Asa's death glare on him.

Also, Ryu is playing with a knife, twirling it like a star with his fingers. Where did he get a knife?

Son of a bitch. That's one of my knives, the little thief. "Ryu," I start.

"Fine," the secretary says, "I'll change your schedules. Let me find out which of the classes your cousin is attending and I'll change all of you. Please, leave me alone."

"We're not going to hurt you," I say.

That's when I notice Tir checking the tip of an arrow with his finger, a manic gleam in his green-gray eyes.

Dear God.

The secretary curses softly, rummages through papers, knocking over a thankfully empty mug. Then he starts tapping on his computer keyboard, his eyes darting from the screen to us and back.

"Guys," I mutter, "take it down a notch, will you?"

I have the urge to snicker and I throttle that urge instantly. This isn't funny. We aren't buddies. Scaring off this poor man isn't cool.

Eventually, he looks up, his hands pausing on the keys. He's sweating. "Done. You are all doing core courses, so that was simple enough, though you still haven't chosen your electives." His voice is practically a squeak. "Meanwhile, I will have to ask the Dean to sign off on this."

"That is all right, mouse-man," Asa says, and I turn to him, my brows lifting. "Go on and ask the leader of this institution. May God's Grace guide you."

Sometimes, I swear...

We're all gaping at Asa.

"I'll be damned," Rook says. "I thought your claims of being a seraph were a steaming pile of bullshit, to be perfectly honest, but then you go and say things like that and make me doubt my bullshit detector."

I agree with that, though... "Electives?" I mutter. "Nobody mentioned electives."

"Yeah," Ryu says, still twirling my knife, "it seems we should choose between languages and arts to improve our cultural knowledge. Never thought we'd get the time to choose, let alone follow through with extra classes."

"Of course. You were supposed to suss me out, grab me and go." I fold my arms under my boobs. "Get in and get out. Like a take-out service."

"Take-out doesn't work like that," Rook says. "Or so I'm told." He frowns. "Was my intel wrong?"

"Wait..." I turn to stare at him. "You're studying the human world?"

A shrug of powerful shoulders. His expression is... sheepish? And mulish. How many animals can he pack in one expression? "So what if I am?"

"Why?"

"Curious, that's all. It's a fucking crazy place. One I'd love to live in one day. So..." He props his hip against the desk. "Our schedules?"

"But they have to be approved and signed off first by.... the dean..." The secretary gestures at the printer where a sheath of papers is being spat out.

"Well." Rook snatches one. "Make copies for us, will you? We might as well start while you wait for the okay."

"...sure." He clicks a few keys. More papers are spat out of the printer.

"Or maybe we can just call the dean to come sign," Asa says. He doesn't budge from his spot but I swear his eyes are burning like stars. "Now."

"Of... of course." The secretary gets up, grabs the papers from the printer, and scurries away, glancing over his shoulder the whole time. Three doors open out from the office, one of them black with a silver symbol on it. He pushes it open and disappears behind it.

"What the Hell, guys?" With a sigh, I turn on Asa. "Are you trying to give the man a heart attack? Easy on the threatening auras, okay?"

Asa frowns. "I don't have a threatening aura."

"Sure, buddy." Ryu slaps his back. "Whatever you say. I, for one, like the way you glare down your nose at everyone."

"... I do not."

"You look about to murder everyone in the room," Tir says. "I've tried to copy the look but it must be something you train at, I guess. Up in Heaven."

Asa turns that death glare on the fae. "Certainly not. We only sing God's glory—"

He stops as the black door opens again and a woman steps into the office. She's dressed in a power suit, matching black jacket and pants, and sensible heels. Her face is smooth, her eyes dark like mine, her reddish hair swept back in a chignon.

Her age and magical race are undetermined.

"Ms. Deveroux," I whisper. "The dean."

"That's me," she confirms, her dark eyes cool as they stop

on me, then move over the guys. "Mr. Adams, our secretary, tells me I should sign off on all of you sharing your classes. Is that correct?"

"I somehow thought the dean would be a man," Ryu breathes, leaning back a little, giving the dean a not-so-subtle once-over.

"Biased much?" I mutter, annoyed, and wait... Am I annoyed because he's checking her out?

Not only, I decide, though, to be honest, even knowing she was a woman—she's the friend Granddad mentioned—I was still kind of startled to see her come out of the office. Stereotypes are damn powerful. I need to work on that.

"Now why should I sign..." She trails off as she properly takes us all in. "Oh. It's you lot."

This time I snort a little. Can't help it. It's the annoyed expression on her face, combined with the sight of the guys lounging about the office, working hard at looking bored but actually kind of smug.

Ridiculous.

They are kind of ridiculous and I shouldn't like it.

"Fine, I'll sign." She has the bunch of papers in her hand. The secretary is peeking through a crack in the black door. "I only ask that you please stop intimidating Mr. Adams, all right? He's a fine secretary and it's not easy to find anyone willing to work in magical academies these days."

Asa inclines his head. "That's acceptable."

"Hey, who died and made you our boss?" Tir mutters, shooting a glare at Asa.

"Don't you agree with my terms, Mr. Verdell?" The dean pins him with her gaze. "I have no choice but to abide by the requests of your Houses but I still run this College and I am sure you wouldn't like me to report to your superiors that you're threatening one of my employees."

Tir huffs. "I'm not threatening—"

"Not Tir's fault he's chicken shit," Rook mutters, "it's—"

"So we're agreed." She nods, turns on her heel, and heads back to the black door. "You have your new schedule, so scram."

"...scram?" Ryu cocks his head to the side. "Really? Does she realize who she's talking to?"

"Some stupid pompous overbearing assholes, you mean?" I grab a schedule from the printer and head out. "I think she knows exactly who she was talking to."

"Hey!" Rook comes after me. "You're supposed to wait for us."

I turn slightly, just enough to give him—and the rest of them—the finger, then manage to get out and slam the door in his face.

It shouldn't give me so much satisfaction, hearing him curse.

And it shouldn't still hurt me inside.

They shouldn't still be able to hurt me just by staying close to me. Their good looks and sexy bodies, their banter and their secrets, every smile and grin they give shouldn't strike me like an arrow to the heart.

I'm halfway through building my walls back up. Almost there. Brick by brick, I'm reinforcing my heart. Soon the fortress will be complete and then no arrow will be able to get through.

For good or for bad.

15

FRANKIE

"Frankie?" Juliette's face when she sees me entering her class is priceless. Shocked but also happy, which is a balm on my somewhat battered soul right now. "What are you doing here?"

"Switched classes to be with you," I chirp, sliding behind the desk next to hers that's thankfully free. Which is... kinda strange, come to think of it. Juliette is a popular girl. "What's up?"

But she won't be detracted from her questioning. "How did you manage to switch? I thought new students were randomly distributed to classes that had space and ours has been full from the start of... Wait a sec... and them?"

I don't have to turn to know who's entering the classroom, but I do anyway. Pretty as pictures, hot as any girl's wet dream, they step inside, one hunk after another, Rook smirking, Tir fiddling with his ear, Asa impassive, Ryu smiling like sunshine, and Kass scowling. "Oh right. They also changed classes."

"To be... with *me*?" She snickers the moment the words leave her lips. "I should be so lucky. Then her eyes widen. They're here because of you?"

"Um. Yeah."

She clasps her hands together, her cheeks coloring. "Aw. That's so romantic!"

I roll my eyes. "Oh God. Julie..."

"But all of them? I mean, I know Mom has four husbands, but..."

"But what?"

"You're right. Why not?" she muses, still ogling them as they scatter around the classroom, taking up every free seat. In fact, I see Rook, Ryu, and Asa going back out and carrying extra desks from another classroom.

Tearing my gaze and attention off them, I scowl down at my notebook. "And why yes?"

Her grin fades. "Franks... you don't look happy about it. Are they quarreling over you? I mean, can't expect every man to say okay, let's all court the same girl and then marry her—"

"Whoa, hold your horses. Marry me? I barely know them."

"Funny," she says. "It looks like you know them well enough for them to change their schedule for you."

I don't know how to reply without giving too much away, so I glance around the class. "Why were there any free seats in the classroom at all? I thought this class was supposed to be full."

"It was." She winces a little. "Never mind."

"Julie? What's going on?"

She shrugs. "Rumor has been going around that you are the daughter of the white witch queen and some students didn't take it well and left the class."

"In protest?"

"Protest?" She laughs low, a little bitter. "No. To avoid me."

"In case being the daughter of the White Witch queen might be contagious?"

She winces. "Shush. It's not just that. They also say you are dangerous, but that's all bullshit. You'd never hurt a fly, I know you better than anyone."

It's my turn to wince. Well, that at least answers my question: she doesn't know anything about my curse. I still wonder if her mom does.

"Look," I say, getting up, "this isn't okay. I'll ask the dean to switch classes again. I hope it's not too late. I thought the guys following me would be the issue, but as it turns out, the issue is me."

"No. Don't." Julie is out of her seat in a blink, grabbing my hand and dragging me back down. "I want you to stay. Who cares what other people say behind our backs? We're family. I'm so glad to have you here."

"What about your friends?"

She sighs. "If they really were my friends, they'd have stuck around."

"Damn, Julie, I am sorry."

"It's not your fault."

But it is, I think. All this is my fault, and the guilt slowly eating at my stomach lining is now compounded by the guilt of getting my family into trouble.

When the professor walks into the classroom, I'm glad to stop obsessing about the what-ifs and what-nots, and focus on the professor's ire.

———

"Does nobody around here consult with us professors anymore before dumping new students into our classes? Do they think we run a factory line? That any newbie can be thrown into a mix of more advanced students and be expected to simply catch up? That's barbarous, and even more barbarous, if you ask me, is our treatment. What am I supposed to do with that?"

He gestures, his hand apparently encompassing all six of us new students.

None of us comments. What are we supposed to say? I

sense a lot of anger in this professor. He should try yoga. It hasn't helped me relax, ever, but who's to say it won't help him? That's what I always say.

The students around me are starting to murmur among each other. Smirks are thrown my way.

"Little slut," one says. "Thought you could bully your way into a more advanced class?"

I make a show of unfolding my middle finger at them.

"Miss *Whatever*," the professor barks at me, "what do you think you're doing?"

"He was asking for it," I mutter between my teeth.

"What was that? I didn't hear you. Care to repeat it?" He's making his way to me and I sigh, prepared to be expelled before the class has even started. "Miss?"

"Seymour," I say, straightening in my seat. "I thought the dean approved the class switch. Is there a problem with that?"

"A problem?" He's now looming over me but I refuse to be scared off by a bully of a professor who obviously has issues. "I'll tell you what the problem is. Are you challenging me, Miss Seymour?"

I stare back at him, not sure what he wants from me. I have the feeling my answer won't matter. Anything I say will be used against me.

"Can we just get on with the class?" Tir says around a yawn, and I regret turning to look at him because he's not just looking tired as Hell but also gorgeous—as always—and I don't need this shit.

I don't need to keep turning every time I hear their voice.

Nope.

"Get up," the professor tells him and points to the door. "Out."

"Aw." Tir makes no move to get up, instead stretching his arms over his head, biceps bulging, and *man* are these boys ripped. "Really? And I thought I was being polite."

"Polite?"

"Sir," Asa cuts in. "The dean really did sign on the class switch. Could we just—"

"I don't know what is going on here," the professor says, meeting Asa's gaze. "But I don't like it. I want all of you out of my class. Starting with miss trouble, there."

"Now, wait a minute," I say.

"What did you call her?" Kass is half out of his seat, eyes flashing. He's sitting the closest to me and I see his face paling as he stands up, a spasm going over his features. His leg must be worse than he'd ever admit to. "Apologize to her."

"Are you serious?" The professor blinks at him, then turns toward me. "Miss Trouble, get out."

"Professor," Juliette starts, and no, I'm not having his ire turned on her.

"I'm going." I lift my hands. "Going. Okay?"

"No, she's not going. Why don't you pick someone your own size?" Rook says.

The professor's glare is icy. "You…"

"I don't need you to defend me, Rook," I say, cross.

"Never said you did, princess."

"And I'm not a pr—"

"Who are you, people?" The professor rounds up on Rook. "Who the Hell are you?"

"Rook Greysill," he says. "At your service. Or not."

There he goes again, Rook I mean, using his name and fame to protect me.

I hate it.

I like it.

I hate that I like it so much.

That I like it for all the wrong reasons, because I know now it means nothing.

"Fuck," the professor breathes. "Rook Greysill the Hellhound? And the rest of you…?"

Rook sweeps one arm theatrically across the classroom. "I give you Ryu Mori-Arnaud, the kitsune. There you have Tirius Verdell of the Wild Hunt. Kassander Massimo di Battista, of the Di Battista vamp mafia. Asariel Nephal of the fighting seraphs from high Heaven. And of course Frankie, the mysterious woman binding us together."

I choke.

Rook turns his gaze to the professor, dark brows drawing together. "Any more questions? Are things clear now?"

"Crystal," the professor says, his voice shaking a little.

So all of them are famous? Famous and scary mercenaries. Criminals most likely. Who would have thought? A sarcastic little voice in my head drawls. It sounds a lot like Rook's. Of course they'd send their best guys to capture me.

I'm the scariest devil in this box.

The professor turns away from us, though I catch the stunned look on his face before he grabs a marker and starts writing on the whiteboard.

The class is deathly silent. Every pair of eyes is on us. We are all standing, I realize, all six of us, like lone trees in a valley, buffeted by a different kind of wind than the rest of the world.

We're not in this together, I remind myself. *They're the hunters, you're the prey. Keep running, Franks.*

"All right, darling?" Rook calls out to me.

"Don't call me that," I reply automatically.

"Okay baby doll. You okay?"

"Stop it. I'm fine." I rub a hand over my face. "I am the *mysterious woman who bound you together*? Really?"

"Aren't you?"

Shaking my head, swallowing hard, I sit back down. "Stay away from me."

Hard to do, seeing as they are in class with me and sleep in the same room with me, but I won't play along and pretend everything's okay. If they wanted to really protect me, they wouldn't give me up. It's silly, I know, the stakes are much higher than that, but I can't help my sadness. I won't play nice when the world is a nasty place.

"Franks," Juliette starts, worry in her voice.

"I'm fine," I say, a little too sharply, grabbing my pen and notebook. "I'll be fine."

Lies. There's no good way out of this, but she doesn't need to know that. For her, to her, I'll be nice, because at least I know she loves me and for that reason, I'll protect her with all I have.

In my world, that's how things work, and screw them once and for all.

―――――

The class was boring—or maybe not, but I couldn't focus on a single word the professor said. It didn't help that he avoided looking at us and rushed through his class only to then rush out of the classroom.

Leaving us students to pack our things and go, the low whispers flying back and forth barely loud enough to break the silence.

This is going to be a new form of torture, I can see it now.

And like before, the last thing I want to do is call Granddad and whine about it, press him to do something to get me out of here, especially knowing he can't. Frigging Heaven has taken control and though an angel, he can't help me. If he had news, he'd have told me.

It's only been a day, Franks, Jesus. Feels like weeks have passed by already.

I rub my eyes. My night was less than stellar, though better than some others. Exhaustion knocked me out for a good part of it, but then the nightmares hit. They were bad.

I remember jerking awake to the five Wonderboys staring at me, and shiver.

As the class ends and everyone files out, stealing glances at the six of us—well, at Juliette, too—I stall, hoping to be left alone for a minute.

"Go ahead," I tell my cousin who's hovering by my side. "I'll be right over. I want to check my notes first."

"You took notes?"

"A few."

I actually didn't. My mind was all over the place but she doesn't need to know that.

With a questioning look at me, the guys also step out, although I'm sure they're waiting right outside the door.

But then a male voice behind me says, "I have a question for you."

"Kass. Dammit." I almost jump out of my skin. "You scared the crap out of me. What are you doing?"

He's scowling. All five of them like to do that, as it turns out, when not trying to woe me for their own ends. "How did you hide your demonblood and your magic from me? I was convinced you weren't the one. All of us were."

Pressing my lips together, I start gathering my things, throwing them into my backpack. There goes my minute alone. "We should get going."

"There's no rush."

"We have class," I say.

"I don't give a fuck about the class."

"Really? I thought we were supposed to continue as if nothing happened." And yeah, it comes out much more sarcastic than I'd intended.

"Frankie..."

"What? I owe you the truth? I owe you something, anything? Tell me, Kass." I turn on him, my backpack forgotten, my hands clenching into fists. "Why should I tell you anything? Why should I even talk to you? Do you think that's fair to ask that of me? I am your job. We're not friends. Not anymore."

He takes a step forward, and sways. He grabs one of the desks, bowing over it.

"Shit. What's wrong?" I'm worried, and I'm so mad at myself for worrying. "You need a blood donor."

"You said I could feed on you," he grunts.

"Not anymore, Kass. Did you hear anything of what I just said? Things have changed. You changed them."

"Frankie..."

"What's going on here?" A shadow falls over us. It's Rook, and his gaze is narrowed.

"Nothing," I say. "I'm going to my classes, and then I am going to the library."

"The library? What the fuck? I have no desire to be cooped up in yet another building. I want to train."

"Then go train," I say, definitely not glancing again at Kass who's slowly straightening, his face white as milk. Definitely not.

"I can't without keeping my eyes on you," Rook says cheerfully. "Come on, Kass. Four eyes are better than two, right?"

"Well too fucking bad!" I hiss. "You're following me, not the other way around."

"That's not how this works. You can't just make your plan without consulting us." He grabs Kass' wrist and hauls him along as he falls into step beside me. "And you know it."

"Fuck you." I hurry, trying to leave them behind, but Rook matches my stride easily. "I'm trying to figure out what I am, and since we're supposed to continue as if nothing has happened, then I'm going back to my research."

"What good will it do? Both Heaven and Hell want you anyway."

"It's important to me. I want to know what I am, what this ability is. Maybe I can... turn it off."

I glance at them and find them both staring at me as if they think I've gone off the deep end.

"Some abilities can be trained, right?" I say. "Like potty training."

"You compare what you can do to going potty?" Rook snorts. "The fuck, lady."

"In a manner of speaking. It was just an example, okay?"

"Sure. Well, we can help you."

My gaze returns to them—to Rook with his arm around Kass, pulling him along without seeming to—and I wish I could just keep staring right ahead, and ignore them. "Help me find out what I am?"

"Yes. Was there something else you were researching?"

I roll my eyes. "Why would you help me?"

"Why not?"

"We're curious," Kass adds, his voice scratchy.

"Right. Make it a game, why don't you? This is my life on the balance."

"You really think you can turn your gift off?" Rook asks.

"I don't know. I hope so. I can't..." My voice cracks and I swallow hard. "Can't go around killing people."

"You have to be the most reluctant weapon I have ever met," Kass says.

"Is this a joke to you?" I demand.

"Yeah, connect your mouth to your brain, dumbass, if you have one." Rook sighs. "We're all weapons, and tell me now if you think we have ever been willing."

Now that's a perspective I'd never considered.

"I thought you volunteered for this job," I say.

"When the circumstances leave you no other solution," Rook says, you volunteer. "But that doesn't mean it was a fair contract."

I heave a sigh. I don't want him to sound rational. To be *right*. I don't want to be given reasons and excuses and feel empathy. He's the bad guy. He's one of the five guys who sold me out. Who played with my heart and without remorse stomped on it, knowing all along that would be the outcome.

But I'm a bad guy, too, a danger, a weapon. And all this anger stemming from fear and guilt isn't helping any. It won't let me accept anything but my own truth.

"Suit yourselves," I mutter, turning my back on them. "I don't care either way."

16

ROOK

"So..." Having hauled Kass to his bed, I turn to her, folding my arms over my chest. "The library. Shall we?"

"Sure..." She glances around the room, slender brows knitting. "Where is everyone else?"

"Your outburst had us thinking," I say, and casting one last look at Kass who has lain down on the bed, I gesture at the door.

"Try not to strain yourselves." She saunters out of the room and I close the door behind us.

"Cranky." I cock my head at her. "Did I tell you that you're beautiful when you're angry?"

"Stuff it, Rook."

"Okay. Too soon. So..." We go down the stairs and start on the path leading to the library. "We decided to split up."

"And who got custody of the kids?"

I stare at her incredulously, then snort. "Well, well. Are you hiding a sense of humor under that jaded exterior, Miss Seymour?"

"Yeah, stored deep inside my black and rotten heart." She

glances right and left as we walk, her shoulders tense. "Wait, do weapons have hearts?"

"No idea? I mean, do demons?" I ponder that as we weave through the campus, heading for the cathedral-like building of the library.

"I thought your physiology was more or less human," she says.

"Emphasis on the less? But yeah, you're right. I just assumed we were talking metaphorically. Heart, the seat of feelings?"

"I have no feelings," she mutters, stomping her feet a little too hard on the gravel. "God, I want to go train, too."

"Then why don't you? Do you really think you can find an answer in the books?"

"You never know. You might get lucky."

"Not me," I breathe, then force on a smile because nobody wants a moody demon around. "Not yet, anyway, but you're right. One has to push on, right, darling?"

This time she doesn't correct me and to be honest, even if she does, I'll probably not hear her.

Because no matter how upbeat I try to remain, this mission has gone to Hell. Who would have thought that, apart from the other emissaries, I'd have to fight Heaven? I mean, Lucifer's fucking balls, man. This is mission impossible. I have to sit on my ass and wait until a negotiation comes through or the dome is lifted, in which case I'll have to be fast like the wind, grabbing Frankie and hightailing it to Hell.

Then she slows down as we approach the gothic metal doors of the library, forcing me out of my thoughts.

"I should call my granddad," she says.

Giving myself a mental slap—why shake yourself if you can slap him upside the face, right?—I consider her words. "You mean, through magic, right? Haven't you had enough of the landline business?"

"I don't... know how to do that."

"... come again?"

She makes a face at me. I'm not even sure she realizes she's doing it, brows scrunched up, and mouth all fucking pouty. "Granddad wanted me to avoid using my magic for anything."

"Riiiight... Well, now there's no reason to hide it, is there?"

"It wasn't about hiding it," she whispers, gazing at the library doors, "it was about avoiding any... incidents?"

"You mean incinerating people?"

"Yeah, that."

"I can teach you how to make magical calls. If you want."

That gets her attention. She squints up at me. "You can?"

"I'm the son of a Duke of Hell. A demon, therefore a child of Lilith and Adam, some say. Created together with the angels, according to others. Forgotten by God in his glory."

"Your point being?"

I give her an annoyed look. "My point is, I know a great deal about magic. I've used it during my long life and I'm seriously wasted on this College of newbies."

"Newbies in magic?"

"Magic, warfare, sex... you name it."

Her eyes go wide. She turns her face away, but not before I see the hot flush on her cheeks. "Right."

"You're not a virgin," I say. "Are you?"

"No. Um. So shall we start..."

"Why are you blushing at the mention of sex, then? Could it be... because you want me?"

"Get over yourself, Rook." Her chin goes up, and fuck, I love her defiance so damn much. "I don't want you. You can rest assured of that. I wouldn't touch you with a ten-foot pole, not even to save you if you were drowning."

Ouch. Okay, I loved it more when she admitted she wanted me.

Message received, loud and clear.

She's right, I tell myself, *and besides which, she's seen your true face. You're hardly a catch, Blackbird. Never were, not even when your face wasn't ruined. Not even before you and the others managed to wound that deeply hidden heart of hers. So suck it up, be a good sport. It's nothing personal.*

Okay...

"I'll just hang around then," I mutter, propping my hip against a massive row of shelves laden with old books and folding my arms over my chest. "And make sure not to drown, so as not to tempt you into touching me with that pole of yours and die of disgust."

She makes a small noise that sounds like disdain or amusement, hard to tell, and walks among the books, trailing a hand over their spines.

Lucky books. Unlucky demon.

Dammit.

———

"Found anything?" I have sensed her approach though I've parked my ass on the floor, my back against the wall, and I'm sort of catnapping. I open one eye. "Well?"

"Nothing worthwhile," she whispers and I open my other eye at the defeated tone of her voice.

"But you found something?"

She's clutching an old, thin tome in one hand. "Maybe? This book talks about a rare kind of vampire that kills with a scream. A Drekavac."

"A Drekavac. Seriously?" I blink. "Well, why not? Even if you are half vampire, the need for blood might be weak."

"Yes, thank you for stating the obvious."

Whoa, my girl is still pissy.

And whoa again, *my* girl? *What the fuck, Blackbird? Backtrack, now.*

"I'll grab a few books with me," she says, "and then we can go."

"What is with girls and books, huh?" I mutter, still comfortably sitting on the floor.

"No idea what you mean."

"You sleep with a book. And you like hanging out in libraries."

"I don't like *hanging out* in libraries." She pauses. Her gaze darts around. She's now actually clutching the book to her middle. "I'm doing research."

"Something the matter?"

"This is where Asa dragged me yesterday, after taking me from Ryu." She shivers. "I still can't..." The wet sheen of her eyes has me scrambling to my feet. "It's also where the shelves almost fell on me and he saved me from certain death. It's all too much to digest, even though I knew what I am, and..."

That fucker gave her a library trauma.

"Frankie..."

She flinches, her mouth tightening. "Ah, why am I talking to you anyway? I'm going to get those books."

"Frankie, wait." I grab her arm and she twists away from me.

"Don't touch me," she hisses. I pull on her, she puts her hand on my chest and shoves. "Don't."

I pull harder and she stumbles into me, the book dropping from her other hand, crashing to the floor. My back hits the wall, and she falls against me with a gasp.

"What are you doing?" she demands, eyes flashing. Eyes that are eye-level with my mouth and are staring at it.

"You want me, sweetheart. I want you, too. It's mutual attraction. Law of physics."

"No." She shakes her head.

"You don't have to like me on a personal level," I whisper in her ear, "to wanna kiss me, doll."

A blush sweeps across her cheeks. "But—"

"Carnal desire is quite separate from matters of the heart. Listen to your local incubus, I am well-versed in sex."

"You are an asshole." She pulls back, making me relax my hold, and then she slaps me. She's breathing hard, her cheeks red, eyes glittering, and I'd have released her, only I can smell how aroused she is.

"Do it again," I groan.

"What?" Her dark eyes narrow.

"Hit me again. You want to."

"I don't like you," she whispers, a little choked, and lifts her hand. "I shouldn't slap you, I should kick you in the balls and punch your face."

I'd like to see her try, honest to Devil, though I have noticed she has some good moves.

And it doesn't matter because I'd let her. Fucking guilt is riding me hard. Who would have thought?

"You're pretty damn pissed at me, my pretty little weapon of mass destruction, aren't you?"

"Fuck you!"

Someone calls out for silence in the library, probably the old lady librarian sitting at her desk in a corner behind stacks of books, and grabbing Frankie, I fling her behind the shelves. "That could be arranged."

"Never." She struggles against me and I let her push me against the spines of the books behind me.

"You're right, I should find another girl or boy to fuck, you're too prickly."

"Prickly? Whatever."

"And dangerous, as established already. Wouldn't want you coming so hard you scream and incinerate me."

"Shut up!"

I want to taste her. I remember her taste. Won't ever forget it. But she's like a wildcat, refusing my touch and my advances.

"Guess I'll be taking things into my own hands while you

hunt down your books. Maybe the librarian would be up for some fun. I'm a fucking demon, baby. I need sex."

"And that's supposed to mean something to me?"

"No, nothing means anything to you, does it? The fact that failing this mission means I'll end up back in the bowels of Hell means jack shit to you. All you can think about is how to go back to your fucking sweet family and go on as if nothing happened. I'm on a fucking roll now, and I try to rein it in but fuck, it's almost impossible. You turn twenty men into heaps of ash and buildings to dust and I take one wrong step and I'm back in the goddamn boiling cauldron!"

This time she slaps me.

I stop, panting, staring at her.

Then she kisses me.

... fuck yeah. Send me to the cauldron, baby, anytime you want if it means your lips on me.

Then her hands are on my shoulders and one leg curls around my thigh and holy fuck, my burning cock is trying to drill through my pants to get to the sweet, hot center of her.

"Frankie," I groan, my voice hoarse, my body tensing everywhere. I have a hand braced on the wall by her head. I use the other to fumble with the buttons of her jeans. Fucking jeans. Why couldn't she be wearing a mini-skirt? Those things were created for a reason: quick fucks.

Jeans were made for cock-blocking.

Her hands slip down my chest and to my fly and my brain kinda zaps and goes white. Her hands are brushing over my hard-on and I'm going to lose my fucking mind.

I'm overdue a feeding of sexual energy, especially with all the fighting and lack of sleep or food. I'd managed to suppress the need until now, but it's like an eager puppy let out to play.

Or rather a massive snake about to combust.

I'm talking about my dick, of course.

Fire races over my skin, under my skin, inside my bones. My balls feel like grenades about to explode.

I shove her leg off me so I can yank the damn jeans down and she kicks them off, along with her sneakers. Her socks are red with pink hearts—incongruous with this sensible, kind of wild girl.

Is it, though? I'd like to know, to get to know her better— and fuck, that dangerous territory, because she's the job, not just a pretty girl.

A pretty girl who's yanking my pants open and taking out my diamond-hard dick as if she means business.

And that's where the last thread of my control snaps clean through. I growl, my demonblood rising, my nails growing to black claws, my black wings spreading over us.

"Oh shit," she breathes, eyes going wide.

At least, the illusion over my damn face is still in place, and that's my last thought before I lift her up, open her legs and nudge at her entrance with my cock.

My pierced cock. I make sure she feels that ampallang. "Feel that, darling?"

"Oh God," she moans. Her hands are back on my shoulders and her mouth falls open as I push the head into her hot, slick pussy. "Oh my God," she breathes. "Oh yeah. Give it to me."

Fucking Hell, this girl.

I'm already drinking in her pleasure as I push into her, inch after inch after inch, not sure she can take it all.

She claws at me, squirming, panting. "Rook…"

And then we fuck.

17

FRANKIE

*H*e shouldn't have said that, about being punished, about being sent back to Hell. Shouldn't have let that sliver of raw truth slip, turning his pretty mouth into a snarl, his words into barbs.

Because those jagged edges made him more beautiful, irresistible. They fit against mine, even cut me a little, poking through my defenses. The façade has been near perfect—both in his behavior and his face, no sign of any damage anywhere, but the fact he lost control even for a second... made him real.

Snagged my precarious discipline, blew through my anger, turned it into white-hot need.

I need to feel those edges.

To cut myself deeper on them, draw blood to soothe the anger and uncertainty.

He's as impatient as I am with our clothes, trying to get closer even as our bodies rub together, separated by less than a fraction of an inch. His thick thighs press into mine as he grabs one of my now bare legs and hitches it up on his hip.

He lifts me up easily with one hand—just how freakishly strong is he?—settling my back more firmly against the shelves.

And then he's pushing into me.

Rough, hard, dry.

Only I'm soaking wet for him and despite the piercing I feel and the girth of his cock punching into me like a fist, despite my writhing as it inexorably pierces me, it's enough to allow it entrance.

God, it's been a while.

I've never been with someone so... endowed.

And pierced.

Or so handsome, because holy shit is he pretty with those arrogant patrician features, the hard jaw, the deep blue eyes, the unexpectedly soft lips currently pulled back in a grimace as he pushes into me. His long black hair is pulled back in a haphazard knot, fine strands teasing his neck and temples and I lift a hand to curl my hand in them.

And the wings!

He growls and crushes his mouth to mine.

He kisses like he's trying to eat me alive, rough and biting, and yet so pleasurable I shake. Or it might be the shock from having that huge, thick cock filling me up.

Feels so damn good.

Mind-blowing.

But make no mistake: this is a hate fuck. That's all it is. Pent-up tension, sexual frustration, fury that needs an outlet.

Remember that, Franks. Remember—

His tongue slides against mine, sending pangs of pleasure down my core as his cock finally slides home, filling me to bursting. I squirm again, impaled on his cock, pinned against the wall like a moth. I have both legs wrapped around him now, my heels digging into a gloriously muscular ass, my mind splintering as sensation grips me.

And it's perfect as my body takes over, as all the maddening, tortuous thoughts fade away, pushed down by the feel of him inside of me, so hot and hard and kind of painful but in a good way.

It's been a while, and I'm now starting to think that what I did, fumbling in the dark with those boys in the past wasn't really sex. It was a joke.

This is the real thing.

The wrenching, overwhelming, piercing, make-you-scream kind of thing.

Scream.

Not good.

I claw at him, suddenly panicking, and he grunts against my lips, pinning me harder against the shelves that wobble a little.

I wrench my mouth away, hissing when he pulls back an inch—only to slam back inside of me.

My hiss turns into a moan as pleasure suddenly pulses through me. His mouth brushes over my neck, his teeth sinking into my earlobe as he starts to rock into me.

Holy shit, I've never been taken against the wall before, and this rough coupling has no right to feel so amazing. I mean, what about foreplay and edging? What about checking if I can take him before slamming his length into me?

"God," I gasp, my pussy clenching so hard around his cock I think I might pass out. "Rook..."

"Give in, Princess," he breathes, ghosting his lips behind my ear, licking me there—and since when is that an erogenous zone? I shudder against him. "Give in and come for me."

I fight it. I'm pissed at him, dammit, and he doesn't get to tell me when to come or generally what to do, frigging demon and his long, thick, pierced cock that's...

"Oh..." My body clenches so hard I groan and the pressure inside me detonates. "God..."

I come so hard I see stars, shaking, my vision going black for a few seconds as my pussy spasms around his hard-on. The pleasure is off the charts, flashing through my whole body, making my nipples ache and my head drum.

Holy... wow...

He's panting in my ear, and it takes me a long moment to realize he's shaking, too. His hips are rolling, small, shallow thrusts. A long strand of midnight hair is tickling my neck.

His cock is jerking inside me, making me clench again.

He came, too.

The thought shouldn't make me smile. My arms shouldn't be looped around his strong neck, my face all but mashed to his padded shoulder, my senses full of his scent, and my soul full of satisfaction that he wanted me so much, that he came so hard he still has to catch his breath.

I push away, reality reasserting itself. He groans a little, the sound making my body clench again, pleasure pulsing through me, and I grit my teeth, annoyed with my traitorous body.

Oh shit, what am I doing? What have I done?

"Get off me," I whisper, then louder, "get off me!"

His wings fold in like a black mantle. His long hair is disheveled, his gaze sweeps down as he draws back a little, pupils dilated, turning his eyes almost black. A light flush colors his high cheekbones, and seeing him like that, open and raw and somehow vulnerable wrenches my heart again, a tug deep inside my chest that has nothing to do with desire and everything to do with feelings.

No.

Not going there again.

"This means nothing," I tell him. "I still don't like you."

He licks his lips and I realize I'm staring at them. "Noted, darling."

I tear my gaze away from his handsome face. "I'm serious."

"So am I. It's not every day I have sex with a weapon of mass destruction."

"Fuck you, Rook."

A black brow arches. "Already done that, girl."

Shit. Shit! I shove at his rock-hard chest again and this time he starts pulling out of me. I grit my teeth, because he's long and thick even when soft, apparently, attempting to lower my legs from around his lean hips, but he's still gripping one of them.

I'm going to have bruises from his fingers, I think distantly, fighting panic and anger and annoyance at myself while still dazed from coming so hard, my body buzzing with pleasure. Fighting this feeling of contentment that is all wrong.

I slap his chest and he scowls, still pulling out of me. Another inch and he's free. Releasing my leg, he steps back, gripping his cock that's half-hard and still... so big.

Stop staring, Frankie.

Stop staring at his big cock with that damn silver barbell in his big, strong hand, stop staring as he stuffs it into his pants and zips himself up. That's not sexy, that masculine gesture, the way the muscles shift in his arms, the way that frigging black strand of hair catches on the corner of his mouth while another curls around his corded neck...

"Had your fill?" I snarl. "All your demonic energy replenished now? This is what sex is about for you, isn't it?"

"Frankie..." The word is a sigh.

"What? Am I wrong?"

"You called it." His handsome features twist, settling into harsh lines as he looks up. "That's all it was to me. A feeding. You were just a snack."

Damn. I don't know why I'd expected any other answer. I grab my panties that came off with my pants and yank them on, then repeat the process with my jeans.

"It won't happen again," I say as I sit down to pull on my shoes. "It was a mistake."

"Right." Now his face is set in stone, shadows playing over it as he props an arm on the shelves and leans against them. His wings drag on the carpet.

"If you want a donor, find someone else."

"Planning on it."

I grit my teeth. I don't want him to agree, I want him to argue, to fight.

For me.

Oh-oh. Going off the deep end there, Franks. Stop it.

Jumping to my feet, I open my mouth and groan as my wound pulls. I place a hand over it, on my side. *Ow.*

His eyes widen and he pushes off the shelves. "What's wrong?"

But I don't get a chance to reply or to appreciate the concern in his eyes.

"Here. What are you two doing?" The librarian steps around the shelves to stand in front of us, hands on her hips, black glasses low on her nose. "When I saw the shelves shaking, I thought I'd never seen anyone browsing so enthusiastically."

"Haven't you?" Rook's voice is a sultry murmur. "You can browse with me, if you like. See how we can shake those shelves real hard."

Her mouth opens—in disbelief, I suppose, even as a dark flush rises in her face. "Are you suggesting what I think you're suggesting?"

"I don't know," Rook says coolly, stepping closer to her, brushing a lock of dark hair out of her face. Those damn wings are still on display. "Are you?"

Oh. My. God. What is he doing? Is he about to bang the librarian against the same shelves he just banged me?

White hot rage washed through me. I shouldn't care, yeah we've covered that, but some respect would be nice. That's it, I tell myself. That's why I'm so angry.

"You're a fucking animal, Rook," I mutter and turn in a huff to go.

"Wait," the librarian says to my back. "I'm supposed to reprimand you. Tell you the library is a sacred place and you're not supposed to bang... against the shelves. If that's what you did. Which apparently it was. Holy crap."

I don't turn back. Let him have her. Suck her dry for all I care. Because I don't give a damn.

That's right.

Though, is it weird I envy her life? She's presiding over a quiet place full of books, and she reads behind her desk unless her presence is needed—like now, to check on the shaking shelves and restore some peace and quiet.

Girls and books, Rook had said.

Maybe he has a point. We do like to read and lose ourselves in stories, find reflections of ourselves in the pages, and make sense of all that happens to us through the heroines and heroes.

Though, what I envy more is how uncomplicated her life is.

Compared to mine.

Steps ring behind me as I bustle through the turnstile and then shove the doors of the building open. Glancing over my shoulder, I find Rook following me, hands in his pant pockets, a dark frown on his face. No more wings.

I can't deny that I'm surprised. Also relieved, but who cares?

"Not going to do her?" I say when he falls into step beside me. *Damn.* I try to outpace him but his long legs have no trouble keeping up.

"The librarian? She's cute, isn't she?"

"Fuck you," I breathe between my teeth.

"But nah. I'm good for now." The cool façade remains on and I want to slap him again.

Franks, behave.

"Was I that good a snack?" I inquire with false calm.

He licks his lips. "Quite filling for now."

"Really?" My anger is turning into cold rage. "For now. You didn't just say that."

He smirks at me. He's so damn beautiful. Such a beautiful jerk.

"Maybe you should bang her," I say as we approach the mensa.

"Come again?"

"Bang her. Fuck her against the wall."

He blinks. "Are you telling me you don't mind?"

"Why would I mind? It's not like I'm letting your dick anywhere near me again. Might as well let you dip it in the first willing female you come across."

He snorts, but his dark brows knit. His eyes flash. "You're fucking with me. You really don't care?"

He doesn't like my lack of jealousy? Interesting. Was it all a play to make *me* jealous?

Well, two can play this game.

I step right into his face, forcing him to stop. I stare right into his dark blue eyes and keep my chin up. "There's nothing between us, Rook Greysill, as you very well know. Why would I care with whom the man who used me gets his dick wet?"

His frown darkens more. "Hey, just—"

"So if you want to get your kicks and snacks, you'd better hassle, demon boy. Just remember: wetting your dick in the shower doesn't count." I wink at him and turn to go.

"Hey!" he calls after me. "Where do you think you're going?"

"Dinner," I mutter. I don't think I even ate lunch. My mind is a mess.

"Wait." He grabs my arm. I try to shake him off but he turns me to face him. "Frankie..."

His expression is hard to read. He looks serious, about to

say something more, but suddenly he stumbles backward, eyes widening.

It takes me a long moment to realize someone has pushed him off me.

"Get your hands off her, Rook," Kass says, glaring. "She doesn't want you touching her."

"Are you so sure about that?" Rook mutters, his smirk making a comeback. "Really sure?"

"What the Hell are you talking about? You..." Kass sniffs, and his brows go up to his hairline. "Son of a bitch. You *fucked*?"

Somehow the crudeness shakes me out of my daze.

"You're both assholes," I tell them. "Go away."

I'm not sure they've heard me. Kass pulls his arm back and punches Rook in the jaw. "You motherfucker."

"Technically..." Rook winces, probs his jaw with his hand. "I've never fucked my mother. *Frankie*-fucker, perhaps?"

In reply, Kass punches him again, and then Rook punches him back, and then they're fighting.

Jesus Chris.

Turning around, I walk away from them, telling myself I don't care if the pair of idiots kill each other. That I don't care about what Rook had been about to tell me, and why Kass got so furious that Rook had sex with me.

18

FRANKIE

*W*hy is the mind such a complicated thing? I ask you. Why can't it stay focused on one emotion but instead has to jump from one to the other without warning? It feels like I have a Ping-Pong ball ricocheting inside my head.

And the reason I feel faint is the lack of food. Must be. I need food and water and everything will look better. More feasible. I don't even know how I missed lunch. Must have been somewhere between fleeing the school building in my rush to leave the stress of having everyone stare at us, saying goodbye to Julie, and rushing off to the library.

I need to train. Need a moment to breathe on my own.

My panties are soaking wet, as are my inner thighs. Oh God, I'm leaking cum all over the place.

Rook's cum.

Crap.

I don't remain alone for long, of course. By the time I've entered the mensa and grabbed some food—I think it's chicken pasta, I'm not sure—Tir comes charging through the door, followed by Ryu.

Awesome.

"Frankie," he starts. "You were supposed to be with Rook or Kass—"

"—but we found them punching one another," Ryu finishes.

They're both out of breath, flushed, and a little sweaty. I can smell their sweat. It's a deep, woodsy perfume that tickles my senses. I'm hyper-aware of their powerful bodies, their striking faces, though otherwise they're quite different, Tir in his gray T-shirt and faded jeans, his pale hair tucked behind his pointy ears, and Ryu with his red hair framing his face and curling at his nape, dressed in a soft yellow shirt and wide, black pants.

I mean, look at all that soft fabric stretched over hard pecs and broad shoulders, the swell of their biceps as they pull back chairs to sit beside and across from me.

Whew.

I can almost hear a suspenseful soundtrack playing in my ears.

Or that might be my accelerating pulse, pounding in my temples.

Not again, I tell myself. *No, bad dog. Sit. Stop panting at them like a bitch in heat. No matter how hot they are, you're not climbing those trees, all right?*

No tree climbing.

No more.

That was a mistake. You said so.

Now two mistakes waiting to happen are glaring at me, exuding vibes of protectiveness and aggravation.

Which also looks hot on them, so...

Stop it, Frankie.

I dig my fork into my pasta and twirl it. They seem to be expecting a reply from me. Not getting it, sorry. *Twirl, twirl, twirl—*

"What the Hell happened?" Ryu asks, putting a hand on mine, pushing down until my fork rests on the rim of the plate.

"May I eat in peace?" I ask calmly. Very calmly.

Tir pulls the plate away from me. It screeches across the table. "Why are you here alone? What are they fighting over?"

"How should I know?" I fold my arms on the table. My stomach aches with hunger. My head is pounding. "They started fighting, I walked away. I'm hungry."

"Hm..." Tir grabs my fork and twirls it, then sticks the pasta into his mouth. "This isn't half-bad."

I'm gaping at him, heat rolling through me. I'm incensed. "Hey. You. That's mine!"

He chews, swallows. Sticks the fork back in the pasta, twirls. "Tell us what happened."

I lean back, scowling. "Ask them. Why ask me?"

"It has to do with you. I'm certain."

"Good for you for being so certain." I watch him eat and get hungrier and angrier by the second. I want to cry but I won't let myself. I'm just so... tired of this.

Ryu is watching me, and suddenly he slams a hand on the table. "You're a dick, Tir. Eating her food is dishonorable." He gets up. "I'm going to get you a fresh plate of pasta, Frankie."

"Is this like... good cop bad cop?" I squint at him as he goes and then turn to Tir. "You act like a bastard and he treats me well so I will open up to him?"

"Know what?" Tir leans forward, mouth tilting in a smirk. "That's not such a bad idea. I'll talk to the others about it. We could try it out, if it will get you to talk."

"Really? To find out why two of you idiots were fighting? Very important, is it?"

"Tir, knock it off." Ryu returns with a plate of pasta and puts it in front of me. "Here, dig in."

Without a word, I grab the fork he brought with it and inhale my food.

"Why are you acting like a moron?" Ryu demands, glowering at Tir as I eat. "Have you considered asking her nicely about what happened?"

I laugh and almost choke on the pasta. "Good cop," I whisper. "I knew it."

"Is that right?" Tir growls. "Asking politely will get her to spill the beans? So easy, is it? Ask her, then."

"You ask her," Ryu snarls.

"Fine." Tir's pretty green-gray eyes narrow on me. "*Please, Frankie, tell us why Rook and Kass were fighting.*"

I stuff my mouth with pasta. "*Bcos Ihud sexy Roof.*"

He blinks. "What? What language is that?"

I swallow. "Because I had sex with Rook."

They both stare at me, brows hitting their hairlines.

"The fuck," Tir breathes.

"But why would you sleep with Rook?" Ryu sounds baffled. "Don't you hate him? Hate us?"

I lean toward him. "It was hate sex. I mean, Rook is so handsome. Don't you think so, Ryu?"

"I'm not... I'm not into guys," he blurts out, his cheeks going red.

"Right. What about you, Tir?"

Tir's cheeks are also reddening. He pushes the plate he stole from me away. He's already eaten most of it, the greedy pig. "What about me?"

"Are you also wondering why I slept with Rook?"

"No. I... Rook is... sexy," Tir says after a few beats.

I'm torn between gaping at him and laughing. "I see..."

Ryu makes a choking sound. "You," he says. "Tir. You slept with him, too, didn't you?"

"What," Tir growls, "you're a mind-reader now?"

"Just answer the question."

But Tir only shrugs his broad shoulders. "He needed to feed. I needed release after they pumped us full of drugs. We took care of one another."

"The buttons," I mutter. "Now I get it."

Ryu blinks. *"Buttons?"*

"He ripped Tir's jeans buttons off." I nod at Tir. "You were sewing them back on. You said you'd fought..."

Tir's jaw works. He looks away, cheekbones coloring more. "I like guys as much as girls. That a problem?"

"For me? No problem," I say, stuffing my mouth with more pasta, because inside, my traitorous brain is going, *whee, guys on guys. Yummy. Especially these guys. I mean, Tir on Rook? Hot hot hot!*

No brain, stop it. It doesn't matter how hot they are, get it? I don't know how else to make you understand... We hate them. Terribly. With a passion. All five of them. Okay?

Jeez.

I mean, one of them just ate my pasta. See? Not nice.

And now I'm having snarky internal dialogues like a crazy person. *Awesome.*

Meanwhile, Ryu is glaring at my plate, his mouth downturned, and Tir is examining his fingernails.

The awkward silence spreads over the table, stifling.

I pretend not to notice, still stuffing my face with food. I bet I'm looking like a chipmunk, cheeks filled with nuts, right now.

That's my sexy look. *Haha.*

Neither of them is looking at me, though. *Thank Goodness.*

I swallow and stick my fork back into the pasta, when Tir decides to interrupt my very literal rumination. Well okay, my chewing and chipmunking.

"Rook said you found something in the library," Ryu says eventually.

Apart from his cock? "He did?"

"Yeah. So tell me about this drekavac creature."

His voice has dropped low, and although I'm aware it's just to discuss a matter that is private, it does something to me, sending a thrill I feel right between my legs. The intensity in his pretty, uptilted eyes isn't helping matters any.

Jesus.

"Funny he told you," I muse, tearing my gaze off his face and focusing on my food. "I thought it was each man for himself now."

"I thought so too." Ryu is watching Tir, a crease between his dark brows.

"Finding out what she is benefits nobody in particular," Tir argues. "Our orders won't change."

"True," Ryu agrees. "This drekavac, then. What is it?"

I swallow something bitter that has nothing to do with my pasta and everything to do with their agreement on my fate.

"A drekavac sometimes predicts death," I say, realizing I lost my appetite after all and dropping the fork on the plate. "It avoids dogs and bright light, roaming at night. And if its shadow falls on someone, then this someone will fall sick and die."

"Sort of like a banshee then," Ryu muses.

"But a banshee is a fairy creature," Tir says.

"Different mixture of demonblood and angelblood, then." Ryu shrugs.

"I don't mind bright light," I say. "And my shadow has never killed anyone."

"Maybe that's a metaphor, like... the shadow of your knife," Tir says.

"I doubt it. Also, I like dogs. Especially the small, fluffy kind."

He blinks at me. "You do?"

"Yeah! Why not? Don't you like them? They love you," I swallow hard, not sure why suddenly my eyes feel hot, "with all their little doggy heart. No conditions, no reservations. What's not to like?"

Tir's eyes widen a fraction. "Frankie..."

"I don't like dogs," Ryu mutters. "Stinky mutts. Always attacking us. Biting the little ones. Dying. Everyone dies. Everyone you love fucking dies anyway in the end, leaving you alone. So what's the use?"

Now we both turn to stare at him. His green gaze is distant, his hands clenched on the tabletop. He doesn't even seem to be seeing us, lost inside his mind.

What use is love? I think. *Is that what he's saying? And what's this about people you love dying on you? What happened to you, Ryu?*

I'm about to ask, throwing discretion to the wind, but I don't get the chance.

Because Tir reaches across the table and grabs one of Ryu's hands. "Focus on the present, abesh. Snap out of it, now!"

"Don't," I start, putting my hand over theirs, "don't push him, Tir, he's remembering something—"

"He's lost," Tir says, his eyes glittering, "and it won't do him any good to stay lost in the woods. He needs to escape and fight in the here and now."

"Easy for you to say," I grumble, "maybe you haven't been through a bad trauma in your past—"

He snorts. Blinks again, his eyes looking wet. "Haven't I?" He reaches with his other hand, takes Ryu's other fist in his, too. Now he's holding both of Ryu's hands, and I find myself joining him, too. I don't know why.

I hate them.

But I can't look away as Ryu makes a small noise and starts.

"What the fuck?" he whispers, blinking. "Where...?"

And I see Ryu return from whatever memory he's been lost in, little by little, *click, click,* his eyes refocusing like the lenses of a camera, until he's looking at us again.

"What did they take from you this time?" Tir whispers. "How did they punish you?"

"They took my violin," Ryu breathes, "and my locket with the photos..."

Tir snarls softly. "May a dragon fuck them dry, those *kerel* shifter assholes."

I nervous giggle makes its way up my throat. It dries up at the look of misery in Ryu's eyes.

For a moment, I forget I should be happy they suffered for taking advantage of me. "Ryu..." I whisper. "I'm sorry. What photos were those?"

"Fuck," he whispers, jerking his hands away from ours. He pulls them into his lap, and he gets up, his chair screeching backward. His eyes have gone round. "What the...?"

"Sit down," Tir snaps, banging his fist on the table, making me flinch. "We have important stuff to discuss."

Ryu sits. Then scowls. "Fuck you."

"That's better." Tir grins, looking pleased to be insulted. "Now back to the discussion at hand."

"The drekavac," Ryu says, his voice so empty it makes my heart clench.

"That's right." Tir folds his arms on the table, pale hair falling in his face, hiding his eyes. "So maybe Frankie here likes dogs, but that doesn't matter. If you're half drekavac, that's not the full form, obviously. You'd only carry some of the features."

"True," I mutter. "Is this it, then? Am I half a vampire? A kind of vampire, at least? Is this the answer?"

"Who knows?"

"So what do I do now?" I whisper. "Drive a stake through my own heart?"

"Whoa. That's kind of drastic. Let's sit back for a minute and think here."

I shrug, pretending not to care that much, even as my chest feels crushed. "Sure."

"They wouldn't be after you for being half a vampire," Tir

says, while Ryu is quiet. "Is this drekavac even that deadly or does it only predict death?"

"No idea. Shit. Doesn't make sense, does it?"

"Let's treat you like a vampire and see what happens," Tir says.

"What do you mean? Feed me blood?"

He tilts his head to the side. "Does it sound appetizing?"

"Hell no. I don't even like my steak bloody."

"No? Barbarian." Tir's gaze flicks to Ryu who's still very pale. "We'll have to talk to Kass about it."

"Great," Ryu mutters.

"Shouldn't that be my line?" I fold my arms over my boobs, frowning, thinking how quickly I fell back into feeling things, being worried over Ryu who used illusions to trick me and get information out of me.

"You think I enjoy any of this?" Ryu glares.

As they make noises about going to find the vampire, I lean forward, propping my elbows on the table, looking at Ryu.

"Would you tell me what you asked for, in case you succeed in your mission? I know already that Tir wants to find his family."

Tir frowns.

"But you, Ryu? Are you doing this for your family?"

And damn me for still trying to understand.

"No," Ryu says, getting up. "I'm not doing it for my family. I'm doing it for myself."

"But what do you want?" I demand, not caring if a few heads turn toward us. "What?"

"An ending," he growls. "To everything." And this time he walks out of the mensa, not looking back, his bushy red tail lashing back and forth as he disappears through the door.

19

TIR

The fox just up and goes, a dark shadow in his eyes that I don't fucking like.

But I'm not stopping him from leaving again. One might start thinking I give a damn. And staying alone with her is a bonus.

Possibly.

I mean, for it to be an advantage, the dome would have to lift off the campus right now, when I'm alone with her, so I can grab her and open a portal to Faerie before Heaven reaches down for her.

Metaphorically speaking.

How many times have I been so lucky in my life?

Exactly zero times, that's how many. And if more assassins were to arrive, she'd be a hundred times safer with numbers around her. With the guys. My pride isn't so high and mighty that I can't admit that. Where is Asa, anyway? Haven't seen him since the morning classes. And what about Rook and Kass? Are they still fighting over her?

Not that I entirely blame them, the stupid idiots, and I almost grin as I glance at her pretty face. Fuck, her mouth looks so soft... funny that I'm the one sitting here with them while they're busting each other's faces.

"Tir? What are you grinning at?"

I blink. "Huh?"

"I'm talking to you." She snaps her fingers in my face, leaning over the table to do so, and wait, is she resting her tits on top of it? Suddenly I can't look away from her cleavage. The black tank top she's wearing has dipped quite fucking low and the mounds of her breasts gleam like white marble. Her mouth moves and I look up, the need to kiss it tearing through me. To make things worse, she's tucked her hair behind her ears and for a fae, that's almost the same as flashing a nipple.

Fuck...

"Tir!" She slams her hand on the table between us. She might have said my name more than once while I was ogling her.

"What?" I swallow hard, my mouth gone dry. I shift on my chair, my dick like a slab of rock inside my pants.

"What do you think he meant?"

"Who?"

"Ryu, of course!" she hisses and rolls her eyes. "Oh my God, what's wrong with you today?"

"As opposed to other days?" I smirk but it's distracted. I am fucking distracted. By her. When I first met her, I thought this pull was curiosity, the focus of my mission, but even then, my body knew, and when my mind entered the game...

"Good point." Her cheeks are pink, her eyes soft. "He just says these... dark things and I don't know what's going on with him."

"He's a broody guy," I agree, getting out of my chair with a wince, because *kraish*, all the cuts and bruises on my body are pulling and burning. "He means nothing by it."

Though I'm not sure about it. He has a dark streak, that pretty shifter, and the way he'd spaced out before wasn't reassuring. His mind goes to dark places and I wish I knew how he expects his mission to save him.

An ending, he'd said. An ending to what? Is he in pain? Is he at an impasse? Is he being used, like all of us, and demanded an end to his slavery in the shifter court? Should I visit his dreams, too, see if I find out?

For shame, Tirius.

He should be the last thing on my mind right now. As should the others. Only Frankie should matter, and not in a I-wanna-fuck-you-against-the-wall way.

"Frankie, wait," I say as she pulls on her jacket and starts toward the door. Marching after her, I scan the mensa with its long tables and annoying students, focused on any sign of danger. "Slow down."

But she doesn't, and grinding my teeth, I follow her. At least I haven't seen the bullies yet, and though I'd fucking like my earrings back, because they're fucking important to me, dammit, I'm glad I don't have to fight them off right now.

Even super-ninja Wild Hunt warriors need a couple of days to recuperate after almost dying, and it looks like the other idiots have really left me to mind her on my own.

Meet the Fae-nanny.

Fuck.

"Frankie!" I bellow again as I step out the door. *Where is she? Fuck!*

And then I catch a glimpse of a pale long ponytail, and cursing some more I start after her. At least some of my energy is back after eating.

When I find the others, I'm going to bust their chops for pulling this vanishing act. Being alone with Frankie is dangerous on too many levels.

Not least of all because all I can think about is burying myself inside her and blocking out the world.

————

"Frankie! Wait up!"

She doesn't. Her blond ponytail bounces jauntily back and forth as I go after her, much like Ryu's goddamn tail.

We all feed off something. nothing comes from nothing. Any energy you expend requires a price.

Vampires need blood.

Incubi need sex.

Demonic spells need blood.

Elemental magic draws life force from living things and elements.

The Fae, well... it is said they draw their energy from their schadenfreude. Maybe the Gentry do, I wouldn't know. I may be half Gentry but I've never spent any time in the Courts.

As for me, I need salt.

You heard that right. Salt. The smell of her pasta had bypassed my rational brain and tapped into the magical subconscious part. And okay, I'd much rather have licked the salt off her skin, but it was a patch-up solution. Having had no food in a while hadn't helped.

Go ahead and laugh. Fairies are famous for craving sugar. Salt is famous for keeping the fairies away. Yet here I am, craving it. I was raised on salty bread. Can't remember ever being given sweets to eat growing up. In fact, I'm pretty damn sure I was not allowed to touch any.

Frowning at the memory I hadn't revisited in forever, pressing a hand to my chest, where the arrowhead was buried only yesterday, I jog after her. Damn girl is fast.

I catch up with her off the path, among the trees. "Hey!" I grab her hand, and she turns to glare at me.

"Stop grabbing me!"

I open my mouth to say *"then stop running away from me"*

but I groan instead as my body informs me that running was a bad idea.

Ow, shit.

"Tir?" I like the sting of fear in her voice, her fear for me, way too much.

"Don't run," I finally manage. "It's dangerous. Falling pots. Stray scale-balls. Assassins. All that."

"Did you see anything?" She glances around. "Or are you just trying to scare me?"

"Not trying to scare you, dammit. But be careful, will you? Dunno where the fuck the others are."

I'm still gripping her arm. Don't want to release her. I want to tear off her jacket, her tank top, her bra. Starting from the top. Working my way down.

She twists and elbows me in the side.

Bullseye.

With a hiss, I let her go. "Dammit!"

She takes a few steps and stops. "Are you okay?"

"Me? Oh. Yeah, great. Just great. Stop trying to kill me, will ya?" Pressing my hand to my chest, I give her the evil eye. I knew she was dangerous, see?

"Shit," she whispers, eyes widening. "That's where the arrow hit you, isn't it?"

"Good thing it's not there anymore or I'd be dead." I chuckle a little because my eyes are watering from the pain. The trick is to keep breathing until it subsides. Trust me, I'm experienced in this.

"I just thought..." she breathes.

"Thought what?"

"Never mind." She shakes her head, her pale ponytail swinging.

"Tell me."

"Fine. When we went through the portal, you... You stopped breathing," she says quietly.

"Did I?"

"Yes!"

"You mean when I almost died?" I say cheerfully. "Nothing can keep a bad Fae down, not even iron poisoning."

"No, I thought you had really died," she says, her voice rising a little. Swallows. Her eyes won't stay on me, her gaze straying to the trees. "You stopped breathing, Tir. What was I supposed to think?"

"Hey, hey." Without thinking, I grab her chin and turn her face back to me. "But I didn't die. I am here, okay?"

She nods, a tiny movement of her head.

"You were worried," I whisper.

I see the moment her expression shutters again. She jerks away from me, steps back, but I won't have it. I follow her, matching her steps, closing the distance again between us.

"Tir," she starts.

"We had a deal," I say.

Her eyes narrow. "We did?"

"I was going to help you train."

"That was before I found out you were after me to tie me up and serve me to your bosses like a gift with a bow on top."

"Tie you up, huh? That can be arranged." And dark desire unfurls inside me at the thought—not only of tying her up but of baring her, touching her, entering her—

"I'm training alone," she spits out.

"Out of the question." *Abesh,* I have to get myself under control. What in Arawn's name is it about this girl that has me so wound up with need? "I'll be there anyway. Might as well give you some pointers."

"I don't want your fucking pointers."

Ducking under my arm, she strides away, leaving me to scramble after her, *again,* annoyed and hard as a rock for her.

Fuck my life.

———

"I didn't agree to you training me," she says but doesn't pull back or punch me in the face—or elbow me and tear that wound open again, thank fuck—when I follow her.

"How did I take the arrow out?" I ask her.

A hesitation. "You didn't. I did."

I open my mouth but can't decide what to say.

"The iron wasn't letting you heal," she whispers.

"I'll... bet. But..."

"I took it out and you stopped breathing. But I'm no doctor. You obviously didn't die."

"Obviously," I breathe.

Her throat works as she swallows, and I'm staring again. My gaze follows her pale skin down to her tits and yeah, I guess I'm a tits lover. Other guys know early in their life, but in the Wild Hunt I never had the time to explore my sexuality or anything much. I fucked and was fucked and then we went out to fight the wars of the Unseelie King again.

Fuck, stop this shit, T.

"Listen... thanks," I say. "For saving my life."

When I had just betrayed her, kidnapped her, and was waiting to deliver her to the House of Air.

"You're welcome," she replies, voice sharpening. "It was a one-time thing so don't get used to it. You'd better look out and not be shot at with arrows again. Or any other projectile, in fact."

A chuckle escapes me. It sounds as incredulous as I feel. "Right."

She stops in a small clearing of the campus park. "This is a good spot."

It's small but it lends the illusion of privacy. "I'll show you some knife work," I say.

"No need."

I ignore that. "Try this." I take her wrist in my hand, moving the knife in an upward arc. I slide my other hand over her waist. "And step forward as you do it."

"I know knifework, Tir."

"But you're not pushing any of your magic into it."

She jerks away from me. "I can't. I'm not supposed to."

"Have you ever considered that a reason why your magic flares so lethally is that you don't use it? It accumulates."

"Not sure it works that way," she whispers, eyes wide.

"But you don't know for sure."

"If I'm a Drekavac—"

"You're not. Even if your father is one, you're different, Frankie. You're powerful."

"Tir..."

I gesture. "Come here. Let's try some knife throwing."

Unexpectedly, she does. She lets me turn her, correct her posture, though she grumbles, "I know how to throw knives."

"I'm sure your granddad did a great job." I force my mind on spreading her legs apart a bit more and correcting the angle of her raised hand. *Mind out of the gutter, Tir!*

"But you think you know better?"

"You can't trust angels to teach you how to fight dirty, and that's how you need to fight if someone attacks you. This isn't a training camp anymore. This is war."

"Ow." She jerks her hand out of my grip. "You're crushing my wrist."

"Sorry." Frowning, I loosen my grip on her wrist. "I'm not used to being careful."

"Who taught you how to fight?"

"The Wild Hunt," I reply absently. I use one of my feet to push her legs just a smidge wider. "Cant your hips a little, find your center of gravity."

"Gee, what would I do without men mansplaining everything to me?"

I snort. "Want me to stop?"

"Center of gravity. Got it. So... The Wild Hunt? They taught you how to throw knives?"

"Among other things," I grind out. "How to fight dirty with every available weapon, and if not, with my fists, my nails, my teeth. And my magic. You don't survive the Wild Hunt until you become a fucking wild animal yourself."

"You didn't like it there."

This time I guffaw. "You could say that. Let me put it this way: I'd do anything to leave the Wild Hunt and go home."

"So why did you join them if you hate them?"

"Like I was given a choice?" I shake my head. "Now show me what you got. Throw the knife at the tree trunk."

"I can see it," she grouses. "Where did you think I was going to throw it? Watch and learn, Wildling."

"Really." I stand back and fold my arms over my chest. "After doing all the footwork, you're telling me to watch—"

She does it beautifully, swinging her weight back, drawing her arm back, perfect form—with my help, I think smugly, but still—and letting the knife fly.

A shadow moves across my vision—someone is there—the knife bounces off him and ricochets before I even move, *holy shit*—

Asa.

Fuck.

20

FRANKIE

"*A*sa!" I start toward him a second after Tir, my heart pounding a sick rhythm inside my chest. "Are you okay, did I hit you?"

But then I stop before I reach him. He looks unharmed.

In fact, he's giving us a stony look, his hands clenching and unclenching at his sides. "I'm fine."

Tir runs a hand through his hair, then gestures at the ground. "But the knife—?"

"Knocked it away."

"Of course." Tir sighs. "Fucking angel. Knocked it right out of the air with your hand?"

"How else?" He glares past us. "Where is everyone else?"

"Wish I knew."

"I walked past the Fae gang as I searched for you. I'm sure they followed me."

"Great. So you've led them right to us? We have enough on our hands without the bullies."

"Maybe you should go distract them," Asa suggests, "instead of putting your hands all over Francesca."

"It's Frankie," I say. "And are you jealous, angel?"

"Yeah," Tir says, "are you jealous, Asa?"

Asa snorts as if that's a ridiculous notion but his eyes flash at Tir. "I've been a very patient man."

"Angel," Tir corrects.

"And haven't kicked your ass to kingdom come despite grabbing Frankie and forcing me to activate the Raziel protocol."

"Oh right. Put that on me, why don't you?" Tir growls. "That was your decision. I only followed my orders."

"But maybe you should go and hang out with the Fae", I say, because I'm annoyed at how much I liked having Tir's hands and attention on me just now. Because I'm annoyed at how attracted I still am to them, as if my body and mind don't like the memo and decided they never got it. "Tir likes hanging out with Jatri, don't you, Tir?"

"What?" he blinks. "No."

"That night we had to clean the storeroom, you went off to that party with the Fae."

"I didn't."

"You came back all bruised. So you lied?"

"Well, it *was* a party." He shrugs. "I just didn't walk there of my own volition. More like, dragged there."

"And beaten," I whisper, remembering his bruises.

Another shrug. "I can tweak truth a little."

"Why did you lie?"

"I don't lie. You all seemed to be so sure I'm an asshole," he says. "So I decided not to break the illusion."

I don't know what to say. Is that true? Didn't we give him a chance to explain, only assumed he had made nice with the bullies? A wave of shame goes through me. But before I open my mouth to say anything, Asa gets right into his face.

"So you lie. How can you do that?"

"I didn't lie," he says. "Didn't you hear what I said?"

"But you have lied on occasion," I say. "I heard royal Fae can lie, but I thought you're not Gentry after all."

"I do have some royal blood in me," he admits. "But I'm not officially Gentry."

I make a mental note to ask uncle Sindri about it. Maybe he knows Tir's story. I have to call my aunt. She must be having kittens by now, though I'm sure Granddad must have told her that he spoke with me...

"And isn't it true," Asa says, now almost nose to nose with Tir, "that you convinced the others to leave you alone with her so you could have sex, jeopardizing her safety in the process?"

"What are you talking about?" Tir puts a hand on Asa's chest. "Back off. Tell him, Frankie. Tell him it wasn't like that."

I tap a finger on my lips. "You did grab me and haul me through a portal, about to deliver me to the Wild Hunt, without a second thought."

His brows draw together. "We talked about that. I was just faster than the others. You—"

"Permission to punch one of your friends," Asa says.

"I beg your pardon?"

"I made you a promise not to hit them without permission."

I gape at him. "You concocted a plan with Heaven and didn't care whether they lived or died, in fact wanted them dead—"

"I never said that."

"—and now you ask for permission to touch them?"

"To *punch* them," he clarifies. "And I only promised not to hit them. Touching is vague."

"You..." I shake my head, stupefied. "So you did. I thought only the Fae were such sticklers for phrasing."

"Oh," Tir says, "angels are worse. Generally worse. Trust me."

"Asa," I say. "Punch him."

He lunges the moment the words leave my mouth and I ignore the tiny snag of guilt in my chest.

No guilt, I tell myself. *You carry enough guilt with your curse. You don't need to carry any guilt for the decisions and actions of other people. No matter how pretty and sexy they are.*

No matter how nice they seem to be on the outside.

You know better than that. Surely, by now you do.

Tir's eyes darken as does his hair, but the horns don't make an appearance, not yet, as he throws up his arms to defend himself from Asa's attack. His head snaps to the side with a hit, blood spraying, then he manages to get a punch in, too, and Asa staggers back.

I take a step back, and another. No guilt, and no disappointment. I had wanted Tir's hands on me, dammit. All over me.

Thank God Asa appeared when he did or I'd have let Tir fuck me, too.

What's wrong with enjoying it, though? I ask myself as I turn and make my escape. As long as I keep feelings out of the way, it's a way to find release and keep my mind off dark things. Not to mention, I could use their attraction to maybe escape once and for all.

I'm not a *femme fatale* or anything, but I have an idea of how men's minds are supposed to work. Big head, small head.

Or rather the other way around.

But I never make my escape. Three bulky-shouldered figures appear, walking toward us, thunder in their eyes.

Kass, Rook, and Ryu.

Shit.

———

"Asa! Tir? What the fuck, guys?" Kass calls out. "Cut it out."

But he's limping and slow. Rook and Ryu overtake him, brushing past me with a look I don't have time to decipher, and pull Asa and Tir apart.

"What did you do to get them fighting like that?" Kass demands, stopping beside me.

"Awfully bold of you to think it was my doing. Don't guys fight over anything other than a woman?"

Kass shrugs. "I honestly have no fucking clue."

"Did you also grow up cut off from the world?"

His eyes narrow. "Why, who else grew up like that?"

"Oh, I don't know. From what I understood, Ryu was a fox for a long time. And Tir was with the Wild Hunt, which... granted, it's the opposite of being alone but he says his fellow warriors are more like wild animals..." I count them off on my fingers, just to piss Kass off. "Then Asa is an angel and a seraph, according to him, which would explain the general rudeness and lack of empathy, since he spent his life as a beam of light chanting around an incorporeal throne... Rook, well... Does Hell count? And then there's you."

He says nothing for a long while, as we watch Asa shove Ryu off him and Tir tries to pick a fight with Rook.

If I wasn't furious with them, I'd be laughing right now. They're like angry kittens, all of them, just... waving their claws at one another and meowing a lot.

At least that's how it looks to me right now.

"What's so funny?" Kass breaks his silence to ask.

"Nothing."

More silence.

Rook has managed to get Tir into a headlock. Asa is saying something about an agreement and rules. Ryu just looks pissed and ruffled.

My mouth twitches. I don't know how long I can hold back laughter.

"I didn't grow up on my own," Kass says and it takes me a moment to remember I asked him a question. "I had a family. And then I had Brody."

"Brody," I repeat dumbly. "That's a guy's name, right?"

"Yes." He takes a step forward. "Guys, that's fucking enough! We have a problem."

———

As it turns out, the problem isn't new, but at least Kass manages to get everyone to stop punching one another and be quiet.

The problem is the bullies.

At least it looks that way.

Frowning, shifting from foot to foot and twirling my knives, I listen as the Kass explains why they left me alone with Tir.

The vampire gang had stalked them and they had tried to shake them off their tail before coming to find me.

"Unlike you." Tir jabs a finger at Asa. "You led the Fae gang right here."

"And where are they then?"

"I think they're trying to figure out what we can do. Thinking about their strategy. Watching us as you give them a show of discord!" Kass's eyes are turning red. "Could you perhaps at least try to look like we're not going for each other's throats?"

"Didn't realize we were supposed to look chummy," Tir mutters. "I missed that memo."

Rook cuffs the back of his head. "Pay attention, pixie boy."

"Don't make me punch you, too."

"We should make love, not war." Rook wags his brows.

"Oh my God that was cheesy," I mutter. "Get a room, you two." And then I shiver when they turn their heated gazes on me. "What?"

"We already have a room," Rook says. "With you."

Um...

"Guys, listen up." Kass is flanked by Asa and Ryu. Asa looks solemn, despite a dark bruise blooming on his jaw and a trail of crimson from the corner of his mouth down to his chin. Ryu still looks pissed and keeps glaring at Asa. "We have to talk about this."

"About the bullies?" I mutter, not paying much attention.

"Yeah. Asa, tell them."

Asa rubs at his mouth, then stares at his bloody fingers with a small frown. "Right... So a heads-up. We don't have to hold back anymore."

Silence greets his words.

"*Nani?*" Ryu is positively glaring daggers now. It wouldn't surprise me to see wounds opening all over Asa from that furious gaze. "Is this a war zone now? Should we try to kill one another and see who wins this game?"

I take a step back. Oh-oh. This isn't good. "Guys..."

"We're talking about the bullies," Kass clarifies, grabbing Ryu's shoulder, shaking him a little. "You're too far gone inside your head, brother. The war you fought is over."

Ryu shakes him off, his breathing uneven. "I'm not your brother."

"Damn right, he's not our brother." Rook lets out a small hoot. "We can do a foursome, baby."

Ryu growls. His fox ears poke out of his red hair. "Keep your dicks to yourselves."

"Back to the bullies," Kass says with a small eye roll that has me grinning against my will. "Let the bullies come at us. We'll take them down. Both Heaven and the four Houses have given their blessing on this matter. The main thing right now is keeping Frankie safe, which means also keeping ourselves safe in order to protect her. We still pretend to be students but we don't have to let anyone step all over us. Got it?"

"Good," I say, "let them come. They have my pendant and I want it back."

"*You're* going to fight them?"

"What, you don't think I can cut it?"

"Rook... are you serious?" Kass turns on him. "She could kill them with one word."

"A scream," technically, I say, keeping my tone light even as my stomach tightens. "And I don't plan on killing anyone. In fact, I never plan on killing. It just happens. And I just want my pendant back."

"Then we'll get it for you."

"No way. I don't want your help. Don't want you around me, period."

"Tough," Tir says. "We're protecting you. That means you don't get yourself into danger."

"I'm still going."

"Then I'm coming with you," Kass says.

"And me," Tir mutters. "They have my earrings."

"Boohoo, poor boy. Did they get your trinkets?" Kass sneers.

"My coming-of-age marks," Tir snarls. "But of course you're an ignorant buffoon, pretending to know everything when you know nothing."

I knew those earrings were important to him. I just knew it.

"Buffoon?" Kass arches his brows. "Is that how you call yourselves in the Wild Hunt?"

"Fuck you," Tir growls.

"*Figlio di puttana,*" Kass spits.

"Hey now, guys, are you going to come to blows again?" Rook huffs. "We're all going, obviously."

"But you can't be with me all the time, not all of you," I point out.

"True. We will ping each other if the bullies attack," Rook says. "Right?"

"Ping?"

"With our magic."

"But I don't—" Something pokes at my chest, like an invisible finger. "Holy shit, what's that?"

"A poke against your magic. A ping. Now you try it."

"I'm not supposed to use magic!"

Rook takes my hand, brings it to his lips. His midnight blue eyes capture my gaze, mesmerizing. "Don't you see, doll, this whole situation has gone off the rails. You can't hang on to everything you were told to do before. That was then, this is now."

"I told her that," Kass says. "She needs to train her magic. That's the only way to tame it."

"And like I told Kass, my magic isn't like a puppy you can potty train," I snap. "It's dangerous."

"Oh, we noticed, honey, don't stress," Rook says.

"Don't stress? Seriously, Rook?" I shake my head. "Good that we're allowed to fight the bullies. The fine print in your contracts really was shitty, huh? I'm tired and I'm turning in for the night."

"It's still early," Asa says.

"I'm tired, too," Kass says before I say something I might regret. "Let's go."

And off we go, me and my unwilling, gorgeous harem, to our stuffy little room where we will try to ignore each other and catch some sleep.

At least that's the plan.

21

FRANKIE

'*D*ear Mowgli,' I write in the margin of my book, dressed only in my tank top and panties, my blanket pulled up to my shoulders. 'Life changes on the surface, but the shit underneath remains the same...'

The guys are arguing.

Again.

"When you were showing her how to throw the knife," Asa is saying, "you should have shown her first how to hold the grip properly before you—"

"I don't need pointers from you," Tir growls, "so you can stuff that sword back up your ass—"

"I can hear you, you know!" I call out. "I'm not deaf!"

"Good," Asa says, raising his voice. "Your throw was clumsy. It's why I was able to deflect the knife."

"Screw you," I mutter, bowing over my book. 'Asa is an asshole,' I write in a bit of margin. I draw a dick and balls beside it.

Rook snickers from where he's eating peanuts from a small box. No idea where he got it from. "Hear, hear."

"Where did you learn about knife throwing and fighting in

general?" Tir asks Asa. "I doubt you do basic training in Upper Heaven."

"I'm a soldier for God's glory," Asa says, deadpan.

I laugh.

Wait, he's serious. Sometimes I forget.

"You amuse our protégé," Rook says.

"Try hostage," I grumble.

"Hey, Ryu, toss me that bottle of water," Rook says, "will you?" Then, after a beat, "What the *fuck* are you doing?"

"Grab your own bottle," Ryu says.

"You're *drawing*?"

"Fuck off."

Curious in spite of myself, I throw the blanket off and sit up on my bunk, almost banging my head on the low ceiling. I turn and glance down, at the crowded room with its two double-decker beds and the two mattresses on the floor between them.

And at the five hunks sucking all the air out of the room.

Because *Jesus f. Christ*, they are all of them sitting around frigging half-naked, as if I'm not about to have a coronary.

Or self-combust.

Or harass them sexually and accept all charges.

Damn.

There is Rook, sitting cross-legged on his narrow mattress, dressed in what looks like black briefs, his pale chest as if sculpted from marble, his long dark hair loose on his back. A memory of him fucking me in the library hits me, leaving me breathless.

I shift my gaze to where Kass is standing by the darkened window, under which a narrow, ancient desk and a chair have been shoved, seeming to be lost in thought. His short black hair curls a little at the back of his strong neck, wild curls crowning him. He's dressed in black pajama pants, wearing a black T-shirt but he seems to have lifted it to scratch his side and it shows a nice swatch of muscular back.

Then we have Tir who's standing, leaning against the ladder leading to the upper bunk of the bed opposite me, clad in black boxer briefs, his muscular legs crossed at the ankle, his pale chest gleaming, painted with bruises and cuts, the terrible wound that almost killed him an angry brown and red cut. The silver hoops in his nipples glint. His pale hair falls in his eyes.

Have you noticed a pattern here? A lot of black clothes.

Yeah, that's the only thing we've noticed. *Haha.*

Except for Asa, of course. Asa is wearing *white* briefs, white and stretched over his crotch and ass and... And I'm left staring at his muscular body where he's doing some stretching exercises on his bunk bed—right across from me, at eye level. Oh boy... He's built like a Greek god, pecs flexing, biceps bulging, his stomach a perfect eight pack...

And then there's Ryu. Ryu likes colors, so I'm not surprised that he's wearing red boxers.

He's currently lying belly down on his mattress, strong legs and golden back on full display. He has those lickable dimples in the small of his back. Gah. His shoulders are broad, covered in freckles, and all those muscles roll so smoothly under his golden skin as he shifts on the mattress.

So much eye candy, despite the cuts and bruises. It's a health hazard.

Especially when you hate their guts.

He's indeed drawing in one of his notebooks, a dark scowl on his pretty face.

"No, seriously, man, what are you drawing?" Rook leans closer to see. "You're damn good at that, who knew? But who are those people?"

"I lost the photos," Ryu grumbles, almost under his breath, "and I will forget their faces, so shut up before I put my fist in your mouth!"

"...kinky," Rook mutters after a moment. "Not today though, honey. Let's leave fisting for another time."

But everyone else has tensed.

Kass turns away from the window, frowning.

Tir pushes off the bed.

Asa stops doing sit-ups.

"Forget whose faces?" I ask in the spreading quiet.

Ryu stiffens, his long back bowing, red hair covering his face. He snaps his notebook shut. "Find something else to kill your time with," he says quietly. "Show's over."

Those people he's drawing are important to him.

His punishment was to lose the photos he had of them.

Not sure why the photos are so important, what kind of distance separates him from them, but it was obviously a steep price to pay.

But you don't care, I tell myself.

That's right. From the bottom of my heart, I don't give a fuck.

Also, I really am tired. Feeling kind of faint. I keep skipping meals—all of us do—and all this tension and uncertainty isn't helping any.

"Aren't you all going to shower?" I say. "What are you waiting for? You stink! Go!"

They cast me uncertain glances. Surprised ones. I bet they're asking themselves what's going on, and maybe also wondering if they really stink that bad and if they really have to go wash themselves.

Which is guys for you.

I don't know why I decide to send them off. It's not to give Ryu some space.

Of course not. That wouldn't make any sense. I mean, I don't give a damn.

Right.

"Surely one of you is enough to watch over me, right? Or did they tell you it has to be a group activity?"

"I don't stink," Rook says, looking offended.

"It's my animal pheromones," Ryu mutters, sitting up and all those muscles shifting in his back are mouthwatering.

Tir sniffs his armpit. "Mm..."

Kass is scowling at the world in general.

"Oh my God. Go wash!" I wave my hands at them. "There's no way in Hell you're sleeping in the same room as me without showering every day. A girl's got some standards, all right?"

Though they smell like hot sexy men, and their sweat does something visceral to me, but I won't ever admit to that.

Ever.

After a long pause, they sigh and start grabbing towels and soaps. Tir has to hunt for his inside his bag—he obviously still hasn't fully unpacked and it makes me wonder whether he thought he'd be out of here quickly, like I secretly thought for myself. Kass heads straight for the closet and grabs his stuff in two seconds flat.

Asa has slid off his bunk to the floor and is gazing at me and Ryu, arms folded over his broad chest.

"You, too, Asa," I say.

He blinks. "I'm an angel, I—"

"Angels sweat, too, and no, you don't smell of roses. You're a very male... I mean a very sweaty angel."

I didn't just say that. And his lips shouldn't twitch into a smirk as if he knows exactly what I meant.

"Just go," I say.

"You could join us," Tir calls out from outside the door.

"Oh my God, I showered today already, unlike you lot." I refuse to acknowledge the invitation in his words and the image it paints in my mind, all of us naked and wet, soaping up one another... pleasuring one another. "Off you go. Shoo!"

I probably *should* shower, after having hot sex with Rook earlier today, but again, not telling them that.

Asa watches me closely for long minutes, thoughts dancing behind the mirrors of his blue eyes. I don't like that he seems to see right through me. Of all the guys, I thought he was the most impassive, the most unemotional, but who's to say he can't read me?

"Fine." He turns toward his bunk bed. Apparently, he's keeping his duffel bag there, using it... as a pillow? *Okay...* He rummages inside but he seems to know exactly where everything is—though I don't see a soap in his hand as he heads for the door.

Meanwhile, Ryu gets up from his mattress on the floor with slow, careful movements. It reminds me of all the wounds and cuts on Tir's chest and that I haven't seen Ryu's to know how bad it is.

It reminds me they're not infallible or invincible. They aren't immortals, even though their life span can get very long, when not cut short by a bullet or blade.

They're as vulnerable as I am.

Brain, you're not being helpful right now. That's not helping me hate them.

"Ryu," I say. "Stay..."

His brows go up. "I thought I stank like an animal."

"Your words, not mine."

He doesn't dispute it. But he stays.

And now we're alone, I don't know what to say. He's looking at me as if bracing for a fight, or a wound, and I'm left disarmed.

What the Hell am I doing?

———

He's quiet, standing there in nothing but his bare skin—and ouch, there are the deep blue and black bruises across his chest and ribs—and his red boxers. They are actually boxer shorts, fitting him like a second skin. They match his hair. They should look ridiculous but look sexy on him. Probably because he's so tall and muscular, and they do nothing to hide the bulge at his crotch where they snugly hug his cock and balls.

And looking at him makes me wet down below.

Frankie. Behave.

Tearing my gaze off his crotch, climbing down from my bunk, I stand and face him. "Ryu."

He says nothing.

"What were those photos they took?" I draw a breath, take two steps closer until I have to look up at him. "Tell me?"

It's only curiosity, I tell myself. Turning off my heart doesn't mean I can turn off my brain, too. And these guys are full of secrets. It's like the proverbial carrot held in front of the donkey. I can't resist.

And now, for some reason, my brain provides an image of the five of them dressed in carroty orange thongs and nothing else.

Oh boy.

I blink. I'm still in shock from everything that's happened. That has to be it.

I look up into his handsome face, my eyes drawn to every perfect line, from the hard square jaw to the sculpted cheekbones and mesmerizing green eyes, the red hair clinging to his temples and strong neck, those wide shoulders and muscular chest. He has silvery marks across one pec and I lift a hand to touch them, wondering what they are.

He catches my hand before I get the chance. "What do you want, Frankie?"

"They took your photos," I whisper, caught in a kind of daze. I'm so close to him his scent winds around me like a ribbon and it's making me dizzy—dizzy with desire, with the need to put my hands on him, on that ripped chest, rise on tiptoe and taste his mouth.

"And my violin," he whispers and his voice is kind of broken, jerking me straight out of my reverie.

It breaks me, too. I never thought I had a soft spot for broken boys but there you have it.

Broken, violent, selfish shifters, I correct myself because *what the Hell, brain? Don't soften their image. Don't erase what they did to me.*

I'm angry. I really am. And hurt. Hurt begets anger, so here we are.

What am I doing? How many times do I have to break my promise to myself and worry?

"The photos," I say again. "What were those photos? The people on them must have meant something for your people to take them away, for you to draw them."

"*My* people." He lets out a bitter chuckle. "My people. The fuck."

Then spinning around faster than my eye can follow, red hair flying like flames, he grabs the chair from the desk and hurls it against the wall where it crashes. I turn and duck instinctively as pieces fly across the room, smashing into the bunkbeds and the opposite walls.

Shit.

And he'd seemed like the sweetest of them all, at first.

Goes to show you can never judge from first impressions.

"Ryu," I whisper, then wince when he goes for the desk, too. "Stop. Just stop!" He's already lifting the desk with both hands, and I just run and throw my arms around his waist. "No!"

He goes very still, while tremors go through his body. He's breathing hard.

"*Kuso,*" he whispers, and I think it's a swearword I know from growing up reading fanfiction online.

"Yeah," I agree. "Shit."

But then the turns and marches me backward, one hand on my shoulder, until my back hits the bunk bed. His eyes flash, more orange than green now, a burning copper.

"Want to know who those people were? Or why I mourn my violin? Huh?"

I nod, kind of speechless as his face *pulls*, stretching, going more catlike as he slams me against the bunk beds. More fox-like.

His hand lifts off my shoulder and slams into the metal frame of the bed. Turning, I see it going black, the fingers gnarled and the nails growing into claws. "Why should I tell you anything?"

"You owe me that much, and I want to know," I whisper. "Please."

Fox ears flick, poking through his hair. His mouth twists, lips peeling back. His teeth are sharp and very white, the canines growing longer as he bows his head over me. I should be scared. The muscles in his chest and arms are impressive, and that's without counting his shifter strength, claws, and teeth. This is a guy who tends to get lost inside his head.

He could rip my head off before he even realizes it.

"They were my family," he growls softly.

It takes me too long to remember my question. "Family?"

"My parents. My wife. My daughters."

"Oh shit. What happened to them?"

He cocks his head to the side, like Tir likes to do. An animal gesture. "They're dead."

I think I kind of expected that, but still, it makes my throat close up. I can't imagine losing my family, or the pain I'd go through. "Recently? What was it, an accident?"

"Disease and old age."

"I'm so sorry." I study his feral face, bent right above mine, the copper eyes and sharp teeth in a mouth split too wide, the too-sharp cheekbones, and a nose that's starting to darken with a shift. "Really sorry, Ryu."

"All of them gone," he growls as if he hasn't heard me, pain in his voice. "I outlived them all. I've almost forgotten their faces."

"But—"

"It's been too long," he says. His eyes half-close.

Then his mouth crashes against mine.

I don't even have time to think *oh shit, those teeth will tear my mouth apart* before he shoves his tongue between my teeth and molds his body against mine. His body is hard everywhere it touches mine, hard abs, hard thighs, and a hard length poking into my stomach, but his tongue shoves pure pleasure into me.

It's as if his touch, their touch, lights me up like Christmas lights and there's nothing I can do to stop the attraction and the need.

He has a hand inside my panties, and then he's tearing them off. *Good,* I think, *good he didn't try to touch me there with those black claws, good God—*

And then he lifts me up, gathers my legs around his hips, so that my most sensitive parts are pressed against his hot length.

"Oh God." My head falls back, knocking against the metal frame of the bunk bed.

I hadn't noticed when he'd shoved down his boxer briefs. I'm pressed against his very hot, very thick, and very naked erection. I could just lift my hips a little, cant them down, and...

"Want me in you?" he grunts, the words barely intelligible.

That's my only warning. The moment I nod, he grabs his cock, slides it down until the broad, flared head nudges at my opening, and pushes into me.

Oh shit.

It spreads it wide as it goes in, splits me open. It barely fits, and yet he keeps pushing, one long, slow thrust that has me writhing and clawing at him. It's rough and it hurts but at the same time, I want it. The burn makes me hiss, but I'm so wet for him it eases the friction, allows me to take him.

More and more, inch after inch, and I do tilt my pelvis up,

impatient. The still-healing wound in my side burns like fire, but I ignore it.

He slides deeper and gasps. I'm gasping, too, wrapping my legs more securely around his hips, sliding a hand around his neck to dig my fingers into his fire-red locks, the other gripping a steel bicep.

My mind has gone into that blank place it seems to retreat to when I have sex with these guys. My thoughts are mere static, a buzzing inside my head. My body feels like a live wire, trembling and shaking with energy and need.

And the burning turns to ecstasy when he rocks into me, bracing one hand on the bunkbed, the other gripping my waist. I feel the pinprick of sharp nails on my skin but I don't find it in me to care.

Then his hand moves up, under my tank top and I have a moment of panic, those claws are damn sharp—

—but they only tear the fabric, baring my boobs. Cool air touches my nipples and they harden instantly, sending zings of need through me.

I wish he'd touch them, put his mouth on them, but even if his face is still fairly human, I'd rather not have those fangs close to my nipples.

Yet the thought makes them tighten more, makes me tighten everywhere.

"Fuck," he breathes and it's almost a growl. "*Kuso...*"

He's rocking into me faster now, shallow thrusts, because he's seated so deep inside me there's nowhere to go.

He feels so perfect in me, so good, a tight fit but oh so right. It won't take much to get me off. I'm already panting his name. Like with Rook, I'm on the cusp almost instantly.

As if there's more than our bodies touching and connecting.

As if I can feel that energy, his energy, brushing against mine, stroking, plunging its fingers into me just like he plunged his cock. Is this magic?

I'm serious.

I'm also too far gone into pleasure to follow up the argument inside my head right now, to try and extricate the pain from pleasure, separate the bliss of his body against and inside mine and this other presence, this other touch that might or might not be magic.

It's insane how out of touch I am with my power. Been suppressing it for almost as long as I've known about it and—

"Oh... Ryu..." I'm coming, pulsing, straining against him, the metal of the bunk bed frame cold against my back, his chest hot, pressing against my breasts as he keeps thrusting into me, his breaths coming in short gasps, his eyes half-closed...

But his gaze is fixed on me, I realize, on my face, the tops of my bare boobs.

It's me he's seeing as his thrusting stutters and he groans, shoving his cock as deep as it can go, pulsing as he comes.

And it takes my breath away.

We're locked together, still rocking, and I realize we're also rocking the bed, a gentle creaking rhythm filling the air. My gaze is caught in his green eyes, my body in the cage he's made with his arms and hips, and there's nowhere to go.

He's still half-hard, buried inside me.

The feeling of bliss and rightness, of perfection and relief, lasts long enough for me to lift a hand to his face, trace that hard line of his jaw with the faint, cat-tongue rough stubble, twine my fingers in the red strands at his temples. I want to kiss him, now that the animal has retreated inside him, the distortion in his face mostly gone, his eyes mostly human and yet still so beautiful...

Clarity returns, like always, a little too slowly, a little too late.

And reality reasserts itself when someone says from somewhere behind Ryu, "That was some hot loving, huh."

Tir's voice.

Shit.

Over Ryu's shoulder, I see the others standing at the door. Their handsome faces are like masks, eyes flat, so dark I can't tell if they're angry or scared or plain sad, but there's emotion there all right. Their half-naked bodies shake with it.

I can't help wondering why they didn't intervene when Ryu slammed me against the bunk bed when his clawed hand crashed beside my head.

When he kissed me.

When he fucked me.

Did they like watching?

How do I feel about it?

But Ryu doesn't seem confused about it. Pulling out of me so suddenly I cry out, pushing my legs off him, he turns around, and wait, is he blocking their view of my body?

Still dazed, I fight to keep upright, my knees like water, and tug on my ruined tank top to cover my breasts—then realize that my panties are hanging in shreds.

"Got an eyeful?" Ryu snarls.

"Hey, man, we didn't know you needed privacy," Rook drawls.

"Fuck you. How much did you see?" A hiss escapes him. "And just how much hear? That wasn't meant for your eyes or ears, *bakayaro!*"

"You forget, we're roommates," Kass says, entering the room, already dressed in a T-shirt and shorts—all black, obviously—"and accomplices, to boot. We have no secrets."

"Or secret trysts," Rook says.

"Ha. Look who's talking," Tir says. He has a small blue towel wrapped around his hips.

Oh yeah, the rest of them are only clad in mini towels, meant to make a girl go insane.

That memo about clarity and reality and hating them?

Right. Better read it. Fast.

"Better put some clothes on you, darling," Rook tosses as he crosses the room to his mattress, his eyes roving over my body. "A guy might think you need some more hot loving."

And for some reason, those words stab me like blades, driving my stupidity home.

"Hey." Ryu is still moving to cover me. "Shut your mouth."

"I don't need you to speak for me," I say coldly, as the memo finally slams home. Turning, I climb up onto my bunk and pull the covers over me, wondering how I lose control every time with them. "I don't need any of you. Good night."

22

RYU

I lie on my mattress on the floor, way too aware of her on her upper bunk bed, curled on her side, her back to us.

Of the absence of her body against mine, the hollowness of mine without her.

Of the other guys.

They aren't asleep. I can hear them breathing, hear their heartbeats. I came this close to shifting, and my senses still haven't returned to the human norm. My dick still hasn't recovered from being inside of her. My body is still humming with pleasure.

Have I lost my fucking mind?

My thoughts are running in a fucking loop. Several loops, in fact, occasionally intersecting.

Frankie.

My mission.

My failure.

My past.

My admissions.

Baring myself to her and unknowingly to the guys, too.

I don't know why I talked to her. Why I fucked her against the bed. Why I lost control like that in every way that counts.

Can't fucking believe how good it felt to be with her.

I almost felt whole for a fucking minute. Fucking sane.

Fucking fine.

But as I lie there, the aches inside my body and mind return like birds returning home to roost for the night.

I feel someone's glare on the back of my neck and I roll onto my back. Can't tell who it is. Maybe it's all of them. I smirk in the half-dark, broken by the faint light coming through the small window, enough for me to see.

What was I thinking? It doesn't matter. Fuckers are jealous.

And why is that good? I ask myself, my smirk fading.

I was living in the moment.

What good is living in the moment when you want to end it all?

I close my eyes and try to catch some sleep. Last night I slept like shit, I'm bruised black and blue from our scuffle with the assassins—now piles of ash the wind is blowing—and all I can think of is how lucky they are.

Fuck.

———

I wake up with a fucking cry caught in my throat, jackknifing to my feet before I realize where I am.

Fuck. Fuck!

"Hey there, *abesh*," a male voice drawls, and I start again, almost falling back down.

"The Hell?"

"Hm..." Tir has his hip parked against the bedframe, arms folded over his chest. He's dressed in low-slung jeans and nothing else, his pale hair loose. "That was some nightmare. Woke me up."

I stare incredulously back at him. "How the fuck did I wake you up? I'm sure I didn't scream."

"Okay, I was half-awake already, to be honest." He yawns widely, showing me those sharp Fae teeth he usually hides.

"*Baka*," I mutter, my heart still pounding unevenly against my ribs.

A glance around the room tells me that Asa is getting dressed by the window, his golden hair like the nimbus of a saint, while Kass and Rook are stirring only just now. Still way too damn early.

"I expected you to wake up with a grin, after getting your dick wet," Tir says. "More...bushy-tailed." He winks.

"Right... Very funny, Tir."

"Thought so too."

I turn away from him, needing a minute. The nightmare is fading, but I still hear echoes of screams and gunfire, and my skin itches. The shift is right below the surface, urging me to change into the fox and run. Tir has no fucking idea how close he hit with his expectancy to find me bushy-tailed this morning... quite literally.

Dragging my fingers through my hair, still not fully awake, I trudge to the corner where I threw my bag when we moved into this too-small room and unzip it, rummaging inside for a fresh set of clothes.

Laundry. I need to do some fucking laundry. *Huh*. I wish I could just pull on my pelt. Living as an animal has a lot of advantages. I haven't had to do laundry in... a very long time.

I frown.

"What actually happened to your family?" Tir has wandered after me, and he startles the living shit out of me once again.

"You're a fucking pest!" I mutter. "Go away."

What did I use to do to wake up after a bad night's sleep where I was human?

Coffee. Right. I had a lot of coffee.

"Did you leave them and then regret the time you wasted?" He moves so that he can lean against the closet, watching me from under lowered lashes, arms folded over his chest once more. Six feet of tall, muscular, maddening ghost.

Not that I'm paying him any attention.

And why did I notice his muscles?

Fuck.

I didn't have a choice, I mutter, pulling a random shirt and underwear from my bag, then my wadded-up towel. "I went to one war. Then another. By the time I was back, a lot had happened."

"What war? Wait... What year are we talking?"

"The world wars."

"You're... Japanese? Wait, no, you speak like an American."

"One-quarter Japanese on my father's side." Born here, and yet never really belonging. That at least hasn't changed. Though I tried. Though I felt like this was my home.

"Wait... How old are you, then?"

"Leave it, be, Tir."

"Wait, wait... I'm doing the math."

"The math?"

"They weren't shifters. Your family. That's why you outlived them. So who turned you?"

I grit my teeth. "I was turned during the First World War. I hadn't realized it at the time. It took a long while for the change to set it."

"So you weren't born a shifter. Interesting."

"Is it?" I ask bitterly. "Not the word I'd choose for outliving everyone who meant a single good thing to me." Grabbing my bottle of soap and my stuff, I turn to the door.

"Where are you going?"

"To shower. You heard Frankie last night. Shower our stinky male bodies or get kicked out of the room."

"Sounds to me like you let her lead you by the nose."

"Said by the guy who didn't waste two seconds to run off and shower last night," I grind out.

He chuckles. "We did stink, it was the truth, and speaking of..."

He lifts a hand and waves, but not at me. I turn to see, and find Frankie sitting cross-legged on her bunk, staring at us.

Same as Rook who's lifted his head off his pillow.

Damn, even Kass and Asa are turned our way.

It snaps something in my mind. "Fuck! Can't you motherfuckers stop eavesdropping all the time on me?" I give them all the finger and stalk out the door, fuming. "Assholes."

Yeah, even to Frankie.

At the end of the day, what does it matter?

If anything did, I wouldn't be here in the first place.

———

Losing my violin and those photos hit me hard, harder than I'd expected. I don't cling to things normally. Learned that early on in my life.

War.

Sickness.

Calamities.

Death.

Loss.

And then as a fox, I kept precious little in my den.

Until I lost that too.

Lost my new family.

Lost my fox clan, and I don't even have photos of them. Never did. Hazards of becoming an animal.

How many lives do you have to live before you can't take anymore? I long for the kind of peace an ending gives you.

And then she was there, kicking everyone out, asking me questions... Touching me.

Frankie.

No, stop thinking about that, about her, about how it felt. That's confusing, and you have made up your mind, so what's the use?

Fuck that noise.

Two guys turn to watch me as I march into the men's showers. Ignoring them, I grab the nearest showerhead, hang my stuff, and turn on the water.

One day at a time. Be ready to fight for what you want.

Be ready to grab Frankie and go.

My brain throws images of her pretty face as I'd fucked her, her eyes at half-mast, her cheeks rosy, her mouth reddened from our kisses. Her moans echo in my ears.

Turning my face into the still-cold spray, I rub at my face, as if that will erase my thoughts. I actually slept better after being with her, and that's insane.

Don't dwell on it, Ryu.

Grabbing blindly my bottle of soap, I squirt some in my hand and soap up my chest, my armpits, my neck, then down my stomach to—

"Need help with that?" a familiar, smug male voice says and I curse under my breath, turning around.

And I find Tir standing right there.

Again.

"Fuck off, Tir. Take a hint."

He gestures down at himself. He's naked. "I need to shower, too, you know."

Damn, he's strong, he's... Why does he have to wear jewelry on his fucking nipples? It draws my attention to them, to his hard pecs and washboard stomach and then lower to where his cock is just...

"What the fuck." I tear my gaze away, getting angry all over again. "Don't tell me you Fae shower every day like it's a ritual or something for you. I know enough about you lot to call you out on your bullshit. Stop following me."

"My lot," Tir mutters, brows drawing together. "Really, Ryu."

Then two more tall figures appear behind him and I want to punch the wall.

Rook is there, too. Oh, and Kass. *Fuck.* At least they're wearing clothes.

I ball my hands into fists. "Want me to rearrange your faces? Go away."

"What you say to one of us, you say to all," Kass says.

Looks like it.

"I mean, that's the only way this is going to work," he goes on.

"Meaning?" I shake my head, water flying. "It's still each man for himself, fuckers."

"Yeah, that's not what I mean. We have to know if one of us has triggers."

"We live in close quarters," Tir says, "and not only carry weapons but have magic, too. Trigger reflexes. Nightmares. Wild magic. Best to know everyone's background."

"Like you've shared about yours with anyone? You're one to talk. Leave me the Hell alone."

———

Rook and Kass are gone by the time I turn back around.

But Tir sure as Hell isn't. He's taken the shower stall next to mine and is... wait, is he stroking himself?

I make a strangled sound before I manage to swallow it down and he turns his head to look at me, a lazy smile on his face. "Wanna join me?"

I clear my throat. I sound like a cat hacking a hairball. "Sorry, man," I say. "I don't swing that way."

"Are you sure?"

"Yeah, I'm fucking sure. I was married with kids. Married to a woman."

"And then you lived as a fox."

"Again, with a female," I feel I have to point out, and the memory of her, my little sweet vixen wife, is a punch to the gut.

"And yet you look at me."

My neck heats. "Get over yourself."

"And not just me. You look at guys."

"Shut up. Decide what card you want to play, Tir. You want to know about me, or you want my body."

"Who says I want your body?" He drags his gaze from my toes to my face, lingering over my crotch and chest. "And who says I have to choose?"

My dick likes that. it likes his proximity, too. It basically seems to like everything about this arrogant fae who gives my body a knowing smirk.

I turn my back to him again, my hands shaking.

Damn.

23

FRANKIE

I'm still digesting everything Ryu said when they all troop through the door and are gone, leaving silence behind.

"Wait!" I scramble down from my bunk, my sheet wrapped around me. "Where are you all going?"

"Frankie," a voice says and I startle so badly I almost fall off the small ladder. Panting, I land on the floor and turn around.

"Asa. Didn't realize you stayed behind," I whisper.

"Someone had to."

"Gee, thanks."

But he's watching me like a hawk from his spot by the window, hands braced on the desk. His face is earnest as it usually is, earnest and breathtakingly beautiful.

I resolutely look away. "So where did they all go?"

"To make sure Ryu is okay."

Despite myself, I turn back around to face him. "Really?" I study his clear eyes for confirmation. "I want to go, too."

"It's the men's showers," he says as if that's the end of the discussion.

"So what? You guys keep walking into the girls' showers all the time! Who will stop me if I go with them?"

"You and I have to talk," he says.

I frown at him. "We do? What about? Did you get any news from Heaven?"

"No. It's not that."

"Then what is it?" I glance at the door, left half-open when the Wonderboys left. I tuck the sheet more securely under my armpits, not to flash him my nipples by accident.

Not that he seems to show any interest, I think, despite that one time he touched me in the storehouse. Heat rolls through me at the memory.

That time he showed a lot of interest. Was it all a lie? His body surely couldn't lie... right?

"Frankie." He closes the distance between us and when I look up, I feel dizzy and hot. He's so close to me, clad only in his white briefs, practically naked, all smooth pale skin wrapped over impressive muscles, and that bulge at his crotch is like a magnet for my eyes, making me feel lightheaded.

My body wants him. My body has been a damn nuisance lately.

"How did Tir survive?" he asks.

"Huh?"

"He flew through the portal with you gravely wounded. Probably mortally wounded, in fact. But he's alive. And you never spoke about what happened while you were with him. You need to tell me what happened."

"Fine," I mutter. "Don't get your panties in a twist."

He frowns at me. "I don't wear panties. I wear briefs."

Great. Here I am, committing one of the cardinal sins—lust —and fantasizing about climbing like a tree, when he's only worried about missing intel. And missing the point.

"Your sense of humor comes and goes, huh?" I sit on Tir's bunk, almost tripping on the sheet. I keep my hands over my boobs, keeping the sheet in place. "Sometimes you sound like you're human and sometimes you sound as alien as the seraph you claim to be."

"You haven't answered my question."

"So observant of you. And it wasn't really a question, was it? You forgot the question mark at the end."

He braces a hand on the top bunk and leans over me. I shouldn't be phased by his proximity after everything that went down—by his scent, his presence, his beauty, the coiled strength in those muscular arms and chest—and yet...

"Frankie."

"Hm?"

"I said, what happened? How did Tir heal?"

"He..." I shiver, remembering the despair I'd felt. "He was really bad off. I thought he wouldn't make it. But I pulled out the arrow from his chest, and I guess removing the iron allowed him to heal?"

"You don't sound so sure."

"I thought he was dying, okay?" I bow my head, letting my long hair slide forward and hide me like a curtain. "I was distraught."

"Why?"

"Why I was distraught? Are you seriously asking me that?" I glare up at him. "I don't want any of you dead, Asa! Who do you take me for?"

"A young woman whose choices have been taken away from her," he says softly. "By us."

I stare at him. "Right. But I still don't want you dead. I generally don't want people dead, despite evidence to the contrary."

He studies my face and I start to get angry.

"You don't believe me?" I demand.

"I believe you," he says, catching me off guard. "You are angry, though."

"Because you used me. You lied to me to gain my confidence. So don't expect me to trust you, be your friend."

He frowns. Opens his mouth.

"Don't tell me that the end justifies the means. Or that you don't understand human sensibilities because I'll scream."

"Frankie—"

"No, I won't scream. Shit." I rub my hands over my face, then realize the sheet has fallen and I am flashing him, after all. I make a grab for the fabric. "Shit!"

"You are beautiful," he whispers.

"There you go," I swallow hard as I gather the sheet over my boobs, "acting like a human again, confusing me."

"It is odd," he breathes.

"What is?"

"The contradiction, like you said. I come from Heaven, and yet sometimes... sometimes it's as if I remember earth."

"Maybe you have spent time on earth before."

"I don't recall any other such mission, any occasion when I had a physical body."

"And you still haven't told me what you expect to gain from this story," I whisper. "This mission."

"I get to go back to Heaven, of course."

"Of course."

"I thought I had already said so."

"It doesn't matter."

"No," he says low, "it doesn't." He crouches down in front of me, his blue eyes riveted on my now-covered chest. "So that was all about Tir? You took out the arrow and he recovered?"

"Yeah. After a while. I thought..."

His hand slides up my body, from my knee to my thigh, then up my side. "You thought?"

"Uh..." His hand is burning a path up my body. Now it's resting right under my left boob. "I don't know..."

"You don't know?"

I struggle to gather my wits. His handsome face is inches away from mine, his mouth so soft and yet firm, the masculine line of his jaw so sexy. "I thought he'd died, Asa, but I was wrong. No mystery there to uncover."

"If you say so."

"I do say so." I can't breathe. It's as if having his hand where it is—still innocently resting on my ribs under my boob—is more than a touch. It's a solid band wrapping around my chest. "Are you using magic on me?"

His brows draw together, his gaze flicking from my mouth to my eyes. "No. Trust me."

"How can I trust a word you say?" The anger flares bright. "You pretended to like me, lying about your real reasons for befriending me, for weeks! And then you went down on me—"

"Goddammit," he breathes.

I open my mouth to say that it's not often you hear angels use that kind of language—and doesn't Heaven punish them for taking God's name in vain?—when he climbs over me on the bed, pushing me back until I'm lying down and our bodies are pressed together.

I gasp because he feels so good pressed to me, his hard bare chest against my now bare boobs, his body warm and solid, his blond hair in those crystal blue eyes fixed on me, his rock-hard erection dragging a moan from my mouth when he does a sort of push up, rocking his hips between my legs.

Then he lowers himself again until he's hovering over me, placing his elbows on the bed on either side of my head.

"I hate you," I whisper.

"Rightly so," he says.

And we're kissing, mouths slanting, tongues warring, teeth scraping as our bodies slide and rock together.

Shit, shit, my rational mind chants, *this is a bad idea, I thought we decided we weren't doing this again.*

Oh yes, yes, my body is crowing, *we want this, we want this angel, we want them all...*

Yeah, rough sex with all of them. They owe me some pleasure after betraying me. That's all this is. Scratching an itch with gorgeous men who also happen to want me at this moment, a break in our hating each other.

That's my excuse, the need for this break, this distraction from the train wreck that my life has become, the physical sensations driving from my mind the thoughts of my family, of the curse, of everyone getting hurt right now because of me.

I grab fistfuls of Asa's hair—it's longer than I remember—and dive into the kiss like it's going to save me from drowning in the dark.

I think it's having listened to Ryu and trying to piece together what he said.

It's Tir whispering to me that he has a family and to tell them he tried.

It's Asa trying to get back to Heaven.

What does it all mean?

I hate you, I think, *I hate you so much. You used me. I loathe you.*

And I want you so badly it hurts.

I don't know what's happening to me and my world, but you're here now, you're real, and you can make everything go away for a while.

Please...

He doesn't seem to have any objections, sliding that powerful body over mine, one hand lowering to caress my ribs, my hip, dive between us, between my legs as he does an almost impossible push-up on one elbow, muscles rippling across his chest—

I gasp in his mouth when his questing fingers slip between my legs, between my wet folds, finding my clit and rubbing it as he continues kissing me, striking sparks off my nerve endings, flooding me with a need so great I arch up and bite into his full lower lip.

Oh God, yes...

How... how does he know what to do with my body, a creature of angelic fire? Last time I hadn't had much mindspace to wonder. Didn't know much about him.

Still don't.

Then I have no more time to question it because he removes his fingers and something much bigger takes their place. Way, way bigger. And my insides clench, empty, needing him.

"Give it to me," I whisper against his lips, going crazy with desire. "Put it in me, do it..."

He growls something I can't quite catch, gripping his cock, pushing into me. He's thicker than Ryu and maybe even Rook, the thought flashes through my head, not sure if that's a good or bad thing.

Thick and hard and scorching hot, his cock wrenches a cry from my throat as it bullies its way into me, spreading my legs wider, snagging my breath in my lungs. Of all of them, I never thought he'd be down for this...

My hands slip from his silky hair to his corded neck and lower, to his hard-rock chest. His cock thrusts deeper and I wrap one leg around a muscular thigh, urging him on.

He groans, slipping even deeper. There's so much of him to take in. Not sure I can take him all. His eyes are unfocused, gazing almost blindly down at me. In fact, they seem to be faintly glowing an eerie sky blue.

Huh.

There comes again that light brush of zinging energy along my senses, like small zaps of electricity along my nerves, and it makes his cock feel even better inside me.

Oh yes. Yes...

It's as if his cock is expanding to an impossible size, filling me up and up and up but in the best way, until I titter on the edge of an earth-shattering orgasm. I'm holding my breath, digging my nails into his pecs, my mouth falling open, and then...

His eyes widen a little and his hips jerk when my core contracts, hard, almost painfully, around his cock. Then pleasure floods me and I cry out again, my head falling back, neck arching as I pulse around his girth.

Feels good...

My eyes start to close, but he bends over me again, capturing my mouth in a searing kiss as he grunts and rocks deep into me, his cock jerking as he comes.

Wow. His elbow is still by my head. His lips are still on mine but he seems to have forgotten we're kissing, his eyes still wide, his mouth going slack. His hips are still gently humping mine, his softening cock still filling me up, sending small aftershocks of pleasure through me.

I float in a haze, my mind blessedly empty, my body buzzing, my limbs loose.

I like sex, as it turns out. I like it a lot.

You like it with these guys, you mean?

Shut up, brain. Always so unhelpful. I'm trying to go into denial here and you're in the way.

You also like this magic thing they do, actual magic magnifying the sensations, making it even more delicious.

Yeah, or maybe I'm turning into a sex maniac. A deviant. A nympho. Maybe that was always my nature. Nothing to see here. Move along.

And then the door opens with a whine and I see a change come over Asa's face. His eyes are still faintly glowing, but now they narrow, and his jaw clenches. He sits up, yanking his cock out of me—ouch!—to stand up by the bed.

Buck naked.

He looks sexy as all Hell, and it's hard not to appreciate the view of him from behind, too, with butt cheeks so tight you can bend a quarter between them, muscular legs, and that powerful back flaring up from narrow hips to broad shoulders and brawny arms.

However, now I can also see the other guys, standing there in a row, staring at us. I can see their incredulous and mostly angry faces.

"Holy fuck," Ryu whispers.

"Did you wait for us to turn our backs so you two could fuck?" Kass snarls.

"Oh, get off your high horse, vampire," Rook says. He's the only one who looks amused. "The kids have a right to have fun."

"The kids?" Kass sounds like he's about to explode into a thousand bats. "What the Hell?"

With a small groan, I sit up. Cum is once more leaking between my legs. It's getting to be an annoying habit.

You should do something about that, a small voice at the back of my mind says. *No condom. You have to talk to someone. The school medic perhaps. Or Juliette.*

And *oh-uh,* Kass is moving toward us. The look he's giving us is truly murderous. I have to deal with that, too.

"What the fuck, Frankie." His gray eyes are blazing, moving from Asa who's standing there like a brick wall—a sexy brick wall, but you get my drift—to me. "You slept with Rook, Ryu, and now Asa, too?"

"Fucked," I say, "that's the word you used, isn't it? We fucked."

"*Cazzo.* Why?"

"Why not? Can't a girl have some fun? Having fed on me doesn't give you rights over me," I tell him. "I don't report to you."

"And what about me?" Tir mutters, stepping closer.

I flick what I hope is a disinterested look over him. "What about you?"

Something cracks in his gaze, something I refuse to acknowledge. "Frankie..."

"Are you going to fuck all of us?" Kass demands. "Is that your plan? Like some sort of weird revenge?"

I glare at him. "Only if you're a good boy."

Rook chokes a little. He clears his throat loudly.

"All of you, listen good. Nothing has changed. I hate your guts. Sleeping with you means nothing to me. You hear me? Nothing. It's just sex."

Rook laughs softly. "That's my girl."

"I'm not your girl," I snap, getting up naked as I am and turning to climb the ladder to my bunk. "I need to grab some clothes. My towel is hanging on a hook behind the door where I put it to dry this morning."

I feel like crying and I'm not even sure why. This is revenge, isn't it? Didn't start out that way, but the way they react tells me they aren't happy.

And they shouldn't be. I hate them, I want to hate them, I don't want to need them or want them or like them. I need my anger to protect myself from them, to keep my distance, to keep my heart safe.

Why is it so hard to do?

24

FRANKIE

*I*t's a relief to be alone. I wonder how they allowed this to happen. How Asa didn't follow me right into the girls' showers.

He's probably standing guard outside the door.

Him, or one of the others.

Walking past two unfamiliar girls showering, I grab a showerhead a bit further in and hang my things on the hooks, then turn the faucet on and wait for the hot water to run.

How do I feel about that? About the guys standing guard outside? I'm annoyed of course. But then why is this strange sense of pleasure at the thought trickling through?

No. Stop it, Franks. I splash my face. This morning feels like a strange dream. Hell, all these past days do, not to mention weeks and months, but... did I really just have sex with Asa?

A throb deep inside tells me that, yes, I did.

I can't fight the tiny smile pulling at my lips. With every guy, it has been different, but always good. So good. And I shouldn't be doing that, but again, what does it matter? Tomorrow is as uncertain as can be and why not *carpe* the *diem* a little and have fun while I can?

Who knows? It might show me that what I thought was feelings is actually only lust.

Scratch that itch, girl. Get it out of your system. Take your pleasure and close off your heart.

I take my soap, squirt some in my palm, but as I lift my hand, another aroma hits my senses.

No way... I lift my wrist to my nose. I smell like Asa.

And Ryu and Rook.

Masculine musk.

It's as if they rubbed the essence of their scent into my skin. I draw their scent deep in an inhale, then let my hand drop to my side.

Damn. Are they wearing aftershave or something? How can their scent cling to me like that? And how can I smell it over the soap? I thought only shifters had that kind of sense of smell.

A Drekavac, I think. That's a vampire. But what if I'm a kind of shifter, instead? No, that's insane. I've never shown any signs of shifting. Plus, what kind of shifter can kill with a scream? None that I ever heard of.

Though there are rare kinds, too. Even kitsune, who aren't that rare, may have abilities I don't know enough about. Like Ryu with his ability to cast illusions.

I shiver when I remember what he did. His conjuring of my cousin was so real... Who's to say there isn't a type of shifter out there who can turn people into piles of ash?

Right on the heels of that thought, a girl's frightened cry rings out behind me and I whirl about, reaching for a knife that isn't there—because in the blur that my morning was, I left my knives under my pillow. Not your usual shower accessory.

Shit!

"Frankie! Where are you?" a male voice I recognize sounds inside the showers. "Hi there. I'm just looking for Frankie."

"Rook!" My heart is pounding. Annoyance burns in my

chest. "What are you doing here? It's girls only showers. Stop bursting in!"

Hypocrisy, I know. I was about to go barging into the boys' showers earlier to talk to Ryu. But guys generally don't feel threatened by a woman's presence, unlike the opposite case.

"Fuck that," Rook says. "Excuse me, ladies. I promise I'm not looking—*much*. No need to turn away." He lifts his hands. "Look, no touching."

He's standing there, dressed in black slacks and a light blue shirt loose over them, his long black hair caught back in a messy bun.

Handsome as a devil.

I roll my eyes. "Rook, what are you doing?"

"Showering with you. Okay, not actually showering, but getting wet, that's for sure. Damn, I should have come naked. Pun intended. Coming naked. Get it?"

I sigh. "Why are you here?"

"You are upset."

"You don't say," I mutter.

"I came to make a suggestion to you."

"To stop having sex with the lot of you?"

He grins. "No, nothing like that. I'm an incubus, remember? Sex is my specialty."

"I remember." I put my hands over my boobs, a reflex move. Somehow it felt weird to be naked in front of him in this context. A non-sexual context. "And you thought you had to talk to me alone? In the girls' showers? Is it something urgent?"

"I wanted some privacy." He rolls his eyes when a girl squeals again and I agree it's quite unnecessary as he has his back to them. I have this weird thought that she wants him to look. From the other guys.

"What for?"

"To talk. Yeah, I know, why not fuck instead, right? But I was thinking... in all your research about your father's identity, have you considered demons?"

"No," I say, "never. What a novel idea. How kind of you to suggest it."

"Frankie." He grabs my shoulders, shakes me a little. "Stop it."

"Stop what? "

"Stop pushing us away. We're all you have right now." Some more shaking. "Don't you get it?"

"Right, I should be grateful because you protected me before—"

"—we delivered you to our handlers." He shakes me again. "I know. We can't unfuck that, and hate-fucking us isn't making you feel any fucking better."

"That's a lot of fucks," I mutter. "And how do you know what can make me feel better? Rook, stop it, you're making me dizzy."

He releases my shoulders, frowns. "Am I?"

"I just need some breakfast." I turn my back to him. I mean, what the Hell, he's seen me naked more than once but like I said, this context feels different. Too intimate. The wound in my side feels hot. It's scabbed over though so it's all healed, right?

"Don't beat around the bush. Tell me what's on your mind. Because you're right, okay? You're goddamn right to be angry but right now, let us help you. Take any advantage you can."

"And then what, I'll fight and escape from Heaven or Hell all by myself?" A hysterical laugh escapes me. I slap a hand over my mouth and hope I won't start sobbing. I'm so scared but of course, I don't say any of that. "You are the eyes and ears of your House, Rook. Don't ask me to trust you, to share information with you."

"Then just listen. Just listen to me. I've seen things in the bowels of Hell few have. Demons have powers that may cause sickness and death. It's their very definition. I know you're looking into shifters and vampires but maybe you should go to the source of demonblood to find your answer."

I look at him over my shoulder. "Do you know of a demon who can kill with a scream?"

"Not off the top of my head, no. But there are ancient creatures down there, darling, ruling all the evils of the world since the dawn of time, like Pazusu and Lilitu and their friends. All kinds of agony, all kinds of death, you just name it."

"But not all demons are that bad."

"Demons are bad, baby, mark my words."

I shiver.

He reaches for me but only tucks a wet strand of hair behind my ear. "Also, demons like sex. That fits."

"All races like sex, Rook."

I think of Asa and have to disagree. "Not the angels, as far as I know."

"And yet."

"Right you are." He lets out a bark of dark laughter. Shakes his head. "Fucking seraph. Didn't expect him to pounce on you the moment we stepped outside the room. Maybe I'm losing my touch. I used to be able to tell who's sex-crazed just with a look."

"You really think he is one?"

"One what? A seraph?"

"No, a flying pig. Yes, a seraph."

He chuckles. It's a warm, dark sound I feel in my core. "Right."

Clenching my thighs, I reach for my towel. "You really should get out of the girls' baths, Rook. You're making them uncomfortable."

"But not you."

No, because I've bounced on your cock, I think, but press my lips together.

"For what it's worth," he says, "I do think he's a seraph."

Ah.

"I think he is one now," Rook goes on. "Not sure what he was before."

By the time I turn around to gape at him, he's gone from the showers.

And I still don't know why he thought coming to talk to me was so urgent.

———

Am I half-demon?

The thought bounces inside my head as I dry myself, wrap my towel around my head, and get dressed. The two girls have already left, rushing to finish their shower after Rook made his appearance.

The boys aren't helping me make any friends.

Which is a stupid thought. What use do I have for friends in a place I won't stay in? I think of that other girl I made in the showers.

Rue, that was her name. She had seemed nice. Feels like a shame not to try and make more friends, regardless of the circumstances.

Granddad would be horrified.

By my lack of mistrust.

By my eagerness to jump onto the guys' cocks.

I almost laugh out loud when I imagine his shocked expression if he finds out. Then I sober up just as quickly. Not that I'd want him to know. Ew. The thought makes me feel embarrassed, and then angry because I shouldn't feel that way. It's just... family. You never stop being a child around them, do you? And anyway...

This isn't funny.

No, but the situation is so ridiculous it might as well be.

"Not sure what he was before."

I said that. It's a gut feeling, a compilation of the things he's said, the things he's done. His double-faced personality. All the weird little things I noticed about him.

What could it mean? I can't think straight. The shower has cleared my head a little, but I still feel a little... fuzzy. A little drunk. It's so strange.

Breakfast. Coffee. That's what I need. I've had too many shocks, too much stress, and also, too much sex in the past twenty-four hours with close to no food. A girl needs sustenance.

Finally covered in clothes, I walk out of the showers, finding Kass of all people waiting outside.

I give him a frosty look, then keep walking. I don't even ask where Rook has gone. They're like revolving doors, following a system I don't understand to keep me safe, or whatever.

Unless they have no system at all, just playing by ear, coming and going, only making sure one of them stays put to babysit.

"Hey. Wait up." He's still limping pretty badly but I refuse to ask the question that is crowding my mouth.

Instead, I keep going.

"Rook wanted to talk to you," he says and curiosity forces me to slow down, despite myself.

"He did."

"He told us you might be half-demon. Rook blabs a lot. But I don't think he's right."

"Why not?"

"You barely have any demonblood in you," Kass says quietly, reaching my side. He's scowling at nothing in particular. "I'd have tasted it when I fed on you."

He looks pale and tired. And beautiful.

"You should find a blood donor," I say.

His jaw clenches. "Look... I'm sorry I reacted so badly. It's just that I asked you to be my donor again, and you refused, but didn't have any trouble taking all the others to your bed."

"I didn't take Tir."

He gives me an incredulous look. "Then better hurry up and do him before breakfast," he snarks, "not to break your streak."

For some reason, that makes me snicker. "You jealous, Kass?"

If his jaw clenches any more tightly, he'll chip a tooth.

Wait... Is he jealous?

Nah, he's a guy. He just wants sex. Probably thinks it's unfair I passed on him and slept with others.

Well, whatever. It's not like I keep a tally. I don't have a plan to do them all.

He curses softly and I realize he's strayed behind. I turn to find him leaning against a wall, his face kind of gray.

"Is it your leg?" I blurt out before I remember I'm not supposed to be worried about them. "Is it getting worse?"

"I'm okay," he blatantly lies.

"What happened to your leg? Will you finally tell me?"

I don't think he will, but after a long pause, he says, "It's an old injury."

"Don't tell me you fought in the world wars, like Ryu."

"Why, does his age bother you?"

"It's weird, is all. He looks so young."

"Huh. And what about me? Are you saying I look younger than him?"

I shake my head, fighting another snicker. I don't know why I'm not glaring at him and stomping around, demanding they keep their distance. All that sex must have loosened me up. Screwed up with my mind. "You all look young."

"I'm not as old as Ryu," he admits. "Not over a hundred, in any case."

"A hundred?"

"He's a kitsune. He's at least a hundred years old. More."

I knew that, but it feels like new information. I absorb it as we make our way to the room. I mean, it makes sense if he fought in the First World War already... "And you?"

"You sure you want to know?" He isn't smiling, though. "Around fifty, I think. Give or take a few years. Been in this business for the past twenty or so."

"This business? Trying and failing to abduct women from Colleges?"

"Fighting for the House of Water," he corrects me, as if it's self-evident. "To stop the apocalypse, the end of days."

"What do you mean? Stop the Antichrist? Isn't that ironic, given you're of demonblood?"

He shrugs his broad shoulders. "There has been balance in the world, since the Coalescence. Disturb it and it all falls apart like a house of cards. Besides which, nobody wants the world to end."

"So you're, what, the balance keepers?"

"They call us The Guard."

I huff a laugh, stopping outside our room, clenching the shampoo and shower gel bottles in my hands. "You're kidding me. You have a name like a boyband? And you're an actual organization?"

"Not as such. We're recruited and given contracts."

"Mercenaries with a cause. And I suppose I am the Antichrist."

He gives me a startled look, then frowns. "Nobody said that."

"Then what am I supposed to be?"

"An undiffused bomb that rolled in the middle of it all?"

"Gee, thanks. And how are you keeping this balance? Who are you fighting?"

"Not sure I should be telling you all this. It's not exactly classified but we don't tell humans about it."

"I'm not human."

"No. You're not. That's true." He leans against the wall by the door, crossing his legs at the ankles, folding his arms over his chest. Going for nonchalant but I'm pretty sure he's resting his bad leg. "There has been a disturbance in Hell. Surges of great power. New demons appearing, armies of them sometimes. It's as if Hell is about... to give birth to something."

"And you think that's me?"

"No, I don't think that. But nobody is asking me, and besides that, I wouldn't know what to look out for. I'm only a mercenary, like you said."

"I don't believe you're just that," I whisper, a little shaken. *The antichrist? God.* "What are they holding over you, Kass? Is it this Brody guy?"

He flinches. "It's not what you think."

"You don't know what I think."

"I failed him. I owe him and I wasn't able to stop his death."

"So he's dead?"

"It's... complicated."

"No, Kass, it's not. Is he dead or alive?"

"Neither and both."

"Stop making fun of me," I hiss, grabbing the door handle and twisting. "Now excuse me. This undiffused bomb has classes to attend."

25

KASS

*F**uck!**

I keep fucking this up.

Is there a way *not* to fuck this up, though? I wonder as I follow her into the room. A way to unfuck it? Can't see it.

Here I'm not only talking about how cold Frankie is, how angry and afraid. I can smell her fear, I can see it in her eyes. And she should be afraid. Antichrist or not, she's the prize both Heaven and Hell are willing to bet on in a battle I can't even see, a war I can't grasp. I may have been fighting in it for most of my life, but the bigger picture is lost on me.

What are the powers that be afraid of? What is coming? Does Frankie really have a role in it?

Be ready to deliver her, the House of Water told me, *when the moment comes.*

Deliver her for what? I thought she'd knew, I thought she'd be evil incarnate, that I'd have no doubts once I met her. But she isn't what I expected, and she doesn't seem to know either.

She has been asking what everyone wants her for and I have no answers to give her. When I posed the question, I was met with silence on the other end. At the time, I didn't have the luxury to question it, to question my decisions and my contract.

And what has changed? I ask myself. *Nothing, that's what. Except you fucked up and can only hope to end up succeeding at least in being the one to have the last laugh.*

The last glimpse of her pretty face, those dark, dark eyes, and that bow of a mouth that's made for kissing, not for sarcasm and scathing answers. That long pale hair that's made for caressing or twisting in your fist in passion, that body that's made for love.

Not fucking.

No, more than that. For worship.

Now I'm half-hard thinking of her underneath me, moaning my name, I think of my fangs sinking into her neck will my dick sinks—

A scent hits my senses and I'm tearing into the room, shoving Frankie aside before the conscious part of my brain even catches up. Someone's there, and it's not one of us.

A man.

Smells like Fae.

"Who are you?" I demand of the fae man who's poking through the covers on Frankie's bunk. "Get out."

He turns around and grins, showing off those sharp Fae teeth.

I recognize him now. "Cirdan," I mutter, unable to keep the hostility out of my voice. The bullies were back in action. I wonder what took them so long, to be frank.

"Who is he?" Frankie asks.

"He's Jatri's second in command. I said get out." I start toward him, feeling my rage build, my fangs lengthening, my vision turning crimson. "Before I tear you apart."

"Woo, scary," he says, voice flat, but his face pales a little and he takes a step back. "Easy now. I'm only here to deliver a message."

"What message?"

"It's not for you, nightchild. To her."

My eyes narrow at him, but before I can stop her, she steps out from behind me.

"So speak, Cirdan," she says, "and get this over with."

He gives her an insolent once-over, a smirk on his face. Now she's in front of me, he obviously feels more at ease. Is he an idiot? She's far more dangerous than anyone in this College and probably the entire country. "Francesca Seymour. Or should I say, Francesca Apollinari?"

"So you've heard the news," she says.

The urge to wring his neck is growing by the second. I have to clasp my hands together not to go through with it. If *figlio di puttana*, speaking to her as if they're buddies.

She's my protégé, and I am her guardian while the others are away. She's my prize, my goal, my target. Mine.

"Greetings from Enbeliar Jatri of the House of Air, Francesca."

"Enbeliar?"

"Not familiar with the fae language? And here we thought you might be one of us, in the end. It means leader."

"You thought wrong," she says coolly and wraps the towel from her head, letting her long pale hair loose over her shoulders.

Now I'm fighting a grin. That's my girl.

And... no, fuck, wait...

"Oh? We thought that your father may have been a member of the Banshee clan, one of the washers and lamenters. A descendant of Aeval."

"I don't wash clothes in the river," she says, "though if I don't do laundry soon, I'll have nothing left to wear. And the only thing I'm lamenting right now is my wasted time, Cirdan of the House of Air."

"So flippant," Cirdan says with admiration.

"And so *not* fae," she counters.

My lips fight to twitch into another grin. *Dammit.* I doubt she can know for sure, in fact as I understand it, she still doesn't know what she is, but her answers to Cirdan tick all my boxes.

Damn, lady.

"Be that as it may," Cirdan says, his face drawing tight with carefully bunked anger, "here is my message."

"Fucking finally," I say.

"Shut up, Batboy."

"Up yours, fae idiot."

Cirdan glares daggers at me, and I glare right back. What, he thinks I'm scared of him?

"If you got something interesting to say, Cirdan," Frankie mutters, walking past us to drape her wet towel over the chair by the desk, "better do it now. I'm kinda busy."

Stifling a laugh, I watch Cirdan's face contort with white-hot fury. He's not used to anyone talking back to him like that. Jatri's second is probably Gentry Elf, a pampered mamma's boy who is used to ruling this College, everyone bowing and scurrying out of his way.

He turns away from me to follow her with his gaze, and I'm ready to grab him and shove him into a wall if he takes another step toward her. "As I was saying, Enbeliar Jatri sends a message, asking you to join him to talk."

"To talk?" I mutter. "Is that Fae-speak for torture?"

Cirdan ignores me which may be the wisest move he's made all day. "What answer shall I convey, Edel Aeval?"

"I'm not Aeval's daughter, like I just said." Frankie combs through her hair with her fingers, also turning around to face Cirdan. "Talk about what?"

"I wasn't told and I didn't ask. He wants to meet in the park, by the white kiosk."

She blinks.

"It's near the lake," I say. "But you're not going."

Her brows draw together. "We will see about that," she says. "And now if you both don't mind, I have history of the magical races to attend. Fascinating subject, don't you think? So much to learn. Goodbye, Cirdan."

———

After the disgruntled fae has left, I grab my backpack with my notebook. My lash is already stashed at my hip.

"We need to put wards on the door," I say, and limp over there to do just that. Biting into my thumb, I use the blood to do some basic warding. "This should do for now. Can't have any more shitheads waltzing in here like the own the place. Not safe."

"How did you do that?" she whispers, coming behind me and she smells of her floral shampoo and soap but also of warm, sweet girl. Sweet blood. Sweet cream.

She traces a hand over the wood of the door and I frown.

"Can you see the symbols?"

"They kind of... glow darkly."

I snort. "Good description. If you see them, that means you do have some trace of demonblood in you." Not a big help, as practically all magical creatures nowadays have a mixture of the two main forms of magic, demonic and elemental. "You need to practice your magic, in case you need me, or one of the others."

"Need you? You mean like I needed Asa earlier?"

Fuck. My brain was slow to catch up but now my body is waking. My dick stiffens more. *Dammit.*

I scowl at her. "I mean, if you're in danger."

"Gotcha." Her grin is cheeky and it transfixes me.

"If you ever need me, ping me." I have to clear my throat. "Remember how to do that?"

"I never learned."

"Fuck. We were supposed to show you."

Her lashes are dark and long, curving over her eyes. I stare down at her face, losing my train of thought.

"We went over that," she says. "I can't use magic."

"You have to try it, Frankie. You need to be able to communicate with us. Stop fearing your magic."

"Easy for you to say." She slings her backpack over one shoulder and opens the door. "You didn't kill all those people."

"I have killed people, Frankie. Wait."

And I'm again limping after her, cursing under my breath. I failed Brody, failed in everything I've undertaken, and somehow being in this College with her seems like the worst fucking torture.

I keep getting dry-fucked.

Dammit.

————

We are an old race, vampires. We walked among the Sumerians and the Assyrians. We forged empires. We put senators in the Roman Senate when Julius Cesar was mucking about the Mediterranean.

But I'm not that old for a vampire myself, my life has been a fucking mess, and to top it all, it never prepared me for the hot feeling in my chest when Tir steps in Frankie's way and she stops to talk to him.

It's the same hot feeling that gripped me when I found her lying under Asa, or when I found out she slept with Ryu and Rook.

It makes no sense. I don't want her. And I don't wish her to want me, because it wouldn't make any sense. I can't stand anyone touching me, anyone under me. I've known it for a stupidly long time, and yet...

And yet she keeps twisting my thoughts.

It's as if she's changing me, and I don't have a damn clue why. She doesn't like me. I don't... well, that's the problem. I don't know what I feel for her. It reminds me of what I used to feel for Brody, what I still feel, but it's less... difficult.

I don't even make sense to myself. My relationship with Brody is fraught with complications and guilt, and with her...

Cazzo, Kassander. As if you have any sort of relationship with her other than that of a kidnapper waiting to happen.

Well, my relationship with Brody wasn't much better.

And then my eyes narrow when Tir grabs her hand and starts pulling her away faster than I can catch up.

"Hey. Hey, *stronzo!*" I break into a jog even if it's killing my hip. "What the Hell are you doing? It's my shift guarding her."

He sneers at me, that perfect mouth turning ugly. His sharp teeth glint white. "You can barely walk, *kerel,* let alone protect her. Sit and rest your leg or you won't be good for anything."

"Won't be or are not?" I put in a burst of vampire speed and reach them. I grab his wrist, pulling his hand away from hers. "Tell us how you really feel about me, then."

"I feel that you are slow and weak. That you shouldn't be trusted to be alone with her."

"Afraid she might fuck me, too, leaving you in the dust?"

"Oh, I'm not afraid of that. You haven't fed. I doubt you can even get hard at this stage."

"Fuck you, Tir."

"You wish, *abesh.*"

"What's your problem?"

"Guys," Frankie says. "Cut it out."

"You almost killed me," Tir says, ignoring her and it only makes me angrier, because who does he think he is, to ignore her like that?

"You grabbed her and ran," I retort. "What the Hell did you expect?"

"I have my reasons. I have a family to go back to."

"And I have a soul to release, so why do you think your reasons are any better than mine?"

We blink at each other.

"A soul?" Frankie asks, her voice hushed. "What do you mean? Is this about Brody?"

Before I can even think of a reply, though, or berate myself for letting that slip, guys appear seemingly out of nowhere, coming at us.

Shifters.

I've been so goddamn stupid, focusing on myself, on this feeling of... of jealousy? Instead of looking out for bullies.

Tir is right, I think as they approach. I suck at protecting her.

"Kraish," Tir mutters, reaching for Frankie again and this time I let him, realizing it's time I faced the music. Tir was right. Without feeding, I'm a liability. And right now...

"We got to lose them," I say, "and with my damn leg I'll only slow you down."

"Kass," Frankie starts and actually reaches out a hand to me, a strange emotion in her eyes. "Don't—"

"Go," I say. "Run to the end of the path, then turn left, around the Charms and Potions lab. Run past the monster stables where they keep the beasts for the arena, and you'll find a storeroom building you can hide in.

"How do you know all that?" Tir breathes.

"He memorized the map of the college," Frankie says.

I nod. "That's right. Take her and go."

"And you?"

"I will distract them."

"No," Tir says, "you should go with her. You're weakened, but my magic is fine. I'll keep them away from you. Ping the others as you go."

"I'm not leaving you here," Frankie says, "Tir. I'm not leaving either of you."

"You hate us," Tir reminds her, pushing her toward me.

I shove her right back. "You idiot, I can't run and you know it. Just go!"

And this time he listens to me. Grabbing a protesting Frankie, he lopes away. I ping the others as I turn to face the shifters, standing in their way, and crack my knuckles, both physical and metaphorical.

I may be weakened, but I'm still a warrior trained to fight. And now fucking *finally* the restrictions are gone.

26

FRANKIE

J told Tir I was invited to talk with Jatri and he almost popped a vein in his forehead.

"You can't go," he'd hissed. "It's a trap."

And then Kass had arrived and picked a fight with him. Okay, that's not really fair. They picked a fight with one another.

Right before the shifters arrived.

"Let me go." I push at Tir but he doesn't release my wrist as he hauls me inhumanly fast away from Kass and the approaching bullies. My backpack is thumping against my side, my injured side, and it hurts like Hell. "You said it. He can't take them on. We have to go back."

"No, he was right. He'd be slow and give them a chance to get to you. You are our priority."

"Stop. Just stop. You're willing to sacrifice him for your own gain?"

"To protect you," he says mulishly.

"Oh bullshit. I'm going back. I'm not helpless."

"You won't even try to use your goddamn magic. That makes you as helpless as a human."

Shit. He's right. But... "I could kill everyone."

"And they could kill you. If you can defend yourself, we'll be less worried."

I stare into his blazing green-gray eyes and make my decision. "Show me." I swallow hard. "Show me how to ping you when I need help for starters."

He pulls me behind a storeroom building and finally stops. "You sure?"

"Yes."

He takes my hand, turns it palm up. "Call on your power."

"Don't I need blood for the—"

"Your elemental power. That's what you used with the assassins. Your mother is a powerful witch."

"But how—?"

"Elemental power draws from the elements. You can either draw from the earth and air, the fire and water, or from creatures belonging to those elements." He holds my gaze. "Like me."

Right. I know all that. I grew up with a witch and studied about magic but I've never tried. Oh sure, growing up, I pulled tricks right and left when playing with my cousins, but my aunt always said she wanted us to grow up normal, and that I'd learn how to use my magic in school.

Then the first incident happened and all talk of teaching me to use my magic stopped. Granddad came and took me away. I was twelve.

For a long time, the details of that day remained fuzzy. To this day I can't remember parts of what happened. But I know that it was the first attack on my life.

"Frankie," Tir says and I blink, finding him closer than I'd expected. I have to tilt my head to meet his gaze. "You have to try."

I'm out of sorts. Kass is back there, surrounded by bullies. I didn't let him feed on me and he can barely walk. And here is

Tir, acting so patient and kind, and where is my hate when I need it? I need to cling to it.

I close my eyes and reach for that place inside me where power pulses like a heart, summoning it, my senses expanding to find the elements I could draw from. I feel the air in Tir, and it's a murmur, a word, a breath, a wind, a name—

He jerks away from me, the connection cutting off, leaving me gasping and dizzy, dizzier than I've been all day. "What the fuck do you want?"

He's not talking to me, I realize after a moment, and turn to see who he's addressing.

Fae. Including Cirdan who's looking smug, twirling a delicate knife between his fingers.

"Tirius." Fancy meeting you here. "As for what I want... Your little girlfriend was asked to meet Jatri but she never showed up. So we take this as an act of war."

"Act of war? Are you insane?" I pull the other strap of my backpack over my other shoulder so that it's resting properly on my back, giving my aching side a break. "I was on my way to meet your kingpin but the shifters attacked us."

"I don't believe a word you say. We're taking you to him."

Tir prepares to strike. It's as if, having tapped into his power, I can now feel it gathering, a storm.

Cirdan's eyes narrow. He flicks his hand and his men start fanning around us. Magic. "So naughty, going against the College rules. Want a fight, Tirius? Want to measure your magic against ours?"

"Tir, don't." I put a hand on his arm.

"Or maybe," Cirdan cuts his gaze to me, "it's Francesca who wants to give it a try? Wild rumors are flying about you. Is it true you can kill with your voice?"

"Want to see if the rumors are true?"

His smirk falls. "You should talk to Jatri."

"Yeah." I sigh. "I think I should."

"No," Tir says through clenched teeth. "You don't have to do this."

"I know. But I want to know what he has to say. And you should go check on Kass."

"The others will. He'd kill me if I left you alone to go help him, and you know it. I'm not leaving you out of my sight."

"Of course you're not." I swallow my next sigh together with my misgivings and fears. "Let's go and get this over with."

———

Crossing through campus, we enter one of the main school buildings. The classrooms are empty, the corridors echoing. Where is everyone? It's as if they were kicked out. Sent away so the Fae could have the building to themselves.

I frown as our path ends in front of a double door. It opens into a lecture hall, a small amphitheater with rows of black chairs. We troop down one of the aisles toward the podium.

Jatri is seated on the desk there as if on a throne, his long legs ensuring that his feet are planted on the floor. His blond hair artfully falling on his forehead, his clothes consisting of an old-fashioned dark blue tunic, belted at the waist, and pants tucked into tall leather boots. As we descend toward him, he leans forward, casual and nonchalant.

"Tirius," he says. "And the girl."

"Jatri," Tir mutters.

"I told you before, it's Enkeleth to you. Kneel at my feet."

"I'm not one of your minions."

Jatri waves a negligent hand. "Make him kneel."

As his minions reach for Tir, I step in front of him and glare at the kingpin of the House of Air. "Stop. You wanted to talk. So talk and stop the games."

"And here is the new fish," he says, rubbing his chin. "But not just any random new fish, are you?"

I glare at him. "What do you want?"

Truth is, my gut is a knot. I keep thinking of Kass, how we left him to deal with the bullies. Did the others arrive on time to help him? Are they okay? I can't even chide myself for caring. I'm too stressed, too distressed. And this clown is making a show of looking me up and down, as if deciding on a price for my pound of flesh.

Unexpectedly, Tir grabs me around the waist. "She's not yours, Jatri, so stop undressing her with your eyes."

"Oh? And you think she's yours?" Jatri's brows lift. "So deluded, *abesh*. And this has nothing to do with you."

"She's under my protection."

Jatri leans back and lets out a laugh. "How is that working out for you?"

"Just fine," Tir grits out. "Come on, Frankie, we're out of here."

"Wait." I dig my heels in. "Tir, wait. We can't."

"She's not stupid, unlike you," Jatri says, his gaze raking over my once more. He's a handsome Fae, like most Gentry, but I feel the need to scrub my skin clean once we're out of here. "She knows this talk is inevitable."

"Is it now?" Tir bares his teeth and snarls, his nails digging into my waist, turning into claws. Black is bleeding into his hair. "We'll see about that."

"Don't threaten me, Tirius. It won't end well for you." Jatri looks unperturbed, but somehow his gang closes in around us and their air magic crackles through me.

Could I draw on it, just like that. not caring about any consequences? Test my magic, taste theirs, see if at least my mother's inheritance is worth something?

"The College is closed off, as you well know," Jatri goes on. "The Wild Hunt won't have your back, if it ever did."

Tir reaches for something at the small of his back. A knife, no doubt.

"Tir," I whisper, "please don't."

"I won't let him toy with you," he hisses.

"Why, is that your privilege?" I hiss back.

He winces.

"If you don't mind," Jatri says, as if picking up a conversation we left off, "my business is with Edel Aeval, not an outcast wild Fae like you."

Tir growls, but I've had enough of this dick measuring contest and slap his chest with my palm. He chokes, mostly I think from surprise.

I nod at Jatri. "Like I told your boy earlier—"

"That ass-licker, Cirdan," Tir says.

"—I don't think I have banshee blood in my veins. My power doesn't seem to fit with what I know about banshees."

"We will see about that," Jatri says, whatever that means. "An eye witness said you turned a bunch of men into piles of ash."

I swallow, my throat dry. "There were eye witnesses?"

"Many men." His brows draw together. "With one scream, you reduced many men to ash."

"Yeah." I shrug, through inside I'm shaking, replaying that scene over and over. My heart is pounding. "I guess I did."

He frowns harder. With his pale coloring and square jaw, he's handsome, I suppose. Funny how I never even noticed his looks until, when my jaw dropped and my panties got soaked the first time I saw Tir and the other Wonderboys.

So strange.

"You are a weapon," he's saying now, "and Tir was sent to retrieve you for the House of Air."

I almost roll my eyes. "So I've been told. But what good is that for you? Heaven wants me."

"Everyone wants you," Jatri says, a calculating look entering his eyes.

Tir growls again and I slap his chest again, more lightly this time. It's like smacking a wall, and damn, I like that.

Bad girl, Frankie. Stop petting the muscular Fae mercenary.

"Go on," I say when Jatri stops. "Everyone wants me. What do you want to do, then? Help Tir?"

"He'd better stay away from you if he knows what's good for him," Tir snarls.

"But won't that give you an advantage?" I ask, turning my head up to look into Tir's handsome face. His eyes are almost black. "Having the Fae gang by your side?"

"If the Fae get their hands on you," he growls softly, "you may wish Hell got there first. So no, thanks."

I blink. "What do you care about that? Don't you want to accomplish your mission?"

"Yeah, Tirius." Jatri smirks. "What is it you really want? Want me to tell your superiors that you're not all in?"

"I am all in, damn you," Tir snaps, his power gathering again like a storm and I'm pretty sure he's got his hand on the handle of his knife again.

"Are you? Whose interests are you really serving?"

"Trust me, almighty Jatri," I mutter, "Tir is all on your side. He's ready to sell me for a handful of silver, so why don't you tell me what you have in mind or let me go. I have classes to attend."

"Wouldn't want you to miss them." Jatri leans back again, eyeing me carefully, like he thought I was a housecat and is now discovering I'm actually a baby jaguar or something. "As for what I want... First of all, to make sure the rumors are right. And second... to make sure you're ours."

An uncredulous laugh escapes me. "What?"

"I heard say," Cirdan mutters from behind us, "that when a woman says 'what,' she has heard what you said but is waiting for you to edit your statement before she eviscerates you."

"Is that true?" Jatri looks only mildly interested in his second's opinion.

"Yeah." I glare at them both. "Make sure the rumors are right? For real? What do you expect me to do, scream until you're all dead? Would that convince you? Shall we give it a try?"

"The rumors," he says, "that every single race, and even Heaven, wants you."

"And how will you find out?"

"By watching. So far, the evidence is compelling. You have a representative of each side following you around like a puppy—"

Tir growls, showing his sharp teeth.

"—from the moment you stepped foot here, plus there's the angel Heaven sent and the Dome placed over the College. I'm willing to suspend disbelief for now, even if the story sounds quite fantastic. I mean..." He gestures at me. "Look at you."

"I don't look dangerous," I say. "I know."

"You don't *feel* dangerous."

"I don't feel dangerous either, but here we are."

"Your magic, *elenyi*. I can't read your magical signature. You don't belong to one of the elements, though your power seems to be elemental, and your demonblood is weak at best, which fits with your story."

"My story," I mutter.

He gestures at me. "Daughter of the white Queen Witch, father unknown."

"How can you tell what sort of magic I have without even touching me or tasting my blood?"

"Easy," Jatri says. "Certain pureblood princes of the Unseelie Court can sense the sort of power someone carries. But with you... it's a near blank."

"You are Unseelie?" I whisper, unsettled. I mean Uncle Sindri is half Unseelie but that was the side of the family who assaulted his mother and got her pregnant with him. Not commendable.

"I'm not." He nods at Cirdan. "He is."

Great. You can never trust the Unseelie. They are Fairy's version of demons, wicked and selfish.

A College filled with the offspring of Fae Gentry and the scions of all the high courts of the four Houses. Who knows what powers they wield. We said we wouldn't hold back if they bullied us, but have we thought this through? Are the Wonderboys' powers a match for these shitheads?

I glance at Tir. He's got his stony face on. "Let's get out of here," he says.

"Yeah," I say. "Sorry, Jatri. Not interested in belonging to you."

"You either come willingly," he says, "or we make you. Your choice. Not letting a bastardly animal steal the glory of grabbing you for our King."

"Charming."

"You forget yourself," Tir mutters, taking a step forward and his hair is now all black, rising in an unfelt wind. His eyes are black too and his horns are rising from his head. Surprised at the sudden transformation, I jerk back. "You forget that what the Wild Hunt is. I won't let you force her into anything."

The Fae go very still. It's that stillness you see when a predator appears, that shock and uncertainty.

"*Enkeleth* Jatri," Cirdan says softly, bowing to his leader. "He's not one of the Hunt dogs. He's a confirmed. Hunter."

"I realized," Jatri says, frowning.

Tir lifts a hand with those black claws and a wind eddy appears, golden dust swirling on his palm. The horns have appeared on his head, solidifying by the moment. "By Arawn's name, I'll gut you and string your intestines across campus if you touch her against her will."

"Now, now," Jatri says, lifting his hands in an appeasing

gesture. "No reason to get over-excited. She may want us on her side until Heaven and Hell work this out between them. This College is about to turn into a battleground. You need to choose a side before the war begins and you find yourself on your own."

"She has us," Tir snaps and it's garbled—probably because his fangs are protruding, different than a vampire's, more curved and thick.

I'm fascinated.

He's fascinating.

My initial reaction so far has been to jump away but there's something about wild, savage, horned Tir that draws me in every time. I want to caress those horns, touch those fangs, explore his body to see what else is different...

"You mean yourself?" Jatri laughs. "Not sure that will be enough, Hunter, excuse my candor. There may be five of you but each one of you is working for himself, as you well know."

I glance between him and this creature Tir has turned into. The bogeyman. Something born of a nightmare. And sadly, Jatri's case is reasonable.

"I will think about it," I say and hold a finger up when Tir snarls at me like a wolf and refuse to cringe. *It's Tir,* I think, *he won't hurt me,* which is a stupid thought, given this whole situation.

"You have until tomorrow to decide, *Edel Aeval,*" Jatri says, his gaze fixed on Tir. "And take your Hunter with you. He's not part of the deal."

"Deal? You mean, extortion? Giving me no real choice?"

But Tir grabs my arm in his clawed hand and I have no choice but to follow him out, gritting my teeth against the pain of that grip.

27

FRANKIE

"Let go, Tir. Ow!" The wickedly sharp tips of his claws are digging into my flesh, and my backpack is thumping hard on my back with each running step. "Stop."

He doesn't release me, though, not until we're clear of the building and out in the open, in the yard between the various buildings, near the fountain where the bullies made us jump into once.

Feels like ages ago.

His claws open and I stumble away from him. The world tilts a little. I bend over, my hands on my knees, waiting for the dizziness to pass.

He paces in a circle, then comes back to me. "Frankie?"

"I'm okay," I whisper, and don't even have the energy to look up, see if he's back to his human-like self or not.

I'm not okay. I'm cold. My side hurts. That's where the wound was, isn't it? When I lift a hand there, it hurts so much I barely keep a cry between my teeth.

Shit.

Slowly I straighten, swallowing bile. "What did he mean,

you're not a dog but a hunter? I thought all Wild Hunt were hunters. As the name says."

"There are ranks in the Hunt. Dogs are those trailing the Hunt, cornering and retrieving prey. And the Hunters are the ones leading the Hunt."

His voice is quiet and has lost its growl, so I risk a look at him at last, and sag a little in relief. He's back to his usual pretty self and it's almost disappointing.

Almost. I mean, he's such eye candy that even with the dizziness and the adrenaline hammering away at my heart, I still want to climb him like a tree and that's saying something with how crappy I feel.

"And you're one of the leaders of the Hunt," I say.

"Nowadays I am, yeah. Wasn't always the case."

"You rose in the ranks," I whisper.

"For a long time, I thought there was no way back for me. That was it, the Hunt. I... lost my soul there. Hunting and killing. Maiming and slaying. Riding through the sky and taking on whoever the Fae King wanted us to kill. Slinking through Heaven and Hell, camping on earth... It's been all I've known for... so long."

"How long?"

"Let's just say... I make Ryu and Rook look young."

Now I'm wondering how old Rook is... But if Ryu is a hundred years old at least... then how old is Tir?

"And the family you mentioned? How are they still alive?"

He shrugs broad shoulders. "Time is different in the Hunt. We're required to fly back and forth to join almost simultaneous events and fights, therefore Hunters move outside of time."

"How is that possible?"

"We Fae are kind of impossible," he says softly, "don't you think?"

"You certainly are."

He grins, one of those devastating, sexy grins, and winks. *God.*

Then he sobers up. "You can't let Jatri and his buddies have you."

"But what difference does it make if you have me or they have me? End result is the same."

"The Fae play with their food. The journey toward an end matters."

I shiver. "What do you care? I thought you'd be happy to have the Fae on your side, keeping me for yourselves."

I'm so confused. I didn't expect him to open up to me. Didn't expect him to give a damn about what happens to me.

But he seems to be reading my thoughts, because he scowls. "I never said I wanted to see you tortured. I only need to deliver you as promised in my contract."

It shatters me. Teaches me yet again not to trust. "Right. Because once you deliver me to your king, he won't *play with his food*, as you said."

His scowl only grows darker. "The king is—"

But I never find out what he is because something in my chest sort of wrenches and it's strong enough to make me gasp. "What was that?"

He grimaces, rubbing at his chest. "A ping. You'll learn to recognize them. They're all different."

"This one... kind of burns. Who sent it?"

"Fire. Must be Rook. Let's go."

———

We run and the stich in my side is turning into a stabbing pain. I'm stubborn, though, so I grit my teeth and keep going until we're running through the park. Black is starting to eat at the edges of my vision and my lungs are working overtime. I have pretty good stamina, so yeah, this isn't good.

Before I collapse on my knees and beg for a break, though, we come to a clearing and there are the guys.

Or some of them.

First, I see Rook, then Ryu and Asa. Asa is helping Ryu up from the ground, and my gut clenches with worry. My lungs feel too tight.

Tir takes the scene in as well and halts. Tilts his head to the side in that way of his. "How's tricks?"

"Fuck you, man," Rook grumbles, turning toward us. His long hair is loose around his face, clinging to his neck and shoulders, and I think I catch glimpses of the scarred side of his face before he regains some control. "Think this is funny?"

"Funny, no. Interesting, yes. What the Hell happened here?"

"What's wrong with Ryu?" I ask. "And where's Kass?"

"Ryu will live. And Kass was taken." Rook's dark blue eyes flash and his voice bites, despite his otherwise relaxed posture, weight on one leg, on arm on a slim hip.

"Taken?" Tir echoes, losing some of the attitude, which is good. I almost cuffed him on the back of the head earlier, Wild Hunt or not.

Or the back of the leg, whatever. On his ass. These guys are so freaking tall.

"By the shifters, we presume," Asa says gravely and despite the reassurances, I hiss when he lifts Ryu to his feet and I see the blood soaking his side.

I mean, they said he'll live. But that's actually not very reassuring, is it? I remember learning that, when grievously injured, shifters need to shift to trigger that super healing mechanism of their bodies. The thought of Ryu turning into a fox is both intriguing—how big of a fox is he, really?—but also sort of worrisome, because will he still be thinking as a man? And how long would he need to remain in fox form for? School and college laws say shifters aren't allowed to shift without permission on campus.

"What did they take Kass for?" Tir steps forward to help Ryu and gets a snarl and a shove from our fox. Undeterred, he grabs his other side, shoring him up, so that Ryu is held between him and Asa.

Rook pulls his long hair back, twisting it at the base of his neck, turning to look toward the campus buildings. "Think, dumbass. They want something from us. Or from Frankie."

"And you let them take him? I told Frankie you'd be on top of this."

"On top? None of us are in top form right now."

"I am in top form," Rook says but that has to be sarcastic. He looks tired. "We should go get him back."

It's easy to ignore the fact that we all scraped by the skin of our teeth just two nights ago. Barely made it out of the attack alive and then each boy turning on the other to steal me...

"We should patch Ryu up," Asa says. "Before we do anything else."

"I'm fine," Ryu says, glaring at us all.

"Oh, is it just a flesh wound?" Rook sighs. "Asa is right, we should bandage that wound before you bleed out. Unless you feel like quickly shifting and fixing yourself now."

So I was right about that. And why doesn't he shift?

"I have some bandages with me," Asa says. "I brought them just in case."

"Ever the good cherub," Rook mutters with a grin.

"Seraph," Asa says, stopping. "Let's look at that wound."

"Get your hands off me," Ryu snarls when Tir lifts his shirt but doesn't fight him.

"I promise not to kiss you," Tir says.

Wait... what? Now I'm imagining them kissing and it's hot.

Too hot. Feels like I'm burning. And seeing all the blood painting Ryu's chest makes me feel faint. Which isn't like me. I'm not afraid of blood.

A shudder shakes me. I should be helping, discussing,

arguing, but I'm still standing there, as if rooted to the spot, my head spinning.

"You, sweetheart." Rook is suddenly turning me to face him, his dark brows drawn over his eyes. "What's this? You're hurt, too. How did you get hurt?"

I blink. "What?"

He takes my wrist and lifts my arm. That's when I notice the bloody gashes.

"Tir's claws," I whisper.

"Tir!" he bellows. "Come here."

"He didn't realize," I object. "He grabbed my arm to pull me out of the building."

"Which building?"

"Where Jatri wanted to talk to me."

"And Tir let you go to such a meeting?"

"Tir doesn't tell me what to do," I say, starting to get cross. "He accompanied me and he and Jatri compared dicks. It was lots of fun."

"Those asswipes," he growls.

But I'm starting to get angry, too—at myself, for softening around them, for starting to care, losing myself back in the lie.

I pull my arm out of his grasp.

"What's the matter?"

"I don't know, Rook, you tell me. Ryu is hurt and you're all concerned. Kass is taken and you're all gung-ho to go get him back. Meanwhile, Tir refused to work with Jatri who wants me on his team. What's going on here? Because there's no way I'm going to believe you give a rat's ass about me. Why are you working together? What's in it for you?"

"I don't trust Jatri," Tir says. "He'll fuck me over."

"Yeah, we don't trust these shitheads," Rook says. "We are independent agents. Our contracts are particular. We don't share."

"Oh. That I can believe. So your best bet is each other?"

"At least here I know where I stand," Tir grumbles.

Relief swamps me. I can go safely back to hating them. This isn't about me, it's about themselves.

"Let's patch Ryu up and get Kass then. What are you all waiting for?"

———

"How did you manage to let them carry Kass away?" Tir grumbles, propping Ryu against his side as Asa produces a package of bandages from a back pocket.

Somehow, I'd expected something more.

"Can't you just... touch him with your Glory and heal him?" I ask. I've sat down on the grass at some point. Can't remember when.

Rook is giving me curious looks, but I'm ignoring him. I'm too tired to pay attention to his looks of concern. A girl can sit in the grass to watch a few handsome guys patch each other up, right?

It should count as a show. The guys should sell tickets for girls and boys to watch them wipe down those chiseled chests and wind swaths of white gauze around them, while glaring.

It's hot. Strangely hot. How is it fair that whatever these guys do is hot? *Jesus.*

"Frankie," Rook says. "Doing okay?"

"Sure." I'm riveted by Asa's strong hands and the play of muscles in his corded forearms while he winds the gauze around Ryu's chest. "Asa, how about—?"

"I can't heal him with my power," Asa says and I blink. Oh. I already asked him that, didn't I? "Divine Glory can't heal those with demonblood in their veins."

"That's... shitty." I sigh, lean back on my hands. I'm content to be sitting here. Don't know where all the urgency went. What was it for?

Oh... right. Kass.

I giggle.

But what I really want to do is cry.

Asa moves away from Ryu, leaving him propped against Tir, and goes down on one knee beside me. "Are you feeling okay?"

"Mm... Been better." But I just lift a hand to trail over his square jaw, the super fine, golden stubble, then higher over his full lips. "Are all angels this pretty? Or only the seraphs?"

"Is she drunk?" Asa asks against my fingertips. It tickles.

Yeah, I feel kinda drunk, and not in the best way. Kind of sick.

"I thought seraphs were kind of monstrous," I go on, warming to my subject. "*Akyast.* The fiery flying serpents. Six wings, body made of copper, filled with fire. Hm... Not as hot as you, though."

"No idea if she's drunk," Rook says. "But we should go get Kass before the fuckheads who got him get bored and decide to toy with him. Shifters aren't exactly known for their self-restrain."

"As if demons are." Ryu bares his teeth.

Aw so cute. I think sometimes he forgets he's not in fox form anymore.

"*Azas.* So be it." Asa takes my hands in his. "Come on, Musen. Let's go rescue the grumpy vampire. This isn't exactly what Heaven ordered..."

28

ASA

She clasps my hand and it's warm, his slender fingers wrapping around me.

When Heaven ordered me to go about like before, I never thought it would mean working as a group, a real group with the other guys.

As if we're friends. Or at least working for the same side. This feeling of camaraderie is... odd and yet familiar somehow. Have I had friends before?

Not possible. Seraphs don't have friends. They don't have bodies, desires, needs—or hobbies or dogs, and again I get that flash of an image through my memory of the white dog running in the grass.

I pull Frankie to her feet, forcing the thoughts out of my head. She's light as a feather. I need to feed her more or she will get sick.

And I know this from my research on humans, and generally human-like creatures, supernatural or not. Not from any memory.

Right.

I pull Frankie up and she stumbles against my side.

Automatically, I wrap an arm around her, to steady her. And she doesn't move away.

Maybe she is intoxicated after all, I think, deciding to keep my arm around her, just in case.

"I should take you to our room," I say, "put you to bed. The others can help Kass without me."

"I don't trust you to put me in bed and don't climb in with me," she says and snorts as if she's said something funny. "Or myself not to climb you."

"Get a room, you two," Tir grumbles, hauling Ryu along.

"We have a room." Rook takes the lead as we trudge through campus. "Our room. And I'd love to see any of you climb one another."

"Or maybe Ryu should take her to her bed," I say, but the truth is, I don't like that and I regret suggesting it.

I frown as we make our slow way toward the buildings. I don't like the thought of lifting my arm off her, of passing her to Tir. Not because I don't trust him.

Another intriguing thought.

How would I feel if I saw her together with Tir? Tir with his arms around her. Her arms around his waist. Kissing, perhaps? Undressing...?

We stumble over a hollow in the path.

"Now who's tipsy?" she crows and hangs onto me as if I'm the only thing that keeps her standing.

None of us are, I think. I don't smell alcohol on her breath. If she has taken something, I can't detect it, though there's another smell about her, I realize, faint but unsettling.

It doesn't belong on her.

"Where the Hell could they be keeping him?" Tir asks, hauling Ryu along, his pale head bent close to the red one. They look like they're going on a romantic walk, not on a mission.

Glory of God, what's wrong with me?

"The shifters like to hold court in the largest auditorium lately, the so-called Grand auditorium," Rook tosses over his shoulder at us. "I've been watching them."

"How did the vampires let them do that?"

"It's a turf war, it seems. They alternate, depending on who has the upper hand in the moment."

"And the shifters happen to have the upper hand now? Why?"

"Chance?" I suggest. "The others are too busy trying to figure out what's going on to care?" I glance at Ryu, a shifter, but he offers no opinion.

In fact, Ryu hasn't said a word all this way. He hasn't pushed Tir away, though, which means he needs the support. Much like Frankie. Can they fight? We're compromised but neither of them seems inclined to follow my suggestion and go to the room to rest.

Something my subconscious seems way too happy about.

We make our way between buildings to the school classrooms and heading for the main auditorium. Frankie is breathing hard and I'm still dealing with that scent about her that bothers me, the feel of her curves pressed to me, waking up my body again.

My cock is hardening and I want to get naked with her again, pin her underneath me and pound into her.

I was told not to touch her sexually, and I went and had sex with her. It's a sin. It goes against my contract. Against my nature. What was I thinking?

Grinding my teeth so hard my molars hurt, I open my stride, following after Rook, all by carrying her along. She protests a little but lets me do.

That's unlike her.

She's sick, the thought hits me. That would explain the strange scent. Humans, even magical ones, can get sick. I've read all about it—*and remember all about it, though that's not possible*—

Someone steps in our way before we make it to the school building.

"Now, what have we here?" a voice says and a girl saunters into view. "Is it the angel and the witch's daughter?"

She's one of Greyson's, one of the few girls at the College. As I understand it, it's simply a matter of demonblood propagating better in males, same as angelblood. A different kind of magic than elemental magic that has always spread through women.

"And what are we, chopped liver?" Ryu mutters because this matter is apparently worth the effort of focusing and talking. "I keep getting fucked and not in an interesting way."

I frown at him. "Not in an interesting way?"

"What about with Frankie?" Rook asks.

"That was... different." Ryu's pale cheekbones color.

"Eyes here." The girl snaps her fingers, a disgruntled expression twisting her broad features. "Don't go spacing out on me or I'll get annoyed, feel me? You came here to find us, correct?"

"We came to find Kassander, the moody vampire," Rook says. "Happen to see him around?"

"Are you fucking with me?" She approaches him. She's chewing gum and doing her best to act obnoxious. Her hair is in pigtails and she's wearing a short dress. My gaze passes over her, instantly losing interest. "We have him."

"There we go," Frankie says, starting to pull away from me, and I'm hyperaware of everything about her. The tiny freckles on her nose. Her soft lips. The perfect darkness of her eyes. The silk of her long hair. The warmth she left behind where her body was pressed to mine.

Is a seraph thinking and feeling like a human still a seraph?

The girl turns to her, eyes narrowing. They're practically the same height. So short compared to us. So easy to squash. One has to be careful.

Be gentle, a voice whispers in my head and I shake it, confused.

"I'm the one you want," Frankie says, pulling herself to her full height, facing the other girl. "I assume Greyson wants to talk to me?"

"You assume right."

"You could have just said so."

The girl shrugs. "The vampire was annoying us."

"Sounds just like Kass," Rook mutters.

"You just don't like vampires," I say.

"Nah, he's just extra annoying. Didn't want to come quietly with us."

"How strange." Frankie grins a little too wide. "Who would have thought."

All sarcasm.

What is she? She's a mystery, and my thoughts scatter whenever she's near.

A mystery wrapped up in a sexy body and a sweet voice, a contradiction in everything she does. She's strong and yet fragile, daring and yet innocent, furious and yet kind.

I feel too much when it comes to her.

I'm not myself, and yet it feels right.

She brings out another side in me.

What's going on with me?

"Greyson said to grab one of you to get you to come over without arguments," the girl says. I'm Madelynn. "I'm his right hand."

"They all say that." Frankie turns to wink at us. "Coming, boys?"

Tir grumbles something, pulling Ryu along.

Rook doesn't move from the spot. "Is Greyson thinking she

may be a shifter? I mean... Maybe it's not a scream that reduces men to ash. Maybe it's fire."

"What do you mean?" Frankie whispers.

"A dragon shifter could do that."

A dragon shifter. I roll that in my mind. Could my intel be wrong? After all, it's still all up in the air. Not even Heaven knows for sure...

"Greyson's mind is his own," Madelynn says.

"By which you mean that he doesn't tell you what he's thinking and planning," Rook muses.

"Something on your mind, demon boy?" Madelynn steps past Frankie, hands on her hips. "Are you testing my patience?"

"You're no match for me, little shifter," Rook says, his voice dripping disdain. "You'd do well to remember that."

"A veteran of the Battle of Adesh, huh? Greyson mentioned it." She gives him an interested once over, an appraising look that manages to also look... hungry. As if she wants to undress him with her eyes.

And it has me bristling, which... makes absolutely no sense. Rook is an incubus. Sex is sort of... his job. His nature. His element.

Rook doesn't... belong to me. With me. He's not mine to shield and protect, not that he needs it, especially from sex.

Only Frankie is, because Heaven commanded it.

The others should be dead by now, stone dead, and I should be feeling nothing.

Nothing at all.

I have to talk to Auria, receive guidance. Ask for any new orders. We can't remain long like this, cut off from the world, from Heaven. She's a threat and she has to be detained and examined for the sake of the world. For the sake of peace. It's an important mission, which is why I volunteered.

Even though I don't quite remember the moment I did that.

It's hazy, going from spinning in chaos, in the Glory, to arriving on earth at this college.

"Asa." Rook is gazing at me, curiosity glinting in his gaze. "Coming?"

An inappropriate response comes to my lips and I swallow it down. Is it their influence, their coarseness rubbing off on me?

For the first time since I landed here, I'm not sure of the answer anymore.

29

FRANKIE

*M*adelynn leads us to the school building, sauntering ahead like this is all so much fun. For her it may be the most fun she's had in years. A party. Wouldn't want to spoil it for her.

I roll my eyes.

Passing by the classrooms, it's almost like a déjà vu of our meeting with Jatri, though strangely I wasn't so scared then.

Now I am afraid to see the state Kass must be in. I really hope he's not hurt any worse.

Turning off feelings is, apparently, impossible.

Even if they are feelings you shouldn't have, born too soon and without good reason.

Ugh.

Good job, Frankie. You were supposed to drown those feelings. Hate sex, remember? All the hate sex.

Yeah, I'm on it. Maybe it's because I haven't slept with Kass yet, that's why I still care.

Sure, look for excuses to sleep with all of them, because that has always solved everyone's problems.

"Here we are," Madelynn says and gestures with a flourish

at a double door that's standing wide open. "Go on in. He's expecting you."

"Of course he is," I mutter under my breath. Asa grabs my arm, though, not letting me through.

"Tir, Rook!" he barks and the two go on first, as if they don't mind obeying his order. "Ryu, with us."

That's how I find myself flanked by a bossy angel and a grumpy, pale-faced kitsune as we enter the largest auditorium of the College.

I have never been inside—mostly because I missed too many lectures—and I can't help but glance around at the vast, three-tiered amphitheater and the gothic, arched windows behind, giving it the feel of a cathedral.

This is an old place. I don't notice it much because of how consistent the style is throughout campus. Very Victorian somehow, with gloomy brick buildings and small windows, the furniture inside mostly varnished dark wood—except for our bunkbeds of course. That's why they stand out, a new addition to make up for the increasing number of students, I'll bet.

But this auditorium is so impressive, it takes me a moment to notice the shifter gang lounging about in the rows of seats way down, near the podium.

And then the double doors behind us slam shut.

"What the fuck," Rook mutters, turning around, his hand going to his hip—to his staff, I assume.

But we have bigger problems.

"Where's Greyson?" I ask, trying for calm. Madelynn is standing in front of the closed door, a knife in her hand, another shifter beside her, and all around us, spread, is most of the shifter gang.

On the podium, just a few feet from us, stands a man I've seen before, though.

He's not a shifter.

Sebastian la Fontaine. The vampire kingpin.

"What is going on?" I whisper. "Where is Greyson? And above all, where is Kass?"

"Kass was just bait," Sebastian says and I realize that among the shifters there are also vampires.

"I know that. But bait for what?"

"Don't be so naïve," Sebastian sneers. "You know what's at stake, all of you. This is beyond gangs and Houses. This is big."

"If you're talking about me," I mutter, you're wrong. "I'm only five feet four."

Nobody laughs.

Ah well. I tried.

"Where is Kass?" I take a step forward and I'm gratified to see Sebastian flinch, though I'm not particularly happy. I'm not going to scream and kill everyone, and he knows it, so what defense do I have?

"So much fuss about a mongrel vampire." Sebastian shrugs. "He was bait and bait dies once it's done its job."

"No..."

"What are you doing, La Fontaine?" Asa says, reaching my side, his deep voice resonating inside the amphitheater. "This isn't a game."

"It sure as Hell is not." Sebastian grins, showing his lengthening fangs. "I've never cared much for the power games in this silly little College. I have bigger aspirations. I have a vision."

"A vision," I repeat, incredulous.

"This place is a microcosm. But the real world is out there and I'm ready for it. For the higher spheres." He clicks his tongue. "You, girl, are my passport to those spheres."

"He's been paid to take you," Asa grinds out.

"Wrong," Sebastian says. "I was paid to kill her. The first time was a failure, but this time we're ready for you."

It was him, all this time, trying to take me down?

"Think we'll let you harm her?" Ryu sneers. "We'll whoop your asses just like we did before."

"Will you? I have you all sussed out." Sebastian lifts a negligent hand. "Bring in Kassander."

———

He's alive, is my first thought as he's dragged into the amphitheater from a back door I hadn't noticed—pay attention to exit routes, Franks, what's wrong with you?—and the relief almost brings me to my knees.

His wrists are bound together with rope, as are his ankles, barely allowing him to walk.

He looks like Hell.

"You can't have her," Tir says and suddenly his bow and arrows are in his hands. I wonder where he kept them. "Let Kass go."

And they're suddenly all armed, Asa drawing his sword, Rook pulling out and extending his staff, making me feel like an idiot for having forgotten my knives. I thought I was going to class, dammit!

Sebastian flicks his hand at his men and weapons are drawn all around. "Are you sure you want to do this?"

Awesome.

"Stop," I say.

"Tell that to your friends," Sebastian suggests.

"I could scream," I say, fisting my hands at my sides.

"And kill your friends?"

"Who says they are my friends? They made deals about me, using me as currency. I hate their guts."

"Right... So if I killed them now, you wouldn't bat an eye?"

"I'd string you by your balls, and you know why? Because you're even worse and I hate you more."

"Nice." He actually chuckles, the psycho asshole. "But you forget one little thing."

"And what's that?"

"Kassander." He arches a brow. "Remember him? Do you hate him, too?" When I don't reply, his mouth stretches into a grin. "Oh. There she is."

"You won't hurt him."

"Do you think I'm bluffing? Put down your weapons and don't even think about using magic." Sebastian gestures for the two men pulling Kass toward us. "Want me to start hurting him to prove to you I'm serious?"

"Oh, I know you're serious," I say bitterly, taking in the new bruises and cuts on Kass. His jaw is swollen and already purple, one eye shut. Blood is coating his face from a cut on his forehead. His arms are black and blue and from the way he's holding himself, I bet he has broken ribs.

"Then come to me," Sebastian says, "or he's fucking dead."

"Think she'll just walk over to you so you can kill her to save Kass?" Asa demands, and I step away from him because that's exactly what I'm about to do. "You forget, we all serve different sides."

"But all of you want her alive. I want her dead. She comes to me, or Kassander and all of you die. Think about it."

"I'm not letting Kass die for me," I say.

"Why not?" Tir sounds exasperated. "Just like us, he will give you up once the Dome is lifted."

It's true. And yet I won't have his death on my conscience. No way.

The thought of him gone from the world is a knife twisting in my gut, though I don't say as much.

"If you don't want to..." Sebastian lifts his shoulders in a shrug and flicks his fingers in Kass' direction. "I won't waste any more time. Kill him."

"No!" I twist away from Asa and Rook who both instinctively reach for me, ducking under their arms, and it shouldn't work with seasoned soldiers but this is crazy and they're about to kill Kass—

"No tricks," Sebastian says, reaching for me, too, momentarily distracted, but my gaze is on Kass and the two vampires holding him. One of them has raised a wicked knife but is blinking as if he's forgotten what he's doing—

The double doors rattle and then burst open with a boom, the shock propelling me forward a few more steps as we all turn to look.

Inside walks a tall, slender woman in a black jumpsuit and high-heeled boots, her long dark dreadlocks falling over her shoulders.

The leader of the demon gang, her demons trooping in behind her.

Kalissa.

She cocks a hip to one side, plants her hand on it, and takes in the scene with her smoky eyes. "Why the fuck weren't we invited to the parlay?"

"Parlay?" Sebastian grabs my arm and opens his mouth wide, too wide for a human, his fangs like daggers, about to go for my jugular. "We're here to deal death, not chat. Welcome to the show."

And all Hell breaks loose.

30

FRANKIE

Throwing back my elbow, I twist in Sebastian's hold, not keen on dying, but I'm sluggish despite the shot of adrenaline, too slow to escape his sharp fangs.

But then something slams into us, throwing me on my ass, knocking Sebastian to the ground. Asa lifts his sword to thrust it into Sebastian's chest—not that would kill a vampire, but it could slow him down—as I roll away, trying to gather my wits.

And remember why we're here.

"No, Kass!" I shout, "they'll kill him! Don't let them!"

But as I turn, I find the men holding him looking strangely confused, looking from him to the knives in their hands. He's using his teeth to cut the rope around his wrists.

He's alive.

Turning back to Asa and Sebastian, I find them struggling. Sebastian has knocked the sword blade away from him and grabbed Asa's leg, his eyes gone red with bloodlust. Shifters and vampires are coming at us, blades and claws at the ready.

I kick Sebastian in the jaw, gratified when he grunts and releases Asa. I pull the angel away. "We should get going. Now."

Too late.

Someone throws a knife, Tir lets two arrows fly, Rook smashes his staff into a group leaping at him, Ryu throws a last shuriken and pulls out his knives.

Chaos.

Asa snaps a warning and pulls me back, swinging his sword in a circle, as if to keep back rabid dogs. Everyone in here is beginning to realize that Sebastian's plan didn't pan out, and they're moving to attack us.

"Their aim is to kill me," I whisper. "Stepping over your dead bodies."

"Not going to happen," Asa says. "Don't you wish now you'd listen to us and trained your magic?"

"Yeah. Hindsight is twenty-twenty."

He slams the flat of his blade into the head of a shifter who leaps at us, already starting to shift into something wolf-like, and I hate feeling this helpless. I want to scream.

And I can't.

Tir is fighting against three guys, his bow now unstrung and used as a staff. It glints, metal bands marking each end. He's pulsing with magic, black seeping into him. I see his black horns solidifying, his lips darkening.

A Hunter.

Rook and Ryu are fighting alongside him. Rook shoots us a look and gestures at the door.

Yeah, we should leave, but...

I crouch a little as another shifter jumps at us, letting Asa kick him out of the way, and find a knife on the floor. Who knows who dropped it but I grab it and stand up, feeling more grounded with a blade in my hands.

My heart is slamming against my ribs like a trapped animal.

The auditorium has turned into a battlefield.

I turn and slash at a girl who comes at me—turn and slash, like Granddad taught me, and she cries out and scuttles away, glaring at me, her sleeve turning crimson.

Oops sorry, not sorry?

Asa seems reluctant to chop off heads, and I'm not trying to, either, but did they really think we'd just let them slaughter us?

Oh right... Kass.

"We should get Kass." I turn to find him undoing the ropes from his ankles. A man is rushing at him down the steps of the auditorium. "Shit. Kass, watch out!"

I start toward him but he already has his whip in his hand and slashes at his attacker. He sways on his feet, and I don't like how gray his face looks, but he's okay.

Then I have my own hands full as more guys rush at us. We fight our way toward Rook, Tir, and Ryu, but I can't help but glance back toward Kass every chance I get.

Asa, the guys who held Kass... they look lost.

They are standing on the steps as he fights with his whip, staring around and at each other, fear written all over their faces.

"What's going on?" I breathe.

"They forgot why they're here," Asa says quietly. "Probably forgot quite a few other things, too, like where they are and what is going on."

"Is that his doing?"

"*Lethe,*" Asa says. "He's wiped their recent memories."

"Kass can do that? I thought only old vampires could do such a thing. Maybe he lied about his age."

"I don't know. Hybrids are full of surprises. Watch out, Musen!"

Sebastian wouldn't stay down for long, of course. We both turn, and I only have the time to raise my knife as Sebastian grabs me and shoves me backward. I slice with my knife as we fall, and I wait for his weight to crush me, for his fangs to drive home this time. The high ceiling of the auditorium seems to fade away as I go down, breaking open to the sky.

I see the faces of my family.

I see men turning to ash and dust.

I see angels swirling up high.

And then... A man's face. Handsome. Pale. Golden curls falling in his eyes.

"Angel," I whisper.

"Frankie! Frankie, are you all right?"

He sounds frantic. I need to reassure him. Because it's Asa, I recall. My angel.

And memory rushes back with a roar.

"Don't worry," I manage as he pulls me to my feet. "Your prize is still alive."

He growls softly. Looking past him, I find Sebastian on the floor. Alive or dead, I can't tell the way he's lying on his stomach, but he's out for the count.

For now.

"What the fuck is going on here?" someone bellows and it's Greyson, flanked by more shifters, come to join the fight.

"Duck!" I yell at him when another blade flies, not even sure why I care.

He ducks. Survives.

Straightens only to stare at me.

"Yeah, I know. Call me crazy but I don't want everyone to die. Some of you are trying to kill me," I explain when he continues staring. "I'm trying not to die, either."

"Understandable," he rumbles. "Which side is which?"

"Your guess is as good as mine. It's a bit of a mess, but stick with us and you're good."

We inch our way toward Tir and the others. Asa and I are fighting back-to-back, slashing and kicking at shifters and vampires, and wait, I'm sure that's a Fae brandishing a dirk and magic.

A wave of power hits me, and the knife falls from my hand.

Then Tir steps right in front of me, one hand raised, and the pressure eases off me. "Careful now," he says as a gust of wind swirls around him, lifting his now black hair, tangling it in his horns. "You need to learn to shield yourself from magical attacks."

Right.

"So," Tir says, "you hate us but hate Sebastian more, so that makes us... allies?"

"Don't get your hopes very high." He grins, a slightly disturbing vision, teeth long and yellow, eyes all black, and turns to thump an attacker over the head with his staff.

"So you're only shielding yourselves from magic?" I duck to avoid a clawed hand swiping at me, kick at the girl who's attacking me. "Not using it to knock all these bastards out? Why? I thought your orders were not to hold back against bullies and assassins anymore."

"Orders," Asa says. "We're supposed to use the minimum of our powers, unless we're losing the battle. No killing, if possible."

"No wonder this is taking forever."

"Why, you're suddenly eager to kill?" Tir asks.

"No. Never." Pressing my lips together, I slash and cut and do my best to defend myself, as Greyson's gang joins the fight, working their way toward us, Kalissa's demons fighting on the other side of us.

I think we may be winning this fight.

Are we winning this fight?

"See?" Asa says. "No fatal magic was required."

"Not sure how dependable those orders of yours are," I mutter. "I don't think anyone cares if you actually live or die. Once you get fatally injured, wouldn't it be too late to call on your powers?"

"... she has a point," Tir says.

"Shut up," Asa tells him, "my orders are never wrong."

"Right, because Heaven never makes any fucking mistakes, my bad."

"Look out, Tir!" I have no choice but to throw my knife at the werewolf leaping at him. I catch the creature—the man—in the chest and he yips as he crashes down. We have a wall of bodies growing around us.

"Thanks. See, you do love us."

"Dream on," I say, anger heating my voice in spite of everything. "Where's Kass?"

"He's wooing the shifters."

"... I beg your pardon?"

"There. They're going crazy over him."

I squint at the stairs where indeed Kass seems to be walking among guys... who are reaching for him only to stroke parts of him as he passes?

"How is he doing that?"

"He's half incubus, or did you forget?"

"I had forgotten. That's... practical," I say. "Unlike your powers, which don't seem to be any help. Or mine, for that matter."

And I can't help wondering why Kass never used that gift on me if he wanted me falling for him and spilling my secrets... did he? No, if he had I wouldn't be so mad at him half the time, would I?

"We don't choose our gifts," Tir says.

"You mean our curses."

"There's much we don't choose in life."

Rook and Ryu have finally reached us. Rook licks blood from a cut on his upper lip. He throws a sideways glance at a girl vampire who opens her mouth way too wide, striding toward us—and she slows down, uncertainty flowing over her features. Her gaze travels over him and her pupils dilate.

"You're one to talk," I mumble, dizzy again. I find myself leaning against Tir's side. "You and Kass could have gotten this entire place lusting after you."

"That could end us, though."

"Hm..." Kass is walking toward us, cracking his whip on the floor. I can feel him, I think, feel the water in his power, liquid and all-encompassing, yet infused with fire from his demon side.

I feel all of them, their powers mixed, augmented. Tir's is air with a touch of earth, Rook's is fire with a whiff of air, Ryu is earth with flames, and Asa... Asa is air and light and... and something I can't quite touch...

"What in Dracula's name is going on here?" a voice booms from the door and I turn to see Jatri and his Fae entering the auditorium, shoving away those guarding the doors. "The girl and I have a deal. She—"

A knife thuds into his chest.

He falls backward, a stunned expression on his face. The fae following him let out a deafening cry, falling to their knees in a wave.

A wave I feel smashing into me, felling me, throwing me down. A shockwave. What the Hell just happened?

"It's steel," Tir is saying, "right through the heart. No way..."

"Is he dead?"

"Stone dead."

Dead... Can't be. Nobody was supposed to die. Defenses... Why didn't he defend himself? I dislike him but that doesn't mean I wanted him dead. Death scares me. I love so many people. I can't imagine the void they'd leave behind in my life if they were gone...

Everyone has someone who loves them, don't they?

And I have taken the life of many.

Darkness is crowding in on my vision. I can't feel my limbs. Ice is flowing through my veins. Hushed voices murmur over me.

"Frankie? Can you hear me? Frankie?"

I hear them, but I'm shivering, shivering so hard I think my bones will break.

"What's happening to her? Is it Jatri's death? Did it affect her?"

"She's not Fae. Air is not her element, so it can't be that bad. She's not bonded with him or anything. Barely knows him. It can't have affected her like that."

"Then what the fuck is wrong?"

"Beats me, man."

Why do they have to sound so concerned? My eyes feel so hot. Any moment now they'll start leaking. They have no right to make me feel like this, so... cherished and needed. I might start believing it. And I can't do that.

I try to speak, but my lips feel numb. Can't feel my face. My eyes are hot, my body so cold.

"Something's wrong," Asa says. "I smelled it on her before, and I can smell it now. We have to get her to the room."

"Or to a medic," Rook says. "She was wounded a couple of days ago. Let me see the wound."

"Not here, not now," Asa says.

"She hasn't complained about the wound," Ryu says.

"She was in pain, though. And dizzy sometimes."

"You knew and didn't tell us?"

"What are you, blind? I thought we all saw the same things."

"Damn you."

"Watch out! Fuck, we're too distracted. We need to get out of here. Greyson! We need you to have our six while we take Frankie out of here."

"They thought we couldn't protect her," Ryu says, his raspy voice tight. "They thought we'd walk in here and they'd just kill her."

"They're idiots," Rook says. "Haven't they heard what she can do? Or were they so confident she wouldn't scream not to harm us?"

"Yeah, stupid," Tir mutters. "I think she just hates killing people."

Such an insight from Tir.

"Well, after this they will have to think twice before they attack again."

"Unless the payment is so good they won't care. I will assume the assassins of two days ago were recruited the same way, across all the Houses."

"Fuck..."

The sounds of battle are still echoing, still way too loud. I miss the next bits of conversation. I'm jostled and moan, my side on fire. When did I catch fire? It's burning inside my chest, eating me alive. It's crackling inside my head, and like a log, I will soon fall apart to ashes and dust, as I deserve.

It feels as if I already am, crumbling on the floor, my hair turning to spiderwebs, my limbs melding with the tiles.

Time stretches. Fades. Returns.

"Frankie," someone says. "Come on. Open those pretty eyes for me. Look at me. You can do it."

It makes me want to smile, the concern, warming me where I'm freezing to death, where I'm breaking apart. Wait, was that Ryu's voice?

"Holy fuck," he says, "she's not waking up. Let me—"

"She's burning up," Tir says. "Have to find the medic, now."

"What use is your Heavenly power if you can't heal her, cherub?" Rook asks.

"Didn't say I couldn't. But it's risky," Asa says, very close to me, his breath warm over my cheek, "because she must have some demonblood in her."

"Asa..."

"If a medic can't help, I'll see what I can do."

"You just want her naked underneath you," Rook says. "Again."

And that's the last thing I hear before darkness swallows me down.

———

I'm stepping onto a sidewalk, hurrying after Granddad. He's giving me a running commentary on my knife work and my throwing technique, mainly all the gaps I leave in my defenses and how I throw without calculating the distance and missing my target—all delivered calmly and kindly, because that's how Granddad is.

Like my own personal Yoda.

Only I wish I were back with my family, with Aunt Mia and my uncles and cousins and not hiding in a dingy little apartment downtown, using an old dojo in a basement to train after hours, and still doing online classes to get a GED. I was homeschooled before together with my cousins and now it's the same, only it's just me and Granddad.

I'm bored. I'm fed up with this hiding and training situation.

It makes me cranky. I'm nineteen now and life should be getting better, not worse.

So I mutter, "I threw just fine when you weren't breathing down my neck." Sounding like a sullen teenager.

"Patience, child."

"Don't patience me. When are we going back home, Granddad? I don't care who my father is. I can't run forever."

"I'm almost there, Franks. I think I almost got it. Give me some more time."

I sigh.

The city is always noisy, in the evenings as much as during the daytime. Our part of the town stinks. Homeless people line the streets. I give them any dollar I save when Granddad gives me money to buy something. That's another thing that bugs me. I'm old enough to earn my keeping by now. It makes me feel dependent and helpless and I hate it.

Patience, he says. I mean, he's right, knowing what I am is important, especially after the incident. But it won't happen again. Maybe it wasn't even me who caused that... that mess.

I shudder and swallow down bile.

It's been years. Surely it'd have happened again already if it had been me.

Right?

But I blink and we're elsewhere, closer to our apartment. The change is jarring and I reach for Granddad.

"What's going on?" I whisper.

"Run, Franks," he says, his voice catching, "they're coming after you, run..."

"Who?" I start to ask but I see them, running down the street, jumping from rooftops and balconies and fire exits, their faces distorted. Bullets and blades fly through the air as Granddad pulls me down an alley.

There's no exit.

We stop and turn.

The scream burns my throat but never comes out. The men freeze in mid-motion, but I can't scream because someone else is there.

The blond man. He's there, watching me, leaning on his staff like always.

What is he doing here?

Favrash... Remember them...

My scream echoes through the street anyway, and I roll in the dust, curling on my side, unable to breathe or speak.

The blond man steps closer to me. "Frankie! Frankie. Stay with me."

"Where else could I go?"

"Come on, Frankie." He lets go of the staff, letting it fall, and reaches for me. "Come back. We need you. I need you."

That sounds dramatic, I think. *It's like a cheesy line from an action movie and it's not like he believes what he's saying, or that I'm dying...*

Is it?

———

When my senses return, I'm not on the street and the blond man isn't standing over me, though his words still echo in my ears. I'm still curled up but it's warm and smells good.

Smells like a man.

And next thing I know, I'm moving, and not under my own power.

Someone is holding me, I think fuzzily, snug in their arms, and I'm pretty sure it's Asa.

"I think she's one of us," he says, and I wish I could speak but I'm too heavy, everything is too heavy, plus I'm cold and he's so warm I want to stay in his arms forever and not move a muscle, not think a thought.

"This way," Rook says, and then "I'll keep them away."

"Leave Greyson and Kalissa to handle that."

"They can't handle everyone." Though Rook seems to move away. "Keep walking," he calls out, then, "Tir, gimme a hand here."

"With pleasure," Tir says.

There's a thump, and another. Someone yelps. Tir curses. A bit of unease stirs in my gut but still I can't move.

A few seconds or hours later, impossible to tell, their steps return.

"All taken care of," Tir says and relief washes through me.

"I'll keep an eye behind us," Rook says, "just in case they decide to follow. Doing okay, Kass?"

"Why wouldn't I be?" Kass grumbles. "We're all fine, except for her. We've failed spectacularly in our task of keeping her safe."

"She *is* safe," Rook snaps. "We still don't know why she collapsed."

"And what about getting caught by surprise, falling into a stupid trap laid by La Fontaine? Like rookies, we fell for it. Unprepared, unorganized, unworthy of our mission."

"Calm your tits, night child," Rook mutters. "We did okay. Her collapse is unrelated to what happened in there—"

"We did *okay*? If the shifters and the demons hadn't shown up to shore up our side, we'd have perished, and Frankie with us."

"He's right," Asa says. "We've been careless. This could have ended badly."

"A good thing she didn't scream," Ryu says, "or we'd all be ash by now."

"Well, this is an interesting thing," Asa says, and his voice rumbles in his broad chest, vibrating under my ear.

"What is?"

"I went and looked. Her scream doesn't turn people to ash."

"It doesn't... What? What do you mean?"

"It turns them to salt."

"... and what does that change?"

"We know only of one creature able to do that."

"We do? Maybe *you* do."

"Come on, Asa, what do you know? Spit it out? What creature can do that? Some rare monster in the bible, no doubt."

Asa slows down, clears his throat. "An angel," he says.

"Shut the door," Rook mutters. "You're not for real."

The others are silent.

He thinks my father was an angel. One of his own.

No wonder Heaven wants me dead or alive.

.   .   .

Ready for book 3? Of Angels and Demons is coming on February 27, 2025!

ACKNOWLEDGMENTS

To Haeley Rochette: lady, you are amazing and thank you so much for beta reading!
To Lainey Da Silva: my friend, I couldn't do it without you, always!
To all bloggers, instagrammers, tiktokers and to all amazing readers: thank you from the bottom of my heart for making this dream real.

ABOUT MONA BLACK

Mona is a changeling living in the human world. She writes fantasy romance and reverse harem romance, and is an avid reader of fantasy and paranormal books. One day she will get her ducks in a row and get a cat so she can become a real author.

Check out her paranormal reverse harem series Pandemonium Academy Royals, and her fantasy romance series Cursed Fae Kings.

www.ingramcontent.com/pod-product-compliance
Ingram Content Group UK Ltd.
Pitfield, Milton Keynes, MK11 3LW, UK
UKHW022324170125
453762UK00010B/449